KINGDOM AND THE GLORY

Anthony Talmage

ISBN-13: 978-1981432202
ISBN-10: 1981432205

About The Author

As a freelance writer I am probably best known for my non-fiction books on psychic matters, the paranormal and the Unexplained. I have published two non-fiction books on this theme, *Dowse Your Way To Psychic Power*, based on my experiences as a diviner and *In Tune With The Infinite Mind*, a look at consciousness and the connectedness of all things. My first venture into fiction was a radio play, an occult thriller *'Ghost in the Machine'*, broadcast in South Africa and Ireland. I have now written three novels – my first was *Ticket to a Killing* in which a serial killer goes on the rampage and the second, *The Kirov Conspiracy*, deals with a loner who takes on the Mafia. My third novel is the one you now hold in your hand, which features a maverick US President who plots to topple the British Monarchy. I have plans for other works of fiction, based on my experiences both in the media and in the field of the supernatural.

ACKNOWLEDGMENTS

To those readers who enjoyed my first book and second books and took the trouble to spread the word and write a kind review. Here are just a few of the comments posted about them:

TICKET TO A KILLING:

'...From the moment I met Emma I was hooked by every twist and turn in her life...'
'...beautifully written book where the storyline never falters...'
'...Would make a great tv drama...'
'...Great escapism. Thank you!'
'...Fantastic read, I was caught up in the plot and found it difficult to put the book down...'
'...kept me guessing to the end...'

THE KIROV CONSPIRACY

'...a classic 'race-against-time' plot which is believable, original and thrilling...'
'...Can't wait for this author's next book..!'
'...Easy to get into and follow without pausing...'
'...Good plot, fast paced and believable. Found the location intriguing...'

Prologue

James Sherborne MP stared, stupefied, at the girl in the passenger-seat of his parked car. She was slumped like a stringless puppet. Her eyes bulged and her tongue protruded obscenely.

Sherborne himself sat with arms outstretched and hands still bent, claw-like, from his struggle to muffle her screams. The inside of the car was silent now, except for his heaving lungs and the rain which rattled in sullen gusts against the windows.

The stormy, May skies had brought twilight on early and headlights from the main road a few hundred yards away intermittently illuminated the two dishevelled figures.

Sherborne's normally immaculate Thierry Mugler pin-striped suit was rumpled, his silk shirt was missing a button and the knot of his tie was wildly askew.

But the other occupant of the car had fared worse. Her blouse was ripped apart revealing a black, lace-edged bra which, itself, had been pulled downwards to bare two firm breasts. Below her waist, the girl's trouser zip gaped open exposing flimsy knickers now tugged and torn, as if by a brutish hand.

Hesitantly, Her Majesty's Opposition Spokesman for European Affairs reached out and placed the tips of three fingers across the girl's carotid artery. No pulse.

He cried aloud, 'My God, no. No, no. Please God, no.' The animal howl of despair which then filled the car's interior penetrated to the outside world as a thin wail and was whipped away into the night by the wind.

It would not have been heard by the driver of the approaching car, whose headlights lit up the bend ahead.

One

The Boomer had confirmed it. The reign of Queen Elizabeth the Second would not last more than another seven months. She was dying of cancer of the pancreas, The Boomer had said.

Robert Pelham savoured the words before giving a thin smile of satisfaction. So, his friends in low places had been right. Now, with their help, Charles the Third would not ascend the throne.

And neither would William, who would prefer not to have the job yet anyway. Seize the day.

Even at this time of night the Palace of Westminster would normally still be abuzz with the comings and goings of politicians of all parties smoothing the way of Commons business conducted in the House earlier. But this was a Friday and Right Honourable and Honourable Members had long gone, back to their constituencies for the weekend. Leaving him to enjoy a rare solitude.

Pelham shifted deeper into his leather, swivel chair, and sipped abstractedly at his House of Commons, own-label whisky. The Deputy Prime Minister was not normally one for self-congratulation. But, now was different.

After all, his whole life had been a preparation for this

moment. Pity he had to share centre stage with that oaf, the President of the United States.

As the spirit burned its way down his throat he thought back over the years. Not for him the silver spoon. It had been one, long struggle: fighting the Establishment's built-in prejudice against the son of a railway signalman; winning his scholarship to grammar school; the long years of self denial ending in an Honours Degree at Cambridge; hawking himself round the constituencies; fighting impossible seats; winning his first election against the odds.

The same single-mindedness had secured his rise through the ranks of his old party, Labour, until he had reached his present position: Number Two in the now Social Democrat Government and the Iron Fist in Ted Lancaster's threadbare glove. Lancaster, The Boomer. He would have no place in the new world order.

Right now, thought Pelham, what Britain needed was a strong leader. He had that strength. He had been called by destiny. Particularly after the shock of the Brexit vote, the Tory leadership coronation and then the protracted years of negotiation, culminating in a humiliating exit, during which the country's fortunes had fallen to almost the level of the Third World. And then, to rub vinegar into a still open wound, the EU had ordered its members to turn their backs on trade deals with their traitorous neighbour, just to ensure that no others in the club fancied their chances as a breakaway state.

This remorseless war of attrition was why the Social Democrats had won the 2021 election: the people were weary of the struggle and wanted the new leftist party to restore harmony with Europe and confidence in the future. But the arrogant EU political classes had poured shit over British heads. Now our history was at a crossroads and about to take a direction no-one would ever have dreamed of. Thanks to me, Pelham thought, smiling to himself. For future generations his name would eclipse those of Thatcher, Churchill, Disraeli, Wilberforce. He was about to reshape the destiny of Europe. Only he could do it.

Pelham knew his long, personal journey had gained him few friends. But he did not care. All he demanded was obedience. And because he was feared and respected in equal measure by his colleagues, he would get it.

While laying his plans he would also have the country behind him. He was seen by the electorate as the toughest potential leader since Thatcher. Someone who would stand up for their interests in an increasingly fractured world.

Thus, his stock in the Party remained high, not because he was liked but because they needed him. And they would need him a lot more by the time he had finished.

Pelham closed his eyes. Mentally, he ran through the scene at this morning's meeting in the Cabinet Room. Senior ministers and a selection of the Party's inner circle, had been summoned for a special announcement.

How The Boomer had played to the gallery. He had even managed a catch in the throat and a dab at the eye with his handkerchief as he had related the details of Tuesday's audience with the Queen.

It was the one thing, Pelham reflected, that The Boomer was good at - talking. Come to think of it, it was the only thing he was good at. The Boomer: virtuoso of the basso profundo. A sounding brass, a tinkling cymbal.

Lancaster had been elected to the Social Democrat leadership two-and-a-half years previously – in 2020 - as the compromise candidate after the Labour Party's disastrous split into a Neo-Marxist rump and a moderate, social democrat majority. Nobody had wanted to rock the boat after that old fool Robbins had taken the Labour Party, and its fanatical, grassroots support base, to unelectability. So the Social Democrats, which rose Phoenix-like from the ashes of Labour, had become the only alternative to the Tories. Ted Lancaster, a Party elder statesman, had assumed the mantle and the kinetic energy that had already been built up in a Brexit-weary electorate had swept them to power a year later.

But almost immediately the cracks had begun to show in their brave new political world. Without a strong commander to keep them in line, recalled Pelham, the hard Left rank and file, egged on by Robbins, had come out of their foxholes and the in-fighting had begun.

Lancaster had found himself under siege from factional interests demanding everything from a return to EU membership to offering Scotland another independence referendum. Deep doctrinal differences had emerged and die-hards ensnared in old ideologies had begun openly to squabble.

But the biggest schism was over Britain's exit from the EU. The Conservative Government's weak compromises had caused bitterness on all sides.

To some extent this had subsided when the Social Democrats had won the election but, gradually, the optimism had begun to fade to be replaced by a disillusionment with all politicians who were perceived as, once again, having failed to turn dreams into reality. But all that was about to change.

Pelham took a long sip from his glass and swirled the amber liquid around his tongue. And, of course, he thought to himself, the defeated Tory ranks had been quick to exploit these divisions. Having lashed their hapless leader Marjorie to the mast, allowing her to go down with the ship, they were now re-grouping around young, progressive thinkers.

Of particular concern to Pelham was James Sherborne, MP for Thamesdown in Wiltshire. He had been one of the few Tories who had increased his majority while others of the same political hue had been wiped out.

Yes, if there was one member of the Opposition who could restore Conservative fortunes, it was Sherborne. And his recent speeches on Europe had hit uncomfortably close to the mark. Garment by garment the man had been stealing the emperor's clothes.

It was because he was dangerous he had to be tamed. And he would be a handy ally to have when the time came, Pelham fancied. He shot his cuff and looked at his watch. Yes, by now the Tories' blue-eyed boy should have other matters than politics on his mind.

Pelham's thoughts turned back to the Prime Minister. As if Lancaster had not got enough to contend with, there was also the vexed question of Ulster. After an uneasy peace following the Good Friday Agreement old tensions between the Nationalists and the Unionists had re-surfaced following the Brexit vote in the 2016 referendum. All The Boomer's attempts at reconciliation had come to nought and mainland Britain had, once again, been under increasing terrorist attack. The IRA were vying with Islamist extremists to see who could break the will of the new political order. There had even been a bomb alert at Westminster that very day.

All MPs had been obliged to use their 'sniffer sticks' minutely to examine the undersides of their vehicles before driving home for the weekend.

So, reflected Pelham contemptuously, while Sherborne and his cohorts revelled in the Government's increasing discomfiture on all sides, Ted Lancaster's answer was to appoint a Cabinet of 'yes men' and take refuge in their sycophantic reassurances. The newspapers were right: The Boomer was a tired old man with failing sight, not up to the job of leading the country as a new, stand-alone democracy with a world of opportunity to stake a claim in.

But, conceded Pelham to himself, at this morning's meeting, the PM's windbaggery had somehow captured the gravitas of the occasion.

Peering myopically over his bottle-end lenses he had told his 30 or so assembled colleagues that, now he'd been able to digest the awful tidings vouchsafed to him three days ago, it was his painful duty to disclose - in absolute and total confidence it must be understood - that, tragically, Her Majesty would not, now, be celebrating her 100th birthday in 2026. She had been diagnosed as suffering from an incurable cancer of the pancreas.

Pelham had known what was coming, of course. But the shock felt by the rest of the gathering had been genuine.

The Boomer's voice had taken on a deep, sepulchral resonance as he had concluded that it was unlikely that Her Majesty would survive more than a few months. It was now up to Her Majesty's ministers to decide on the road ahead.

So, Pelham resolved, I have less than half a year to turn the nation round and set a new course. In some ways it was a shame that Lancaster would not be around to witness his triumph.

Three short raps at his door startled the Deputy PM out of his reverie. That would be Dresner. Dresner his facilitator, his fixer, his conduit, his minder. Dresner, the best in his field. Dresner, his link with the President of the United States.

Harry's return would mean all the building blocks were now, finally, in place. All that was left was a simple sleight of hand with some eye drops. Brilliant!

The figure who entered the handsome, wood-panelled sanctum was in his early thirties, of medium build, broad at the shoulder and narrow at the hips.

He stood silently for a moment before crossing to the hospitality cabinet and reaching in to where he knew a certain bottle would be. He splashed a triple measure of JD into a glass and slowly took a sip.

Finally, looking directly at his English boss for the first time, he shook his head. 'It was a goddamned screw-up.' His American accent contrasted incongruously with his surroundings.

Pelham's smile collapsed and his face darkened as if a light had gone out. But, before he could comment, Dresner held up a placatory hand. 'But if you've done a deal with Old Nick, he sure is keeping his side of the bargain.'

'Meaning?'

'Meaning. It's going to work out just fine.'

Pelham's frown lifted. 'His claws have been drawn?' Dresner nodded. 'And how.'

Pelham gave a long, satisfied sigh. 'So, no more pre-emptive speeches. The routed Tory rump loses its wunderkind.'

Dresner raised his glass in a mock salute. 'Four down and just the Big One to go.'

Pelham emerged from behind his desk and waved Dresner to one of the arm chairs grouped around a mahogany coffee table. He sat in another opposite. 'So what happened?'

For the next 20 minutes Dresner related every detail of his journey, from the time he and his companion followed their quarry out of the House of Commons car park until his return, alone, four hours later. He left nothing out, just as he had been trained. He even spoke of how the rain squalls had worsened the further he got from the city.

His listener sat in silence, occasionally nodding. But when Dresner came to the nub of his de-briefing, Pelham sat bolt upright. 'My God, the bloody fool.' Then, sinking back thoughtfully he added, 'Well, well. How very obliging of him.'

Dresner replied drily, 'As I said, Bob, the Devil looks after his own.' Pelham stretched out his right thumb and forefinger. 'We're that close, Harry...'

Dresner coughed. 'Thanks to a little help from your friends.'

Pelham blinked away his rising elation and gazed levelly at his companion. 'That goes without saying. I take my hat off to your people. Intelligence gathered at the flick of a switch, a nation's secrets snatched seemingly out of the air, peccadilloes laid bare, incriminating dossiers assembled to order. I sometimes wonder if a man's very soul is safe.'

'Yeah, well. I guess Uncle Sam's got most of the world by the balls.'

Pelham chortled. 'I'd like to know whose trousers the DOI's hands were down for this one. Even her Britannic Majesty's First Minister got his information fourth-hand.'

'So it's been confirmed. How long?'

'The Boomer says she'll be lucky to last six months. Which chimes in perfectly with our timing. Hobart awaits my signal after which all his newspapers, TV and cable stations will speak with one voice.'

Dresner said, 'And 60 million people here and billions across the rest of the globe will get the message, "Pelham for President".'

The corner of Pelham's mouth twitched. 'It does sound...in tune with the times.'

Dresner's face cracked into a rare smile. 'Yeah, goodbye

the Windsors - and so long the other Krauts and their pals.'

'No complacency, Harry. As tonight's events prove only too convincingly, nothing in this life is certain.' Pelham bounced from his chair. 'But there are ways of improving the odds in one's favour. Belt and braces and all that.'

Pelham reached for the phone. 'So if you'll excuse me, Harry, I think a call to our very co-operative Home Secretary is in order. And after that I shall beg a small favour from a friend at the Yard.'

Two

'Autocide' was how the physicist from the Metropolitan Police Forensic Science Laboratory had described it. Another import from America, he had said.

Shrugging with awkward sympathy, Det Insp Jack Lockyer's Scotland Yard colleague had explained how autocide was the growing practice in the US of going crazy behind the wheel and taking your own life.

Usually the resulting smash killed the driver. The advantages, apparently, were less distress for the loved-ones, who believed it to be a genuine accident, and a healthy cash bonus for the dependents, courtesy of the insurance company.

So, the would-be suicides closed their eyes, pressed the accelerator to the floor and drove into any poor bastard who happened to be coming in the opposite direction - never mind who else got killed.

For the thousandth time Lockyer wondered which god had decreed his wife should be one of the first British victims of this twisted logic. But, whoever the gods were, they had a warped sense of humour. Because Jennie's killer, a lovesick, 25-year-old, whose girlfriend had kicked him out, survived a combined, head-on impact of 95mph with just a broken leg and three cracked ribs.

The forensic team had found the metal pattern from the crashed car's accelerator imprinted by the impact on the sole of the driver's shoe. Which proved he was urging his vehicle on at the point of impact. Subsequently a court had found the man guilty of manslaughter.

After a year's detention under the Mental Health Act the prisoner had been released and had later married the girl who had thrown him out. That was all six years ago, since when the numbness of Jack's grief had become a habit, imprisoning his feelings behind an impenetrable shell.

He was respectful of his seniors and considerate to his juniors. But he was honest enough with himself to realise that the long, obsessive hours he dedicated to his job was an arid substitute for a swathe of his life now missing. He found it lonely but, ultimately, more comfortable that way. The light had gone out in his life and he just had to accept it.

On the odd occasions when any emotions threatened to mutiny and batter his defences down, he took himself off with a bottle and drank himself into a stupor.

This latter fact, of course, had not gone unnoticed by his superiors at the Yard. Give them their due, they had tried everything suggested by the psychologists. Later, they had given up and had left him to nurse his grief in his own way. With the occasional wagged finger about throwing away almost certain promotion. And only a fool finding solace at the bottom of a glass.

Wearily, Lockyer pushed aside his half-consumed bowl of cornflakes. How was he going to fill two whole days off? Usually, he volunteered for any task, on overtime or otherwise, so long as it filled the space between getting up and going to bed. His bosses knew he was always available. Which made Lockyer especially popular with his younger colleagues, who had learned there was another world outside the detection of crime.

But, this weekend had been one of those rare occasions when there was nothing on offer. Lockyer grimaced. Which meant no excuse for not tidying the flat. But time for that later.

He poured a second cup of instant coffee and added two heaped teaspoons of sugar. Good job Jennie couldn't see him now, he thought. She'd be tutting about his weight and putting him on a diet. No, that wasn't true. How often had she said she loved her grumpy bear as he was, cuddly or otherwise. He smiled at the memory. If only...if only...

He unfolded his copy of The Century and groaned. Wouldn't they ever tire of bashing the royals? The front page headline screamed, HARRY AND MEGHAN TO PART...Bust-up No 4 makes it a Royal Flush.' Alongside a story soberly rehearsing the reasons for the collapse of the marriage, the editor had penned a leader under the words: UNEASY LIES THE HEAD THAT WEARS THE CROWN.

It went on to posit that the Monarchy, an institution which had weathered the end of feudalism, continental invasion, the industrial revolution, two world wars and innumerable Royal scandals, was now hanging by a thread. And the near centenarian Queen (God bless her) could not be expected to steady the ship yet again – not at her age.

In conclusion the leader thundered, 'The only thing now not wrong with the monarchy is the monarch. Serious questions will be posed should - God forbid - anything happened to our Good Queen Bess.'

Lockyer turned inside. Page two carried an item about yet another IRA bomb threat. This time at the heart of government itself. He could not help smiling to himself at the thought of all those pompous windbags crawling around on their hands and knees looking for non-existent bombs.

Because non-existent they had been. It was a typical terrorist tactic: cry wolf enough times until everyone got so fed up they got careless. Then strike a devastating blow. Jack sighed. Fifty years and it was still going on.

He looked for some light relief but found instead another tub-thumping issue. Pages three, four and five were devoted exclusively to The Century's other current obsession - the EU and its threat to British sovereignty, despite the country now no longer being a member of the club. Stories mixed laughable examples of bureaucratic lunacy with strident warnings that Britain was being intimidated into becoming obeisant to a Teutonic superstate.

'As a nation,' another Opinion column trumpeted, 'we are sleepwalking to unconditional surrender. What neither the Armada, nor Napoleon, nor Hitler, nor Stalin, nor any other of our foes could achieve, is now being accomplished by a faceless, soulless army. And they have a secret weapon: that accursed coin The Euro which waits in ambush for our pound.' The writer claimed the European bloc was manipulating its currency to trash sterling.

It fulminated, 'Wake up, Prime Minister, the Kingdom is under siege. It is time for the British bulldog to bite back, to defend the realm paid for with the blood of our ancestors. Ted, they are saying you are a lame-duck PM. If it is true, we give you fair warning now: IF YOU HAVE NO STOMACH FOR THE FIGHT, WE KNOW A MAN WHO HAS.'

Lockyer tossed the paper aside. Good knockabout stuff, he supposed, but a shade hysterical. Still, if all Ben Hobart's papers espoused the proprietor's own rabid republican views, Lancaster would never survive the barrage. And who would take the Party over to see the country through the post-Brexit challenges? Probably the Deputy PM, Robert Pelham, he surmised.

As far as he could see the other three possible candidates were totally uninspiring. Howard Ingleby, Chancellor of the Exchequer, had never previously held a government post; Austin Willis, the Home Secretary, was a nonentity despite the high opinion he had of himself, and Roland Sinclair, Chief Secretary to the Treasury, had views on returning the UK to a federal Europe, which were diametrically opposed to the stubborn opinion of the country.

So, his money would be on Pelham. But, who'd be a politician, Eh? He felt sorry for poor old Lancaster. He was being sniped at from all sides. And it wasn't as if he was a fit man. They said he suffered from glaucoma, which meant he had to carry drops around with him all the time. Some reports suggested Lancaster was obliged to absent himself from important meetings and lie down in a darkened room while the medication took effect.

And he hadn't the resilience of a young man, either. By all accounts he was gradually wilting under the combined pressure of his own party's squabbling and the Tories' pack instinct for the smell of blood. Her Majesty's Opposition had certainly bounced back after being trounced at the polls.

Lancaster did not seem to have an answer to their twin charges that the divisiveness on the political left was seriously harming the country as was their submissiveness to the Euro-federalists.

Shadow minister after shadow minister were scoring palpable hits across the Dispatch Box. They claimed that despite Brexit the government's signing up to the European Social Chapter had cost jobs. And Britain's continued contributions to European institutions had gone up while grants in the other direction had all but disappeared. And all this was in order to help our European partners to bale out the economies of new EU members from the old Eastern Bloc who brought little to the table but begging bowls.

The Conservatives had sensed the nation's mood and, wrapping themselves in the Union Flag, had promised to repatriate all British contributions as soon as they were back in power. And they had the Social Democrats on the run.

And with their new, youthful-faced rising star, James Sherborne, fronting the attack, Lancaster's party had continued to degenerate into factional disarray. The country was baying for blood and, in a miraculous bounce-back from near annihilation, the Tories' fortunes were riding high across the country.

To stand a chance of keeping office, Jack mused, the Democrats would have to come up with a block-busting master stroke. And, as far as he could see, their cupboard was bare.

His thoughts were interrupted by the phone.

'Lockyer.'

'Sorry to disturb you, sir, on your day off - '

'- Claire, always a pleasure to hear from you.'

'Sir?'

'Never mind, Sergeant Bishop, lowest form of wit and all that. What can I do for you?'

'A body's been found, sir. In Wiltshire. It's of a young woman - '

'- Wiltshire? But that's out of our patch?'

'I know, sir. But I've been asked to say it's been agreed as a Yard investigation and I'm to pick you up and take you to the locale immediately.'

Jack smoothed the bristles of his greying moustache with his left thumb and forefinger. Now here was an immediate oddity. For a death in another force's jurisdiction to be taken over by New Scotland Yard meant deep offence to the boys and girls whose manor it was on.

Which meant that someone very high up had ordered it so. Which seemed to indicate it was no ordinary homicide.

'It is murder I take it?' Lockyer said eventually.

'According to the Wiltshire Scene Of Crime Officer, sexual assault followed by strangulation. But Dr Jackson, from forensics, is on his way - '

'Jackson? You mean old Hamish's been dragged away from the golf course? To go all the way down to Stonehenge-land. I hope his passport's up to date.' Lockyer grinned down the phone. 'Get here, quick as you like, Claire. I needed an excuse not to do the housework.'

Three

'As far as I can tell, there's nothing to connect you with this girl. You...we...must bluff it out,' Elizabeth Sherborne said firmly.

Her husband shook his head vehemently. 'I'll never get away with it. Someone's bound to have seen something. And how could I possibly carry on as if nothing's happened?'

The two were standing in - rather pacing - the kitchen of their country home in Hinton Magna, Wiltshire. A kettle was gently simmering on the aga and the dishes from breakfast were yet to be cleared from their French oak, farmhouse table.

They had discussed the events of the previous night for hours during which James Sherborne's demeanour had swung between profound shock, disbelief, anger, fear and self-pity. His wife had taken command of the conversation and was now analysing their chances of covering his tracks.

'Go over it just once more,' Elizabeth pressed.

'No, no, no. Not again, for Christ's sake? I've told you everything. It makes me want to vomit every time I think about it.' James Sherborne's visage crumbled as the horror hit him afresh. Abruptly he flopped down exhausted in a kitchen chair. Cradling his head in his hands he began to sob.

His wife's face softened. She placed her arms on his

shoulders and leaned downwards. 'Darling, remember the children. They're only in the sitting room. If they come in and see you like this...'

James reached into his pocket, took out a white, linen handkerchief and scrubbed at his eyes. He looked up at Elizabeth with a weak smile. 'Sorry. Of course you're right. Damned stupid of me.' He took her hand. 'My God, Lizzie, I don't know what I'd do without you.'

'You'll never have to, you know that. I love you, James. I always have and I always will. That's why I'm pushing you so hard right now. I must know if we've overlooked anything.'

Glancing at the door which led to the hall and the other rooms in the house, she sat down opposite her husband and lowered her voice. 'Now tell me if I've got anything wrong...' Painstakingly, she went over, once again, the happenings of the night before.

'...You were driving your usual route at the usual time for a Friday. As you turned off the A338 to take the back roads to Hinton this girl stepped out in front of you, apparently from nowhere. She was bent double as if in pain?'

Her husband nodded. 'The bloody rain was sloshing down. And the sky was so dark I nearly didn't see her.'

'You pulled up and she unbent and walked round to the passenger side. You wound the window down and asked her if she was alright. You then realised she was crying and obviously in distress so you told her to get in out of the rain.'

James interjected bitterly. 'If only I'd just driven away then. But I couldn't just abandon her, could I? She was in the middle of nowhere and seemed to be in a terrible state.'

Elizabeth continued, 'She asked if you could drive her to her parents' home in Hungerford. Because it was only 15 minutes out of your way and, because of her condition, you agreed. As you drove off, intending to take the next turning left, she became hysterical.'

James said, 'I was so shocked. One minute she was this pathetic bundle and the next she was this hell-cat yelling obscenities and tearing at herself.' He looked pleadingly at Elizabeth. 'You do believe me, don't you. Tell me you believe me, Lizzie.'

Elizabeth replied softly, 'Of course I believe you, James.' Then she said, 'So, the girl had become hysterical accusing you of trying to rape her. By this time you'd pulled into the side of the road and were trying to calm her down, yes?'

James's eyes grew large and filled with tears again. 'But nothing I did seemed to work. She was yelling and screaming like a mad woman. She was spitting and ripping at herself and me, as though fending off a real rapist.'

'So you tried to quieten her?'

James sighed heavily, 'There's only so much screaming and hysteria a person can take and I suppose I just snapped. I reached out to put my hand over her mouth and then next thing I remember is her bulging eyes and her tongue sticking out like that...' James mimicked the face of a hanged man. 'It was obscene.'

James ran both hands through his unkempt hair. 'When you read about people being frozen in horror, it sounds a cliche. But that's exactly how it was for me. I was petrified. God knows how long I sat there with this...thing next to me, like something from the Chamber of Horrors.'

'And you're absolutely sure the girl was dead? She couldn't have fainted?' James shook his head. 'I tried to find her pulse, but there was nothing there.'

'So, what happened next?'

'I suppose instinct took over. I just wanted this obscenity

out of my sight. So, I waited until there were no cars around and opened the passenger door and she just fell out.

'I tossed her handbag and umbrella out after her and drove home as if the hounds of Hell were after me.'

He flicked a look across the table. His wife's face was full of compassion for his ordeal. He shook his head. 'I can't take it in. I keep thinking I'm going to wake up in a minute with my biggest problem being the next dreary constituency surgery.'

His dark brown eyes took on a look of longing. 'Right now, I'd swop a hundred years of that tedium just to put the clock back 24 hours.'

James watched as Elizabeth, a slender and dark-haired woman, paced the same area of the floor he had earlier. As she walked she folded her arms and hunched her shoulders in an attitude of deep thought. Through their 16 years of marriage, he thought, she had always been there for him. His rock. And he had never needed her more than last night when he had arrived home a blubbering, incoherent wreck.

After piecing his ravings together she had given him two of her sleeping tablets and, eventually, he had fallen into a fitful sleep. She had been there this morning, when he had awoken to realise the horrific images in his head were not the product of a nightmare.

One moment of madness and all their lives were changed for ever.

James was brought out of his introspection by the sight of his wife, who had stopped her pacing and was now looking determinedly across the table at him.

'I haven't changed my mind, James. For your own sake, as well as mine, Daniel and Sarah's, you've got to pretend last night never happened. Telling the police won't bring the girl back. And you and I both know it was a terrible accident. No less so than if you'd knocked her over when she jumped out at you.'

James gazed at his wife uncertainly and whispered, 'I'll never get away with it.'

'Why not? Think about it James. A dark night in the rain. A lonely road. No-one would have heard or seen anything. The girl was a stranger with nothing to connect you with her at all. You just happened to be the unlucky victim of time and place. Now that girl is dead, probably because of drugs if the truth were known.'

James shook his head, still unconvinced. 'If I don't go to the police now, and later they find something to connect the girl to me, they're bound to assume the worst. You and I know it was an accident but if I was caught trying to cover it up, I could face a murder charge.'

'But what could they find to connect her to you? First, they've got to have a reason for even questioning you. And even if they did as a matter of routine, there's absolutely nothing to link you to what everyone will assume was the murder of a hitch-hiker whose body was driven to a quiet road in the middle of nowhere before being dumped.'

His wife's analysis had a certain logic. For the first time the fears that clouded James's face began to lift. 'Do you really think I could get away with it?'

His wife nodded. 'I don't think we have any alternative. If you went to the police, like the honest upright public figure you are, it would be headlines in every newspaper in the country within hours.

'You know what hypocrites people are. They'd say there's no smoke without fire. The tabloids would crucify you, even though you're innocent. You'd be finished as a politician. Everything we've both worked for since before we were married would be in ruins. And think of the effect on the children. No, it's unthinkable. We must keep our nerve and pretend it never happened.'

Four

Tessa Jordan, The Examiner's first woman editor, stared without enthusiasm at her screen. The computer image of tomorrow's lacklustre front page matched her mood exactly, she thought.

Last night's row with Josh had drained all her energy and she could not shake off a feeling of impending doom. Both her professional and personal lives were out of control and heading for disaster.

Reluctantly, she dragged her attention back to her monitor. There were two holes yet to be filled before Sunday's paper could be put to bed. Par for the course for a Saturday morning.

Sometimes, when there was a running story, they would keep changing the entire layout right up to the deadline, with contract staff in remote print rooms in Manchester, Edinburgh and Plymouth grumbling about working unpaid overtime. She reflected that before modern computer technology it would have been the distribution department panicking about lost rail connections. The sooner they went fully on-line the better, she thought. At least they could update stories on a minute by minute basis. As it was she had to juggle both versions without giving one undue advantage over the other.

But today they had their lead and it was only a piece under the shoulder and a bottom double that was missing. She looked again at the splash: PALACE DENIES ROYAL RIFT said the headline. Beneath it was a piece by Hubert Treglown, their Royalty Correspondent, rehashing the ritual response which had followed the story in today's Century.

The trouble was, there was nothing in The Examiner's follow-up to distinguish it from any of the other Sunday papers. The tabloids would scream all kinds of sensational nonsense to gain an edge on their rivals. Meanwhile the more sober broadsheets, hers included, would rake over the entrails and pontificate soberly. All very dull.

And there, she thought, was the rub. She was not providing the inspiration to her staff or readers that made for a unique, circulation-building formula. She'd had the job for just over a year and in that time sales had drifted down from 320,000 to 280,000.

She had given it her best shot, but she was failing. Any time now one of El Supremo's hatchet men would summon her to the Penthouse Suite and hand her the dreaded, brown envelope.

And at home things weren't any better. Poor Josh. She had given him a hard time again last night. And it really wasn't his fault. It was the old cliche of incompatible personalities. She was the strong one and he was the charming, but feckless, weakling. How she longed, at times, for their roles to be reversed.

Wouldn't it be wonderful, she pondered, if he, just once, announced he had booked a theatre and a meal and would brook no argument. Whatever engagement she was obliged to attend in her official capacity, he demanded she spent a romantic evening with him instead.

But Josh wasn't like that. He was quite content to defer to her requirements. To drift along in his job as a sales executive with a Mercedes distributor, which meant he earned large commissions for little actual effort. She grinned to herself. If you worked for Mercedes, you were a sales executive. No doubt at a Ford distributers, you would be a plain old second-hand car salesman.

She and Josh rubbed along together in a comfortable sort of way but she now knew he wasn't what the real, deep-down Tessa needed. Which was someone strong and confident enough in himself to be able to take her into his arms and reassure her. To tell her that, however high she rose, or low she fell, she was loved for her own sake. And that he would always be there.

But that wasn't Josh's style. And, to be fair, she was probably a domineering bitch at heart and would resent someone else telling her what to do. She sighed heavily. Bloody hormones, she thought.

Her introspection was interrupted by the arrival of Frank Dutton, the one colleague she trusted and could count as a true friend. His air of calm assurance was a balm to her troubled spirit.

He closed the office door shutting out the Press-day cacophony of shouted conversations and clacking keyboards in the newsroom. 'By the look on your face you're indulging in a bout of mental self-flagellation again,' he said looking in a fatherly way over his half-moon glasses.

Tessa smiled up at her news editor weakly. 'Is it that obvious? I was actually wondering whether I'd be clearing my desk before, or after, I had no-one to go home to.'

'Another bust-up?'

' 'fraid so. And I feel so guilty because it's always my fault.

I get so frustrated with Josh's un-fazability that I end up trying to goad him into anger - just to convince myself that we're both still alive. Does that sound crazy?'

Frank grinned in sympathy. 'Well if it is then half the couples in London are mad as well.'

Tessa said reflectively, 'Lots of women would be only too happy to have someone like him. He's reliable, faithful - I think - he makes me laugh and he's good in bed. What more could I want?'

Frank replied drily, 'What indeed?'

'But, I suppose because I play "Ms Irondrawers" here all day, I need to go home to someone who...well...I can be myself with. Instead, with Josh, I end up making all the decisions for him too.'

Frank was about to say something when Tessa burst out, 'And he's so...so damned...shallow. Last Sunday I was in the middle of some soul-bearing outpourings on relationships when, just when I thought I had got through to him, he stopped me in mid sentence, looked at his watch and leapt out of the kitchen yelling he'd missed the first five minutes of Match of the Day. I wouldn't mind but he was recording it anyway.'

Frank smothered a smile. 'Sounds fairly typical of what passes for connubial bliss. You two really ought to get married.'

Tess flicked a stray strand of hair back behind her ear. 'I'm not ready for that again. I tried it once and found I preferred my face the way it is - not re-arranged according to the whims of a psychopath.' Tessa expelled her breath in a long sigh. 'And, besides, the real me is scared of making a commitment...' She eyed Frank sardonically '...But, at the same time, afraid of ending up a dessicated old maid. Am I ever going to sort myself out?'

Frank gave her a considered stare. 'Of course you are. You're young yet. There's plenty of time. Things'll work out. Meantime, you've got enough to worry about here.'

Tessa grimaced. 'You're right, of course. Stop being self-indulgent, Tessa, and get on with the job you're paid for - albeit for not much longer. Sorry, Frank, it's only one of my moods. I shouldn't dump on you like this but it's comforting to talk to a wise old owl.' She added brightly, 'Every crazy, mixed-up kid should have a Frank.'

Frank grinned and wagged a finger at his boss. 'I won't disagree about the wise, but less of the old if you don't mind. I may be pushing sixty but to the Ancient Greeks I would have been in my prime.'

Tessa adroitly switched the subject. 'And I wouldn't mind betting the Ancient Greeks could have knocked up a better front page than we've managed to. Haven't we got anything better for a splash than a Palace Press Release re-write?'

Frank scratched his thinning hair. 'It's what the great unwashed'll be Facebooking and tweeting, or even talking about in the saloon bars of Britain tomorrow.'

'I know, Frank. But they won't be talking about the sensational new angle in The Examiner. Is there nothing else happening that we can go for instead of all this Royalty mush?'

'Well, there is something coming in from a stringer at the moment, on a body being found in Wiltshire. But, on the face of it, it sounds pretty routine. A bog standard murder these days might just about make a par on an inside page so I can't see it displacing the Harry and Meghan show.'

Tessa leaned forward and tapped a few commands into her terminal. Immediately, a story filed via a freelance's laptop 80 miles away, scrolled onto the screen. The details were sparse. The body of a girl, believed to be a hitch-hiker, had been discovered in a ditch in a lonely lane in Wiltshire.

As Tessa read on she began to experience a growing interest. The local police had handed over the investigation to Scotland Yard who had sent a top detective and a forensic scientist to examine the body. This was no run-of-the-mill death, she thought. If the Yard had been called in, it had to be something special.

Abruptly she made a decision. 'Frank, I'm going to put the royal stuff in as second lead. Get me as much as you can on this body. We'll run with that at the top tomorrow. If nothing else, we'll at least be different.'

Frank's grey eyes glimmered with amusement. 'It's the ability to take just such bold decisions that's got you where you are today, while we play-it-safe old stagers can only gape in admiration.'

He leapt through the door and closed it behind him before Tessa's rubber stressbuster could hit its target.

Five

Delicately for such a big man Dr Hamish Jackson, Senior Pathologist at the Metropolitan Police Forensic Science Laboratory, lifted the corner of the blue plastic sheet.

'Death was due to asphyxiation caused by strangulation,' he said formally. 'The body was face down in the ditch. I had to get the lads to lift it out before I could make my examination.'

Lockyer and Claire Bishop peered down. The girl's top half was covered in mud while her legs were scarcely marked, making the corpse seem like two disconnected parts of a mannequin fitted clumsily together. The bulging eyes and protruding tongue were testament to the victim's fight for oxygen in the last seconds of life.

'Definitely murder then, Hamish?'

'Oh yes, Jack. No doubt about it. It looks as though the hyoid bone, at the base of the tongue, has been crushed. And with considerable force I'd say.'

'Anything else?'

'Well, she was not virgo intacta. Which is, of course, nothing unusual these days. But, judging by the state of her clothing, and the finger and thumb marks around her throat, I'd hazard a guess that she'd been raped, strangled and then dumped here - most probably from a vehicle. Unfortunately, there are no tyre marks. But, I'll be able to tell you more when I get her back to the lab.'

'When did she die?'

'I'd estimate no less than 12 hours ago and no more than 18.'

'Which means she was dumped here somewhere between 6 o'clock and midnight last night.'

Sgt Claire Bishop noticed the girl's clothes. Expensive. The sort of gear you would wear to impress: ivory hipster, bootleg-cut trousers and matching flared jacket over a black, figure-hugging shirt. On the feet were patent-leather, high-heeled, court shoes.

When alive the girl would have turned the head of every man in the room. In death she had been transformed into a repulsive carcase, a balloon face partially veiled by a curtain of lank hair. One arm was still raised, as if reaching for the large golfing umbrella, which was in the ditch a few feet away. Claire shivered.

Hamish opened the girl's handbag, the ivory leather now smeared with mud. 'I'm no detective, Jack, but I'd say you can rule out robbery.' He pointed at a roll of banknotes, held together with an elastic band. 'All twenties. I'd say there's at least a thousand there.'

Carefully, his gloved fingers reached in and pulled out a screwed-up piece of writing paper. 'Another clue for you. This was tucked among the usual female accoutrements.'

Hamish smoothed the wrinkles with his thumbs and held the sheet out for Jack to read. Jack's brows knitted as he recited out loud. 'PA 4PM.' He stooped to look at the other side. It was blank. Hamish popped it into a polythene bag and sealed the top. 'I'll do the usual tests to see if there are any other significant indentations, but I doubt it. I'd guess that this was ripped from a notepad after someone had jotted down the time and place of a meeting.'

Lockyer repeated, 'PA 4PM. Could be a time and place - '

- 'Or it could be a person's initials and a time,' suggested Claire.

Jack folded his arms and stroked his moustache. 'Hmmm. Could mean anything at this stage. First things first, though. We'd better find out who she is.'

Lockyer looked around him. The rain had stopped and a watery sun was breaking through the clouds. The area had been cordoned off by Wiltshire police whose senior officer in attendance was hovering, waiting for a word. Jack moved across to speak to him.

The local man greeted his colleague from the Met with a friendly grin. 'Hello, sir. I'm the Investigating Officer. I don't suppose you remember me but I first met you at Bramshill. I was on the sergeants' course and you were lecturing us on your favourite theme...' He screwed up his eyes, trying to remember. '...I've got it: you called it "Perspiration is better than inspiration".'

Jack looked the speaker up and down. He couldn't place him at all. But then it had been a long time ago. Out of politeness he said, 'I seem to remember your face.'

'Passmore, Keith Passmore. I'm an Inspector now with Wiltshire CID.'

'My pontifications didn't blight your career, then?' Jack said drily.

Passmore replied enthusiastically, 'They weren't pontifications, sir. Not from the man who cracked the-bodies-in-the-trunk case, or collared the Thief-row Airport Mob. You may not realise it, sir, but us younger coppers held you in awe.'

'You make me sound like Methuselah. I'm only 48 now and couldn't have been more than 34 then. Incidentally, no need for the "sir", we're the same rank.'

Passmore shifted uneasily. 'OK...er...Jack.' He laughed. 'It still doesn't seem right. You were pretty well a legend, you know.'

'I still am, Keith,' Lockyer said wryly. 'But these days more in my own lunchtime, as it were.'

Passmore looked at Jack for a moment. Then he said diffidently, 'We were all really cut up about what happened to Mrs Lockyer.' He added fiercely, 'What a bloody waste.' Lockyer laid a hand on the other man's shoulder. 'I appreciate your sentiments, Keith. I know they're sincerely meant.'

Any awkwardness either felt was dispelled by the arrival of Claire at Lockyer's side. After introducing the two, her chief said briskly, 'Right. Down to business. What can you tell me about this body, Keith?'

'Well sir...Jack...it was spotted early this morning by a postman. As he drove his van past he saw the legs sticking out of the ditch. At first he thought some weirdo had dumped a shop window dummy there. When he had a closer look he pretty near fainted on the spot.'

'Not surprising. Then what?'

'He dialled 112 on his mobile. We got here in half an hour by which time we had orders that the case was being taken over by the Yard and to touch nothing until you arrived. The Chief Super was not best pleased, I can tell you.'

'Hmmm, curious that. Where did the orders come from?'

'Must have been from pretty high up; Commander at least.'

'And you've no idea who the dead woman was?'

Passmore shrugged. 'Not a clue.'

'OK Keith. Soon as Hamish is finished here, we'll leave you in peace. If you get any enquiries from the media refer them to me. Meanwhile, if we come up with anything, I'll keep you informed personally.'

Passmore's face brightened. 'I'd appreciate that. Thank you Jack.' He added confidingly, 'I bet you didn't know this but the Wiltshire Force is the only one in the country with a 100 per cent clear-up rate for murder.

'That's why my bosses are pretty pissed off about the Yard taking things out of our hands. In fact, between you and me, they told me to keep a handle on what's going on. So if we can liaise, that'll keep them happy and out of your hair.'

'Consider it done, Keith. And I'll do my best to maintain your record. I'll be in touch.'

On the way back to London, Claire did the driving leaving Lockyer to gaze unseeing out of the car window. Occasionally he glanced at his young assistant. Attractive girl, he mused. Bright smile, laughing eyes. And one of the new breed of fast-track graduate recruits, so nobody's fool.

Twenty years ago she was the sort who would have intimidated him. He would have been tongue-tied by her self-confidence. After an inept attempt to engage her in conversation, he would have given up and slunk off, leaving her to flirt with more brash companions.

As they passed the M4/M25 intersection she broke the silence. 'Any early thoughts, sir?'

'I'd like to hear yours, Claire.'

'Well sir the first thing that strikes me is that she was no hitch-hiker picked up randomly by a homicidal motorist.'

'Go on.'

'For a start, she wasn't dressed for thumbing a lift. The

sort of outfit she was wearing was more suited to displaying her best assets under soft lights and even softer music. Not standing in the rain hoping for a passing motorist to take pity on her.'

Lockyer nodded. 'So..?'

'So I think she had a date and whoever it was with killed her.'

'But why dump her body by the side of a road where it was bound to be seen? Why not drive it to some woods and bury it, or at least drag it into the undergrowth?'

'Because, sir, our killer wasn't thinking straight. He was in a state of high emotion; maybe anger or even panic. So, as soon as he realises she's dead he chucks her out of his car and drives off.'

'Hmmm...There's something else that backs up your non-hitchhiker theory too. It was raining and blowing a gale all evening yesterday. Yet, she wasn't wearing a raincoat, or any wet weather gear. The only thing she had was a brolly...'

'...Which suggests she only expected to be walking to and from a car in the rain...'

'...Which, in turn, suggests she was driven to the locale by the killer.'

'But why that particular spot, sir? I mean it's on the road to nowhere.'

'Well, it's not far from the M4. The driver could have been looking for somewhere quiet to...er...press his attentions...'

'But it still seems an odd place, sir. I mean, a quiet lane yes. But it's so narrow that any vehicle coming along would have had to manoeuvre carefully past. Not the ideal sort of place for uninterrupted passion.'

'So, Sergeant Bishop, are you suggesting that whoever

dumped her there had already killed her and just wanted a quiet place to push her out of the car?'

Claire shook her head. 'I really don't know. There are so many things that don't add up.'

Lockyer said, 'How about this for an explanation? Our victim has her assignation, her soft lights, etc. But, on her way home, has a row with the boyfriend who turfs her out of his car in high dudgeon. And that's why she's forced to thumb a lift from a friendly motorist. Only the motorist is not so friendly. He makes advances to her. She rebuffs them. He rapes her and then strangles her to cover his tracks?'

'That doesn't ring true. It's too pat.'

'I agree,' Lockyer acknowledged good-humourdly. 'Thank God for forensic science, that's all I can say. Hamish will point us in the right direction. In the meantime, try to crack the code of PA 4PM - it's got to mean something. And something significant, I wouldn't mind betting.'

Six

Anyone attempting to listen in to Tom Ginsberg's transat phone conversation would have heard a meaningless Donald Duck squawking.

The encrypted satellite link had been installed specially for 'Operation Dunkirk,' a codeword suggested half-jokingly by some wit in the CIA's Department of Overseas Intelligence which had stuck.

Ginsberg, the DOI's Deputy Director, was finding it difficult to conceal his elation. His window in the Langley Headquarters looked out across acres of Virginia parkland and in his mind he fantasised a switch to the White House lawns and the scenes of celebration that would ensue there after he had brought off the biggest coup his service had achieved in its entire history.

There would be marquees, champagne, flunkies and the greatest gathering of dignitaries the world had ever known. They would be there to celebrate the end of a thousand years of British history and a new beginning for a nation plucked from the quagmire of Europe.

At least that's how Robert Pelham was supposed to perceive it. But the President, Sam McGovern, regarded it somewhat differently. He had a different vision for so-called

Great Britain. But that was some way off - after a struggling and exhausted UK had been squeezed into submission. The first step, though, was Dunkirk.

But if 'Dunkirk' went wrong, thought Ginsberg, he and the operation would be disowned. He would be dubbed a renegade and thrown to the wolves. That was why he was keeping on top of Dresner's every move. Why he insisted on a daily briefing, even though some days there had been nothing to say. But, today? Today, Dresner's report sent a tremor of excitement, almost like a physical pain, humming through him.

'So, Harry, the old dame's finally admitted it?'

'Yeah. Meanwhile, Lancaster's got his finger up his ass and the Cabinet are sitting around like dummies.'

'But the way's open for Dunkirk?'

'Yup. The Man's all set. The timing's perfect.'

'I have to brief the President, so let me get this absolutely clear, so there are no mistakes. After Pelham's...er... neutralised Lancaster he takes over Number 10 and hits 'em with the Queen thing. He says it's the end of the line for the Monarchy and it's time to go for broke - become a republic and give Europe the finger at the same time?'

'Got it.'

Ginsberg said drily, 'But he doesn't, of course, go so far as to suggest himself as the first President of the Commonwealth of Great Britain?'

Dresner failed to detect the note of irony. 'Naw, the Brits ain't as up front as us. He'll talk about having greatness thrust upon him... He'll say the nation's standing at the crossroads of history...a tide in the affairs of man...awaiting the will of the people and all that crap...'

'And what is the will of the people, Harry?'

Dresner replied, 'Pelham's no fool, sir. He'll play on the

current mood like a violin virtuoso.'

Ginsberg controlled his irritation. 'And the current mood is..?'

'Exactly as the White House and Pelham predicted. Most people are totally pissed off with Royal freeloaders. And even more voters hate their balls being squeezed by Johnnie Foreigner across the Channel.'

'So our man thinks they'll jump at the chance of closer links with Uncle Sam. Even if it's only to put two fingers up to the Krauts?'

'That's how we read it, sir.'

A confederation of two republics, united by a common heritage, Ginsberg mused. It was all coming good. He could see the union flag and the stars and stripes fluttering together over the White House now.

'Sir..? Sir..? Are you still there?'

'Sorry, Harry. I was just thinking. It seems OK so far. But, it all depends on Lancaster's...er...retirement. How goes that?'

'All in hand.' Dresner laughed humourlessly, 'He doesn't know it yet but those eyes of his are gonna be the death of him.'

Ginsberg frowned at the phone. 'There's going to be one Hell of a schemozzle. Are we buttoned down real tight on this, Harry? I mean, Extreme Prejudice involving the British Prime Minister. Is Pelham solid?'

Dresner hastily reassured his chief. 'No worries, sir, honest. Pelham's a cold-hearted mother with an Intel processor where his feelings should be. And we've planned everything from the dosage to the autopsy. We've supplied Pelham with the "how" and the "what". All he's got to do is put the "when" into his schedule.'

Ginsberg still wasn't happy. 'Is there no other way, Harry?

Can't the old guy be persuaded just to hand over to his deputy?'

'No chance. For one thing Lancaster hates Pelham. He only made him his Number Two because the suits told him it was the only way to hold the Party together. And for another the dumb-ass has a sense of duty. The only way to shift him out of Number 10 is in a casket.'

Ginsberg sighed. 'OK, I guess we've got no alternative. But you know if anything goes wrong you're on your own?'

Dresner said grimly, 'I guess you've made that pretty clear, sir.'

'Good. Now, what about the other pretenders?'

'All gagged.'

'Including Mr Snow?'

'Especially Mr Snow.'

'Harry, don't be cryptic. This is a secure line. Paint me the picture.'

'Sorry sir. Well, we'd set up the trusted "in car rape scenario" but the stupid bastard killed her.'

'Jesus H. How?'

'Strangled. Then he must have panicked and dumped the body. When I first went back to pick her up, the car was parked with its lights off. I made one pass, waited a while and then turned round and went back. By the time I got there, the car was gone and she was lying in this ditch bug-eyed, blue in the face and very dead.'

The elation Ginsberg had felt earlier evaporated and a cold fist clutched at his stomach. This was not part of the plan. It could bring all kinds of complications out of the woodwork. Jesus H, it could even screw up Dunkirk.

He kept his voice steady. 'I know I don't usually ask for the sordid details of your activities, Harry, but I think you'd better fill me in on this. And start at the beginning.'

Dresner's exasperated sigh was compressed by the transponders and signal boosters on the satellite's up and down links and lost in a hiss of static. 'Sir, there's absolutely nothing to worry about. It'll work out even better than we planned...'

'...Dresner, shoot...'

'Ok, Ok. It's like this. We'd been using a couple of high-class hookers in the usual honey-trap operation.' He added with a note of wonder in his voice, 'It's the oldest trick in the book but they still fall for it. Anyway, we got enough on Ingleby, Willis and Sinclair to take them out of the picture.

'But Mr Snow was different. No skeletons, no money troubles, a happy home life, no obliging "researcher" tucked away somewhere in Bayswater. In short, the kinda guy to give politicians a good name. So we had to adopt a more...um...pro-active initiative - '

' - Get to the point, Harry.'

'We wanted him on a hook not even the Pope could wriggle off. So, we set up one of our girls to hitch a lift and then cry rape. The idea was she'd grab something in the car like a glove or handkerchief, which could be used as evidence against her attacker.

'Then, after ripping her own clothes in a frenzy, she'd jump out looking like she'd done a couple of rounds with a fairground wrestler. Just as a friendly motorist – me - happened by. She'd scream "take me to the cops" or some such and we'd beat it into the night...'

'...Meanwhile,' suggested Ginsberg coldly, 'our Good Samaritan realises immediately it's all a set-up, goes straight to the cops, and blows our plans out of the water.'

'Wrong, sir. Yeah, he knows it's a phoney deal all right, but he also sees all the headlines and his career going down the john. He knows whichever way he jumps, he's in the shit. Besides, it would be her word against his and in these PC days the presumption always favours the woman...'

'So, he waits for the sky to fall in on him..?'

'Which, sir, he later discovers won't happen because his friends in high places have put a lid on his unfortunate lapse...'

'...which lid will stay on so long as he does as he's told? As you say, Harry, crude but effective. So, what went wrong?'

'Nothing - for us. It was a bonus. I dropped her off just ahead of the target. She waved him down as arranged, got in his car and then...the long goodnight.'

Ginsberg winced at Dresner's movie slang. 'Sherborne's not the killer type, surely?'

'I wouldn't have said so. But you can never tell. Maybe he panicked. Maybe he flipped. Maybe he enjoyed throttling the life out of her. Who knows?'

Ginsberg swung away from the window and stared into the darker interior of his office. 'What I do know, Harry, is this is a serious departure from the plan. Presumably Sherborne's not going to be stupid enough to confess?'

'No sir. We predict the poor bastard'll keep his mouth shut and his head down. As I said, it should work even better for us. We know he's a killer. But he doesn't know we know. To him it's just one of those crazy things life throws at you.

'When he thinks he's got away with it, we'll play our ace and he'll come on side, with the rest of his people thrown in, as an enthusiastic supporter of Pelham's vision of a new Britain.'

'Hmmm, sounds all very well in theory. But, aren't you forgetting one thing: the cops. What if they track Sherborne down? Everything could unravel.'

'Unlikely, sir. You see Pelham got the case transferred from the local police to Scotland Yard -

' - Scotland Yard? Is he crazy? Aren't they supposed to be the best there is?'

'Yeah. But this crime's gonna stay un-busted. Guaranteed.'

Ginsberg sighed heavily down the phone. 'You're now going to tell me that Pelham's got the Metropolitan Police Commissioner in his pocket, too.'

'Er...no sir. But the next best thing. Don't forget, Operation Dunkirk's been Pelham's obsession for 30 years - ever since the Thatcher brand of British Nationalism got swamped by the wimps and fudgers. He might be, ideologically, on the other side of the fence from Thatcherism, but he's one hundred percent against an EU federal superstate - just like Maggie.'

Ginsberg contained his impatience as Dresner got into his stride. 'In fact, in 1986, there was actually a majority in the Labour camp who wanted to pull out of the EEC. While some have swum with the tide since then, Pelham's never wavered.

'Now he sees himself as a New Messiah offering to free an increasingly disillusioned electorate from, as they see it, a fresh onslaught orchestrated by the Krauts.'

'...Yes, yes, Harry. Let's drop the history lesson, shall we? What's all that to do with the cops and this homicide?'

'Sorry, chief. It's just that Pelham's spent years salting away any dirt he could find on anyone who might be useful to him when the revolution came. One of his finds was a Superintendent Forsyth at Scotland Yard, who was on the take. So he kept the file in his drawer for a rainy day.'

Dresner added with satisfaction, 'The guy's now a Commander and the rainy day's come. Result: Pelham calls all the shots on the dead hooker case. So he's got Mr Snow by the balls.'

Ginsberg shook his head in admiration. 'Jeez, that guy

Pelham's something else. OK, Harry, I'm convinced. But keep on top of developments. I want to know the second there's a problem.'

Dresner replied, 'You've got it, sir. But there won't be.'

Seven

'Jack, I'm begging you. When I left, our entire print room were singing "Why are we waiting." Meanwhile, I'm trying to cobble together something different on this body-in-the-ditch story before they all down tools and bugger off.'

Lockyer smiled. He liked Frank Dutton. His terrier-like tenacity could be irritating. And sometimes, in order to stay one step ahead in the cut-throat media jungle he inhabited, he would occasionally give a sensational spin to the facts.

But despite these blemishes Frank had integrity. Which made a change these days, Lockyer thought. And, in all the 20 years he had known the journalist, Lockyer had never heard him swear. Quite a novelty for a veteran of the old Fleet Street. So his lapse just then, Jack reflected, was a mark of Dutton's desperation.

Jack looked across his desk at the worried figure slumped in a chair opposite. Frank was staring at him beseechingly over his glasses. Jack had just received the pathologist's preliminary report when his old sparring-partner had walked through his door.

Claire had offered to drop Jack off at Putney, but he had preferred the Yard. There was some company there, despite the usual weekend skeleton staffing. And he could get a head start on this investigation which was becoming more intriguing by the minute.

'...So, if you've got anything new, Jack, anything at all...I just need something I can hang an exclusive tag on. Your Press Office has handed out its usual verbiage. Covers a page but says nothing we haven't already had from our stringer on the spot.'

'You know I can't show favouritism towards any member of the media, Frank,' Lockyer said with mock severity. He picked up the file in front of him. 'However, I have only just had the forensic report which does add a few details we didn't have before. And, since you've taken the initiative to be here...Well, I can't help it if your colleagues haven't seen fit to do the same.'

'Jack, you're a gent. So, what've you got?'

Jack opened the file and flicked through Hamish's notes, written in ink in a meticulous hand. How long would it be before even Hamish was obliged to input his findings direct onto a memory stick? Jack wondered. Knowing Hamish, probably never.

Hamish was nearing retirement and was not likely to bother now with new technology which, he had openly confessed once over a pint, he found incomprehensible. Jack shrugged to himself. But what Hamish lacked in keyboard skills he made up for in experience.

Jack decided to give Frank Dutton a few tidbits but for the time being he would keep to himself the screwed-up paper containing the cryptic message. And there was something else about the report which puzzled him. He would salt that away for later as well.

He scanned a copy of the Yard's official Press Release. He could see why Frank was frustrated. Body of a young woman...postman on his early-morning rounds...ditch in Wiltshire...no identity as yet...believed to have been the victim of a serious sexual assault before being murdered...death by asphyxiation...Appeal for any witness who might have seen anything suspicious.

Nothing about the roll of banknotes. Or the man's glove which SOCO had found half submerged in the ditch. And certainly no mention of the mysterious scrap of paper. Which was not surprising, as Lockyer had held those snippets back when briefing the public relations people.

'I can add a few details to this,' he told Frank. 'For instance the victim was a good-looking woman. Her handbag contained £1,000 in used notes and a man's black, leather, left-hand glove was found near the scene.'

'Phew! A thousand quid? So that rules out robbery?'

Jack nodded. 'Which fits in with our theory that the girl knew her attacker. She's not likely to have risked being alone with a strange man with that kind of money on her.'

'Unless, of course, the man himself gave it to her,' suggested Frank.

'Then why leave it behind? No, the man didn't know of the money. And we know it's a man because of the glove. We believe at the moment that the couple had arranged to meet -

' - a lovers' tryst. Gets better and better - '

' - I didn't say that. Who knows what the meeting was for? But, the girl got into the car, was driven to a lonely spot where she was murdered. Or perhaps she was murdered and then driven to a lonely spot...'

'...A layby?'

'No, that's the puzzling thing. The body was dumped by the side of a narrow lane with hardly enough room for two cars to pass. Not the sort of place conducive to romance if other road users are trying to squeeze through all the time.'

'So, more likely the driver chose that spot just to throw the girl out of the car?'

Lockyer nodded. 'Possibly. Or he simply panicked, opened the car door and shoved her body out. Also, the state of the girl's clothes would suggest she'd been involved in a lengthy struggle which, if it took place in the aforesaid conspicuous place, must have happened unexpectedly.'

Frank tapped his teeth with his pen. 'This thousand quid, Jack. Could there be a drugs connection?'

'No evidence so far. No traces in her body or handbag.'

Dutton checked the tape on his pocket recorder to make sure it was still running. 'Let me see if I've got this right. A beautiful woman is raped - '

Lockyer held up his hand. 'According to the lab report, not necessarily raped. There was evidence of recent intercourse but that might not have been an actual rape.'

'But, it's more than likely?' Persisted Frank. Jack shrugged.

'Ok...A sex murder anyway. And money was found in her handbag and a man's glove nearby. Where, exactly, was the body found?'

Jack prodded a map he had just stuck on the wall behind him. 'Just about...there. One of the back roads north of Hungerford.'

'Who uses this particular lane?'

Jack peered more closely at the villages and hamlets within a five-mile radius. 'I suppose anyone who lives in Foxton, Garford, Chilton Foliat or Hinton Magna.' At his mention of the last name, Frank squawked. 'Hinton Magna. That's where James Sherborne lives. You know? Sherborne, darling of the Right, Europhobe and scourge of the Social Democrats' Front Bench.'

Lockyer shot Dutton a warning look. 'You can't tie him in with this. It's just a pure accident of geography that his home happens to be in the vicinity of a homicide.'

'That's as maybe, Jack. But to a journalist it's manna from heaven. The body of a strangled woman found just a few miles from the front door of a political high-flyer who's always on the box about law and order and the Socialists being the criminal's friend. It's too good to miss, my old mate.

'Anyway, I bet he'll love it. It'll give him another chance to bang on in the House about..."The curse of a violent society afflicting even my own corner of this once green and pleasant land"...'

Jack sighed. What was he thinking earlier about integrity? 'Well I can't tell you how to write your story I suppose.' He took a photograph out of Hamish's file and flicked it across the desk. 'This should add to its impact though.' Dutton stared at the picture. It was the sort of likeness you would get from a passport photo-booth. It showed a lovely but expressionless face.

Jack explained. 'That's the girl. The picture was taken in the morgue and photoshopped by the lab. It's the best we can do in the circumstances. There was nothing in the girl's handbag to identify her, so we hope someone'll see your paper and recognise her. And, it might jolt a few people, particularly the murderer, into the bargain.'

Frank whistled. 'Now, that's what I call an exclusive. Thanks Jack. All I need now is a quick quote from Sherborne and we've got ourselves a very respectable front page.'

'SEX MURDER RIDDLE AND A TOP TORY.' James Sherborne's hands shook as he picked The Examiner off the pile of Sunday papers scattered on the doormat.

Elizabeth peered over his shoulder. She had been dreading this moment. All day yesterday she had been propping James up as he flagged under the weight of fear and depression. Sarah and Daniel were used to their father's wildly swinging moods and had thought nothing of his irascibility. They had both taken themselves off and had only appeared at mealtimes.

But Elizabeth had been there while James alternated between elation and despondency. At first, as each hour passed and there had been no call from the police, James had become more confident. He had even managed a laugh with the kids over lunch.

They had all collapsed into giggles at Daniel's earnestness in declaiming: 'Dad will be Prime Minister one day.'

Elizabeth smiled to herself. It had been this unswerving, childlike faith that had inspired the children's Christmas present to their father several years previously. Daniel and Sarah spent months saving their pocket money until they had £20. Elizabeth had not told them she had been obliged to add another £200 to it in order to secure the finished product.

But, it had been worth it. James had been beside himself with pride. He had threatened to go back up to London there and then and drive up and down outside the Commons just so other MP's might see it. Now, it had become part of the folk-lore of the House.

So, lunch had been fun. But later, when James had heard the local radio news bulletin announcing Scotland Yard had taken over the Wiltshire body-in-the-ditch murder enquiry, he had plunged into despair again.

The only newspaper to have rung him was The Examiner. The reporter asked him if he had any message for the Home

Secretary now that the tentacles of violent crime had reached almost to his own quiet back yard. Once again Elizabeth admired her husband's chameleon ability to shed one persona and adopt another.

As soon as he knew it was a journalist at the other end of the phone, James had discarded his mood of dejection and had become the commanding, confident MP. He was appalled by the incident. It was another human tragedy resulting from the government's inept handling of the crime and punishment issue. He was saddened that even his own, rural idyll had now been invaded by the obscenity of murder.

Now, Elizabeth noticed, Mr Hyde had replaced Dr Jekyl and James was shaking all over. His lips were moving silently as he read and re-read the story. A picture of the dead girl stared out of the page. Elizabeth reached out and steadied the juddering paper.

She read, 'The body of a beautiful young woman was found in a Wiltshire ditch yesterday, just a few miles from the country home of Shadow Cabinet member James Sherborne, tipped by some as a future leader of the Conservative Party.

'The girl, aged about 20, had been raped and strangled. Police believe her attacker was the driver of a car in which the victim had been a passenger. They speculate the couple might have met earlier in the evening and later had a violent row in which the girl's clothes were ripped and she was forced to have sex.

'Among the victim's belongings was £1,000 in used notes which, say police, rules out robbery as the motive for the murder. Among other clues the police are examining is a man's left-hand black leather glove, found at the scene.

'The gruesome discovery of the girl's body was made by Clive Strutt, a postman on his early morning rounds...' The story went on to quote a breathless Mr Strutt explaining how he had first mistook the corpse for a mannequin. But when he had realised it was a dead person he had nearly fainted and fallen into the ditch himself.

The report went on, 'Mr Sherborne, MP for Thamesdown, whose Elizabethan estate is just five miles from the narrow country lane where the body was dumped, said last night that he was shocked and appalled. "It is a mark of the Socialists' failure to toughen their stance on crime, that this kind of human tragedy now invades even the quietest backwater,'" he said.

'He added, "I shall ensure the police spare no effort to bring the perpetrator to justice." Wiltshire Police have called in Scotland Yard and the investigation is now in the hands of Det Insp Jack Lockyer. After receiving a preliminary report from the Yard's forensic department he said that, despite the large sum of money found in the victim's handbag, there was no obvious drugs connection. "I believe this murder took place after an assignation between two people rather than a gangland killing," he said'.

The story went on, 'At present the girl's identity is a mystery. Police are appealing for anyone who might recognise the face printed on this page to come forward. They would also like to hear from anyone who may have seen anything suspicious in the vicinity of the A338, just north of Hungerford, on Friday night between 6pm and midnight.'

James looked up from the paper and stared with haunted eyes at his wife. 'Well, that's it. That bastard of a reporter has virtually accused me of committing the crime - '

' - Absolute rubbish. All he's done is embelish the scant details he's got by adding your name to the story.' Elizabeth added firmly, 'James, you must not be paranoid.'

James laughed harshly. 'Don't be paranoid, Eh? Look, it's alright for you, you're not the one in deep shit. Which ever way you look at it, this article clearly links my name with a girl found murdered. It's not going to require a giant leap of the imagination for someone to realise there might just be something in the theory.'

'James, you've got to stop this,' Elizabeth retorted angrily. 'You're distorting the meaning.' She waved her hand at The Examiner. 'All the reporter has done is capitalise on the co-incidence that James Sherborne, champion of stiffer penalties for violent crime, lives just a few miles from where such a violent crime apparently took place. It's nothing more nor less than that.'

James looked at her pleadingly. 'Do you really think so?'

'I'm sure of it.' Elizabeth took the paper and dropped it on the hall floor. Then she held James's hands and gazed searchingly into his eyes. 'You...we...must keep our nerve. The Examiner's story might result in a flurry of enquiries from the media, or even the police. But, that could work to our advantage. Once you're in their minds as the crusading politician, you'll be out of their thoughts as a suspect.'

James's face was flooded with relief but it was almost immediately replaced by an expression of hopelessness. 'But, what about the glove? One of mine must have fallen out when I opened the door of the car. They could trace it back to me.'

Elizabeth shook her head. 'I very much doubt it. Yesterday, I went over the car inch by inch and vacuumed it out. I found a button off your shirt and one glove. I guessed you'd lost the other, so I burned it. There's absolutely nothing to connect that young woman's death with you. Trust me, darling...'

Eight

The editor of Consolidated Media's ailing Examiner swallowed her last bite of toast, brushed the remnants from her nightdress and smiled determinedly. Josh Hamilton, Tessa Jordan's partner, who was sitting up in bed beside her, smiled back.

Tessa stretched and said, 'Ah, it's wonderful to have a whole day off. No phones, whingeing staff or Ben Hobart's apparatchiks lurking in sinister fashion.' Josh made a show of leaning over and looking under the bed. 'No, you're absolutely right. There's no-one there.'

Tessa screwed up her face and hit him with a pillow. 'Idiot. You know what I mean. What shall we do today?'

Josh shrugged. 'Anything you like. Whatever.'

'Oh, Josh, can't you just once make the decision?'

Uh-oh, thought Josh, here we go again. Everything he did or said recently seemed to get on Tessa's tits. Nothing seemed to please her. He felt a sadness inside that their love was slipping away.

Tessa looked at him sideways. She knew what he was thinking. Poor Josh. Living with her had become such a disillusioning experience. They had shared her flat in St John's Wood for nearly a year now. During that time she had come to realise that their relationship was going nowhere.

Their growing apart was probably all her fault, she reflected. In the first flush of their time together she had enjoyed Josh's easy-going attitude to life. He had been such a contrast to Oliver, her late and unlamented wife-beating husband. But, after a while, she had found Josh's laissez-faire nature an irritant. The more he tried to please her, the more irritated she got. God, but she was a bitch.

It was probably The Examiner that was doing it. She was so determined to show that a woman could be just as good an editor as a man, that she pushed herself to the limit and beyond. But she was not making the grade.

That made her angry with herself and angry at those around her. This, in turn, brought on the guilt and shame, which made her unhappy. And she had fallen into the habit of taking her unhappiness out on poor, blameless Josh. Hell!

And she also hated the way the job was turning her into a control freak. The free spirit had become a virago driven by the will to succeed and ruled by appointments, schedules, lists. And lists of lists. In short, she was beginning to hate herself.

Josh certainly did not deserve to suffer her moods. He was a good man. He was reliable, faithful and he made her laugh. But, was that enough to prop up the relationship for a lifetime? Probably not. Especially, as her self-loathing was causing increasing friction.

So, where did they go from here? She was 34, divorced, with a demoralising number of heartaches behind her and an increasing preoccupation with time's winged chariot.

Her future as an editor depended on the whim of Ben Hobart, El Supremo to his staff who, it was rumoured, had in mind cutting his losses with The Examiner and closing it down. Or simply publishing it exclusively on line thus cutting out the expense of printing and distribution. So, her career was as uncertain as her love life.

Josh's voice cut into her ruminations. 'You've got the best story on this body in the ditch...' He waved his hand at The Examiner's rivals scattered across their legs '...Not one of them's made the connection with Sherborne. And yours is the only paper mentioning a thousand quid in the girl's handbag and a man's glove found at the scene. Good stuff.'

'It's not bad is it? She agreed. 'But not enough to impress bloody Hobart. He doesn't care about the journalism; it's the bottom line with him. And The Examiner's bottom line is written in an unappealing ruddy hue at the moment, which means my "...Dear Tessa, it is with regret..." letter could appear on my executive desk any day now.'

Josh gazed at her uncertainly. 'Is he really as ruthless as people make out?'

'He'd chop off your hands if he thought it would save money on soap.'

'Charming fellow. But, I suppose you don't get where he is today without being ruthless and single-minded.'

Tessa put her plate on the bedside table, underneath her now empty teacup and saucer, and gestured at the litter of papers. She said grudgingly, 'I suppose you've got to hand it to him. From one clapped-out weekly newspaper in Sussex to global media tycoon in 25 years is going some.'

Tessa went on to explain to Josh that Ben Hobart - an ex-pat Australian - was now reckoned to be bigger than Rupert Murdoch with media interests in the States, Australia, Canada and Eastern Europe. Plus satellite and internet TV and radio.

His latest venture was in digital broadcasting. Tessa said sombrely, 'He's an extremely powerful man and the one figure governments and heads of state want to keep on the right side of. And at this moment he's probably licking down the flap on my brown envelope.'

Josh shook his head and grinned. 'He probably employs someone else to do his licking for him.' He hunched forward and drew his knees up to his chest. 'I wonder what makes people like him tick? With all that power and money what ambitions can he have left?'

'Oh, he's got ambitions all right. He fancies himself as a latter-day Cromwell and would love to see the end of the House of Windsor. He hates handed-down privilege and can't see why, because of an accident of birth, one person should lord it over everyone else. He's been campaigning on and off in his newspapers but he can't get enough politicians on his side to make it stick.'

Josh said, 'But, when the revolution does come, he'll be manning the tumbrils.'

Tessa snorted. 'More like pulling the handle on the guillotine. Except that's a French device and he wouldn't want to be seen approving of anything Continental.'

'Sorry?'

'Apart from power, money and being an anti-monarchist he's got one other obsession. That's the EU. He reckons turning the European Economic Community into the European Union was a bureacratic con-trick which nobody noticed until it was too late. He thinks Britain is far better off out of it and we editors have been instructed to take that line at every opportunity.'

'Do you mind?'

'What, toeing his line? Well, as it happens...' Tessa smiled crookedly '...and I would say this wouldn't I...I think he's got a point about Europe.'

'So, you go along with his "Sack the Queen" and Little

Englander views?'

'Well, not entirely. For instance, I believe the Queen's done a good job in her time. But, I think Charles has blown it. In fact, the antics of the Royal family from Charles down have lost the nation's respect. William and Kate have redressed the balance a bit but not quite enough. So, God knows what will happen when the Queen finally shuffles off...'

'Charles will become king, surely? You know...the king is dead, long live the king and all that...'

'Charles is not popular in the country. People either think he's a weird eccentric or plain bats. They're not eager to see him step into Her Majesty's shoes.'

'So could the succession rules be changed and William become King?'

Tessa shook her head. 'Hardly likely. The nation might just tolerate King Charles the Third as he's getting on a bit now and wouldn't be monarch for that long.'

Josh said, 'I suppose it would emphasise Britain's distinctiveness now that we're out of the EU. We can do our own thing and no-one to tell us otherwise.'

Tessa nodded. . 'I'm sure El Supremo would agree...'

'...El Supremo?'

'That's what we call Hobart - El Supremo. El Supremo supports anything that gives two fingers to his hated European superstate - even if it features his slightly less hated Royal Family.

Josh was relieved the conversation had turned from the personal level to safer territory. 'Why does he have it in for Europe?'

'El Supremo believes that as regional identities are swallowed up and the fittest nations like Germany start to dominate, unemployment will grow in the smaller satellites and resentment will build up.

'The "big brother" element will creep in and the stronger will get stronger and the weaker, weaker. This will lead to a suicidal downward spiral of the entire supra-national entity.'

Josh reared back, grinning. 'Ooooh, most impressive. Supra-national entity, eh?' Tessa grimaced and prodded his arm playfully. Josh said, 'OK, so what's the alternative?'

Tessa replied, 'Hobart believes that instead of an amorphous mass of dissolved social and cultural identities we should go for small regional communities, each with its own distinctive character.

'They'd be city or regional states like Catalonia, Scotland, Wales, England. In all there'd be about 100 in the continent of Europe and these would compete and trade with each other, none becoming particularly dominant.'

'Hmmm. Sounds vaguely medieval.'

'I think that's where he got the idea actually. He reckons going back to "small is beautiful" will work. Quite a lot of politicians here are starting to see it his way, too'

Abruptly, Tessa laughed out loud and looked at Josh mockingly. 'What a pair. Here we are, enjoying a lazy breakfast in bed on a Sunday morning, and our conversation sounds like two boring pundits on a TV discussion programme. Couldn't we think of anything better to do to pass the time?'

Josh grinned sheepishly. 'Sorry. But I thought I'd try to take an interest.'

Tessa face softened. 'I appreciate it, really I do Josh. I'm sorry if I've been wrapped up in things. To be honest, I'm finding it hard going at the moment. I don't think I'm cut out to be the boss.'

'Nonsense, you love telling other people what to do. That's why I'm so meek and submissive.'

'Why you...' Tessa squealed as she made to dig him in a ticklish spot. Josh held up his hand. 'Don't you dare. You know it always gives me hiccups.' He grabbed her wrists and gazed into her eyes. 'Seriously, though Tess, what's going to happen to you if Hobart does close The Examiner down?'

She gently disengaged herself. 'I'll take whatever handshake is offered--golden, silver or otherwise, pour myself a large gin, and take stock. I suppose I could always go back to freelance reporting. One thing about being a journalist these days, the world's so media-mad, there are always jobs.'

Josh reached out and took her hand. 'I'd look after you.'

'Josh, darling, I know you would. You're a good man...'

'...But not one you'd want to become beholden to.'

Tessa looked at him sadly. 'Not one whose life I would screw up. Oh Josh...it's...it's not going to work...I mean...between us...I think we ought to face it?'

Josh withdrew his hand and stared fixedly at the duvet. 'Why do you say that?'

'Because I'm a bad-tempered bitch and you deserve better...'

Josh replied with false jocularity, 'Well, until that someone better comes along let's stay together. Please. After all, someone's got to go round the supermarket while the upwardly-mobile executive of the house is running the world.'

Tessa eyed him steadily and then nodded in submission. Once again, she was going to take the line of least resistance.

Coward.

Nine

That same Sunday morning, if Jack Lockyer had forsaken his office and walked down Victoria Street to clear his head with a stroll by the Thames, he would certainly have noticed two particular people enjoying a seemingly companionable amble in the Spring sunshine along London's Victoria Embankment.

One would have been a familiar face to Jack and the other a stranger. Lockyer's practised eye would quickly have spotted the pair being 'boxed' by two characters in sharp suits.

As the anonymous trackers kept pace, but remained discreetly out of earshot, they occasionally pressed a colourless plastic earpiece and muttered something into their lapels.

Most members of the public would take them as security men of some kind. But Lockyer would have recognised them as hard cases from Scotland Yard's SO19 Firearms Unit, whose job it was to ensure the continued good health of Her Majesty's ministers, including the Deputy PM.

Since the re-establishing of a hard border between the Republic of Ireland and Ulster following Brexit, violence in the province and on the British mainland had erupted again with increased ferocity. Every senior politician was on the IRA's death list, but only those in the Cabinet received round-the-clock protection.

Though MP's were publicly united in their disdain for the people of violence, deep down they were all afraid of history repeating and they would be blown to bits in their cars like former MP and friend of Prime Minister Thatcher, Airey Neave, or shot to death in their own homes like Ross McWhirter, co-founder of The Guinness Book of Records.

Nothing would have struck Jack as unusual about the government's second to top man, and an acolyte, taking an hour or two off for a stroll. But, if he could have overheard their conversation, he would have been astonished to discover it providing the key to his body-in-a-ditch investigation.

But as it was, he had not left the dreary surroundings of his allotted square of New Scotland Yard in Broadway. He was too busy working on the riddle of a strangled woman, a cryptic message, a man's left-hand glove, £1,000 in used notes, a high profile MP, and why the case had been tossed into his lap.

'The President's got a burr up his ass on this, Bob. Screw it up and his re-election goes down the tubes.'

Robert Pelham hid his irritation at the trivialising of his life's ambition by the blatant self-interest revealed through the vulgar, transatlantic metaphor. And it particularly irked him because they were taking him for a fool. That oaf McGovern was being just a shade too co-operative.

It had not taken Pelham long to work out what the President's end-game really was. He wanted glory. The glory of subsuming a dependent Republic of Great Britain and Northern Ireland into the United States itself.

From the frying pan of the EU into the fire of the US. Pathetic, Pelham thought to himself. McGovern would find out, albeit too late, that I'm not that stupid.

But I'll string him along while it suits my purpose, he thought. Then, after the President, in his eagerness to hook his quarry, had signed enough guarantees, I will pull the plug on him and treat with his successor as an equal. One step at a time, though. One step at a time.

He turned to Dresner. 'With the greatest respect to your President, Harry, he might lose an election but I could end up, metaphorically, sewing mailbags for the rest of my life - hardly the way I plan to go down in history. You can tell Sam McGovern from me that I, too, have a stake in Dunkirk's success.'

Dresner cleared his throat awkwardly. 'Sure you have, Bob, don't get me wrong. It's just that he's getting jumpy now we're so close. He wants to be part of it but he knows he dare not support Dunkirk until he's sure of which way the cards are stacked.'

'You mean he's keeping his head down while I do the dirty work. When I'm in the clear he rides over the hill leading the Seventh Cavalry.'

Dresner looked uncertainly at the Englishman. You never knew when he was joking. Admittedly, Pelham was doing all the dirty work. And the work couldn't get much dirtier than taking out the Prime Minister of England. But, if anyone could get away with it, Pelham could. He was such a cold-hearted bastard.

And, Dresner reflected, another of the man's virtues was to be able to set an objective and carry his people with him. He was respected as a street fighter par excellence. In this land still riven with class-consciousness, Robert Pelham had clawed his way from the bottom of the totem pole almost to the top.

After that, Dresner thought darkly, a mere assassination was a shoe-in.

Besides, if Pelham followed directions and did his part as agreed, the chances of anyone finding out were minimal. Nah, this guy wouldn't let the President down.

'When do you plan to...er...retire Mr Boomer?'

Pelham glanced casually at his two minders - one behind and the other about 20 yards ahead. No chance of them overhearing. He looked past his companion to the Thames. Its dark waters swirled past unheeding.

'Soon. Very soon. I can't let him make the announcement about Her Majesty. That would spoil everything. Are you absolutely certain your people have made their calculations correctly?'

'The lab boys have checked and double-checked. A man of his age and constitution should keel over in minutes. It'll look like a heart attack brought on by stress.'

Pelham gazed levelly at his companion. 'You'd better be right. If he realises what's happening and starts to blab before going under, the whole thing could blow up in our faces.'

Dresner said, 'But not in the President's though, Eh? In the worst-case scenario he'll disown me and denounce you as a deluded psychopath.'

'I'm well aware of that, Dresner. It was a figure of speech. You do realise I'm placing a great deal of faith in your department's expertise? I presume the President is cognisant of their role in all this?'

Before Dresner could answer, Pelham continued, 'And you may not be brought to justice on this side of the water but, by God, I can't see Sam McGovern forgiving and forgetting if it's the DOI's mistake that costs him his re-election and his place in history.'

Dresner replied stiffly, 'Yeah, the Department know it's their asses on the line, too.'

Pelham smiled brightly. 'Good. Good. So long as we all understand one another.'

Dresner said, 'So, since we are in it together, could you run it past me one last time, Bob, and I'll get our side to triple-check, just to make sure nothing's being left to chance.'

Pelham gazed straight ahead as mentally he ran through a plan which had taken seed as a wild idea years ago but had become possible only after a presentable young American had got into conversation with him when he was leading a trade delegation to the States six months previously.

It turned out later the young man was in the employ of the Central Intelligence Agency. But, at the time, he seemed like just another White House aide. But he had dropped just enough hints about the Queen, and the future of the monarchy, to awaken Pelham's interest.

At a later session cards had been put on the table and Pelham had also outlined his thoughts on hitting back at Europe. At the same meeting he learned, for the first time, that via intercepted telephone calls and intelligence work on the ground in London, the CIA were now certain the Queen was seriously ill.

He was discreetly sounded out on what he thought the future might hold for the House of Windsor. He had confessed his long-held belief that, when the present sovereign died, Britain should change from constitutional monarchy to democratic republic.

And, from that conversation had evolved the operation both countries were now covertly embarked upon. Within two weeks he would either be in jail or be changing the course of history.

Instinctively, he lowered his voice. 'Tomorrow, Dunkirk begins. Discreetly I let it be known that The Boomer is not a well man. Indeed, he has valiantly struggled to conceal his failing eyesight and his weakening heart. He'll deny it, of course, but once the Commons rumour-mill starts grinding - '

' - But some of it's true. I mean the eyedrops and all...'

'Quite. And that comes later. Meanwhile, as the disinformation gains credence, Hobart's papers will clamour for the lame duck to step down. And his TV and cable stations will not be backward in coming forward with the suggestion that the Party already has a ready-made replacement - me.'

'What if Lancaster outmanoeuvres us? Suppose he agrees to stand aside - in favour of someone else, but not you?'

'As you well know, there won't be anyone else. There can't be because there's no-one left we haven't got in the palm of our hands - thanks to the DOI. Our dossiers on the only possible contenders for the job will be produced, by me, to The Boomer on Thursday.

'I shall tell him either he confirms the stories about his health and endorses me as his heir apparent or my friend Mr Hobart will let his hounds loose on the fraudsters, adulterers and pederasts in his Cabinet.'

Dresner asked, 'What if he calls your bluff? I mean you and I both know those dossiers are mostly fiction with a bit of fact thrown in for authenticity.'

Pelham clasped his hands together in a gesture of admiration. 'Ah, but they're such beautifully-crafted files, who wouldn't believe them? I despise Lancaster for being the shambling weakling that he is but he does have the best interests of the Party at heart. And he knows, once the headlines start, we won't get back into government for another decade. He won't dare take that risk.'

'Ok, so then what?'

'I also prevail upon him not to make his announcement

about our ailing monarch - I shall do that when I'm in Number 10 and while the nation is still reeling over our leader's tragic demise.'

Pelham eyed their two bodyguards. Both were about 50 feet away and attempting, unsuccessfully, to blend into the background. He coolly ticked off on his fingers. 'First, the nation will be stunned by the fatal collapse of their Prime Minister, killed by the pressures of office. Next, they will be mortified by my disclosure that our sovereign will soon be joining her erstwhile First Minister.

'While an emotionally-vulnerable nation mourns, I shall softly-softly suggest that there could be no more fitting a tribute to the woman who has ruled over us for almost 70 years, than to acknowledge she was unique. The last of her kind. Irreplaceable.

'And, perhaps the people might agree, now is the appropriate time for a referendum along the lines: Should our dear Queen Elizabeth the Second be the Kingdom's last monarch?'

Dresner arched an eyebrow. 'Which proposition, of course, Hobart's papers and all his social media outlets will support to the hilt?'

'Exactly so. As the clamour grows, and people are contemplating a major change in the constitution, I shall suggest - again with Hobart's backing - pulling out of all those stultifying European Union commitments which they blackmailed us into after Brexit and become a proud, independent nation once again.'

'Which the opinion polls already show most people are now in favour of,' interjected Dresner.

Pelham wheeled towards the railings and paused to look across the river at the stark outline of the Festival Hall. 'If we get our timing right, we can swing the nation behind both propositions.'

Dresner said wryly, 'Not to mention a ready-made first President of the new Republic of Great Britain and Northern Ireland.'

'I detect a note of irony in your voice, Harry. But I do not do this for myself alone. I sincerely believe this is the way ahead for GB plc. As does your own President, who sees it falling very nicely in with thoughts of his own.'

Dresner said, 'Only kidding, Bob. You'd make a great president.'

Pelham nodded in acknowledgment. 'Now it's your turn, Harry. Just confirm to me how Sam sees his part.'

Dresner looked at Pelham reproachfully. 'Geez, Bob, you know very well what the Old Man's promised.' He laughed hollowly. 'You nearly drove him crazy insisting on dotting every "I" and crossing all the "T"s.'

Pelham inclined his head. 'Just the essentials...just to be absolutely sure.'

As the two began to make their way back towards the Houses of Parliament, Dresner said slowly, 'As soon as The President is sure the wind's blowing in the right direction, he'll come out of the closet and back you with everything he's got.

'He'll offer to replace the shackles of the EU with a free trade zone without tariffs covering the whole of the US.

'Initially, we - the United States - will underwrite any deficit through loss of inward trade - we reckon about £50 billion initially...'

Pelham interrupted '...But I immediately save another £20 billion in ending contributions the EU insisted on as a price for a very meagre trading arrangement.'

Dresner nodded. 'Big bucks, Bob...'

'...And I also save by opting out of the Social Chapter again, which means we become more competitive...'

'...And, on top of all that, the President will take over Britain's world-wide defence commitments...'

'...All of which, added to the £20 billion windfall dissolving the monarchy will give me,' said Pelham reflectively, 'will provide enough spare cash to rebuild the National Health Service, keep our promises on an increased national living wage, cut taxes by at least 2p in the pound, lower interest rates, improve education at all levels and boost pensions. A paradise compared with the mess we've got now. How could any sensible electorate refuse?'

Dresner said phlegmatically, 'Which will guarantee at least another five years of a Social Democratic government...And President Pelham another five years at the helm.'

Pelham retorted, 'Plus another four for President McGovern due to his part in gaining a ready-made springboard to a European Economic Area of half a billion people. Not to mention, of course, the warm glow he'll have given everyone through a new brotherhood with their British kith and kin.'

'Everyone's a winner,' said Dresner.

Ten

Jack Lockyer never suffered from the 'Monday-morning syndrome.' To him coming to work was a pleasure. It preoccupied his thoughts and provided just enough human contact to keep at bay the loneliness which hovered permanently at the fringes of his consciousness, even after six years.

'Sir, we've identified the dead girl.'

Jack looked up as Claire's eager features loomed round his door. 'And?'

'We had the usual smattering of calls after the pic in The Examiner. But only three matched up: a neighbour, her flatmate and a very distressed mother.'

'Oh Hell, what a way to find out. Damn, damn, damn.'

Claire's features took on an expression of sympathy. 'I know, sir, it's awful. But I suppose the only thing you can say is it must be better than your loved one disappearing and there being one, long silence. It must be even worse not knowing.'

'Is someone looking after the mother?'

'Yes sir, a family liaison officer's with her.'

Jack stared at his assistant. What did she know about grief? She couldn't be more than 26 or 27. Probably never felt the hurt of real loss; the gut-wrenching agony when it happens;

the shattering shock; the disbelief; the depression and then the numbness.

Even now, in his more introspective moments, the pain of remembering would pierce his armour and the futility of Jennie's death would hit him over again. Then he would kill the pain with alcohol.

'So, sergeant, who was she?'

'Linda Burchfield, known as Lucinda. She shared a flat up the West End with a girl called Rebecca Ward, known as Bekky.'

'What's all this "known as..?"'

'Ah well, sir, apparently they were partners in a sort of two-person escort agency - offering their services to lonely, rich men, in exchange for £1,000 an evening, tax-free.'

'Your use of the word "evening" is, presumably, a euphemism for "night" I take it?'

'Judging by the rent they'd be paying on their address - Duchess Mews off Wimpole Street - I'd guess Bekky and Linda were providing more than just conversation and companionship, yes.'

'So, the thousand pounds in Lucinda's handbag could have come from a punter?'

'But, if that client killed her, sir, why leave his money behind?'

'Probably because the murderer wasn't a client. More than likely it was someone else she arranged to meet later in the day.'

'You mean PA 4PM?'

'Exactly. I wouldn't mind betting that whoever PA is, he picked her up in his car, drove her down to Wiltshire and, for whatever reason - perhaps jealousy - strangled her.'

'Hmmm. Sounds a bit too convenient a theory, sir. '

'A tip, sergeant: never reject the obvious, just because it is the obvious. Right, now let's get over to Ms Ward and see if she can help us pull a few of these strands together.'

'So what you're telling us, Ms Ward, is that you have no idea who PA might be. Or who Linda was due to meet at 4pm last Friday. Or who might have written this cryptic message?'

'Look, Inspector, I'd like to help but I really have no idea. Lindy and I didn't live in each other's pockets. Sometimes we'd chat, and compare notes, that sort of thing...'

'...what about a regular boyfriend? Did she have one?'

Rebecca took out another cigarette and lit it from the one she had nearly smoked down to the tip. Lockyer and Claire had been at the apartment for half an hour and so far they had heard nothing which might throw any light on Lucinda's murder.

Jack gazed round. Nice. Very nice. Expensive, reproduction walnut table and bureau, a scattering of Bokhara rugs on the floor and original oil paintings by some 18th century Dutch artist on the walls.

He and Claire were seated on a beige sofa and Bekky Ward was perched nervously opposite them on one of two matching chairs.

'Look, Inspector, Lindy didn't have a relationship as such but she did meet regularly with a creepy American guy.'

Claire leaned forward. 'Creepy? Why creepy?'

Bekky shrugged. 'I don't know. It's just a feeling. I saw them together a few times and each time I noticed how...well...he seemed to...dominate her. It's hard to put into words. I suppose what I'm trying to say is he acted as if he owned her.'

Anthony Talmage

'Do you know his name, Ms Ward?'

Rebecca shook her head, 'Sorry. Lindy didn't talk about him and I didn't push it. But I got the impression that he was calling the shots and Lindy was doing what she was told.'

'Have you been able to come to any conclusions about what part he might have been playing in Linda's life?' Lockyer pressed.

'Not really. I just got the impression that he was using Lindy and paying her very well for whatever it was she was doing.'

Claire asked, 'How do you know he's an American?'

'I don't. Not for sure. But on the odd occasion Lindy talked of him she called him "The Yank."'

'So, Miss Ward, we have a mysterious American who hired Linda regularly for some purpose not connected to him personally for which he paid her well. Could it involve blackmail do you think?'

Bekky puffed nervously at her cigarette and blew a column of smoke towards the ceiling. 'It could, I suppose. The reason I say that is because she always did the Yank's business somewhere else, Chelsea I think, and sometimes when she came home she'd have the smile of the cat who'd had the cream.

'Once she just couldn't keep it to herself. She said if only the voters could see what she'd seen, they'd chuck out the caterwauling lot of them.'

'Hmmm. Which suggests politicians, up to something…um…disreputable...'

'...so blackmail's a fair supposition, sir.'

'Ms Ward, I don't suppose Linda kept a diary?'

Lockyer noticed Bekky clutched her knee with one hand to stop it shaking and with the other she mashed her cigarette in the ashtray. 'Not that I know of, Inspector. But if I find one, I'll let you know.'

'That would be very helpful Ms Ward. Well I think that's all for now. We'll see ourselves out.'

When Jack got back to his office, he was surprised to find his boss waiting for him. Commander Ernest Forsyth was staring absent-mindedly out of the window at the wall opposite.

As Lockyer walked in Forsyth turned and switched on an unconvincing smile. 'Don't know how you can work in surroundings like this.' He indicated with a manicured hand Lockyer's dented, grey metal desk, the matching filing cabinet and the long dead spider plant draping forlornly down its side.

'I'm used to it, I suppose, sir,' Lockyer hedged.

'Quite. Um, how's the body-in-the-ditch investigation going. Any leads?' Lockyer kept his face expressionless. 'Not a lot so far; early days yet.' Was it his imagination or did a look of relief flicker across Forsyth's face?

'I want you to report to me personally anything you come up with, Jack.'

'Might I ask why, sir? I mean, a young woman strangled and dumped is hardly unusual these days.'

Forsyth's face tightened. 'No you may not ask. I have my reasons and I don't expect to be cross-questioned. Just do it, please. I want daily reports of your progress.' Then he relaxed again. 'Sorry, Jack. Under pressure. Aren't we all... Keep me in touch, eh?'

When he had the office to himself again Lockyer lowered himself into his chair and swivelled it to stare thoughtfully at the map on the wall behind him. Politics. Forsyth never showed an interest in run-of-the-mill investigations. But, if politics - or a politician - was involved, that would be a very different matter. And that could be why the Yard had been called in over the heads of the local boys.

Jack recalled Frank Dutton's lurid - and misleading - headline in yesterday's Examiner: 'SEX MURDER RIDDLE AND A TOP TORY.' In Jack's opinion, linking the two had stretched journalistic licence too far. The only connection the MP had with Lucinda was an accident of geography. Or was it?

On impulse he picked up the phone and dialled Keith Passmore at Wiltshire Police Headquarters in Swindon.

'Keith, it's Jack Lockyer.'

'Jack, great to hear from you. My boss has been asking me what the latest is on the ditch murder. He's really pee'd off at having to hand the case over to you. He can't understand it.'

Jack said philosophically, 'Ours is not to reason why...To be honest, I'm just as baffled. Anyway, we've got an ID. She doesn't come from your patch, although her mother lives just over your border at Hungerford. She was a Linda, also known as Lucinda, Burchfield with a flat in the West End here. So at least you can tell your Chief Super there's no local connection.'

'That might sooth the savage beast I suppose.'

'But having said that, Keith, you haven't by any chance come up with anything at your end putting James Sherborne in the frame?'

'Sherborne? Oh, I get it. The Examiner's story yesterday. Talk about a smear campaign. That was an outrageous piece of journalism. Someone's obviously got it in for the poor guy. Normally I don't have much time for politicians but I happen to know Sherborne and, if it's possible these days to have an MP with integrity, he's one.

'Although he's always on the box and is obviously one of

the Opposition's Great White Hopes, he still manages to work damned hard in the constituency here. In fact he's just won a battle to keep the A and E Unit at the local hospital open.'

'So you don't reckon he could be connected in any way with this murder?'

Keith hesitated. 'No, not Sherborne. He's as straight as they come. It's just the over-active imagination of some reporter putting two and two together and coming up with five.'

Jack recalled his conversation with Frank Dutton in his office and felt a twinge of guilt. He said neutrally, 'You're probably right. It's just this business of transferring the case to us. It would make some kind of sense if a top politician was involved. I mean Westminster would want to have the case handled in their own back yard.'

Keith replied, 'But why, Jack? You're not going to cover anything up any more than we would. So what would be the point of calling the Yard in?'

'That's exactly what I'd like to know, Keith.'

Eleven

The Metropolitan Police information line was not the only one telephoned by those who thought they could identify the expressionless face of the late Linda Burchfield. Some of her former acquaintances preferred to confide their knowledge to their favourite newspapers. Who knows, the Press might be willing to pay something. The police certainly wouldn't.

And that was how, after Lockyer and Claire had left Rebecca Ward's apartment that Monday, having been furnished with the address of the two flat sharers, journalists from two national tabloids and one broadsheet turned up at various times in Duchess Mews asking for pictures and interviews.

Although she had felt a genuine affection for her flatmate, and was deeply shocked by her violent death, Bekky was a pragmatist by nature. So she decided to reveal just enough about their 'escort' service to provide an appetiser for the rest of the media.

Maybe then she could sell everything she knew to the highest bidder. And, after finding Lindy's little pocket diary, thought Bekky, she had a lot to offer. But she would probably go to one of the Sundays and cut out the grubby shits who had patronised her with their 'bit more cleavage, love' and 'skirt a bit higher, sweetheart.' She would rather throw the diary in the Thames than give those chauvinist bastards anything.

It was the Inspector and his pretty assistant who had made her realise what a pot of gold she might be sitting on in the flat. Bekky knew that Lindy had kept a record of her appointments, particularly those connected with the Yank. But it was only after that copper had asked about a diary that Bekky realised it had to be in her flatmate's bedroom somewhere.

If it had not been in Lindy's handbag, or at the scene, or the murderer had not taken it, there was only one other place it could be.

Within 10 minutes of Lockyer and Claire leaving, Bekky had discovered Linda's diary under the lift-out compartment of her jewellery box. As Bekky had thumbed through the pages she had gasped and her face had flushed with excitement. Jesus, she thought, if these initials were who they appeared to be, some paper would be willing to pay a fortune.

Later when each hack, accompanied by his faithful snapper, had trooped into her living room, Bekky had blinked back the tears, posed demurely on the sofa and talked about a respectable, above-board escort service she and Linda had provided for...certain individuals.

Asked bawdily whether these...clients...might be alarmed to find their activities headline news, Bekky professed innocence. But, by an arch of the eyebrow, suggested there was more to the agency's clientele than she was prepared, at this stage, to disclose.

All in all, she thought after they had gone, she had handled things rather well. She knew the journalists would sensationalise everything she said. And when the next day's papers hit the streets she was not disappointed.

'DEAD LINDA'S LOVE NEST SECRET' screamed The Sun, 'MURDERED GIRL IN SEX-FOR-SALE SHOCK' said The Mirror and, more soberly, but just as titillatingly, The Telegraph intoned, 'MURDER VICTIM OFFERED CALL-GIRL SERVICE TO LONELY BUSINESSMEN.' There followed a melange of fiction spiced with the odd fact gleaned from their interviewee.

Apart from their regular duties, the thousands of employees of the CIA's Department of Overseas Information are charged with eavesdropping on other people's conversations. They listen in to phones, radios, satellites, carrier waves, microwaves, faxes, the Internet and the increasingly bewildering number of social media outlets. Nearly all of this effort was in response to the rise of Islamist and a resurgent IRA terrorism.

All the data garnered is poured into a computer which analyses millions of individual snippets and produces an assessment and recommendations for action.

Just one cell in this complex, global network exists in a humble basement under St George's Hotel, opposite the BBC's Broadcasting House at the top of London's Regent Street. This particular Tuesday morning one normally diligent listener had forsaken the tedium of checking the computer screenshots and printouts and was instead examining the pile of daily newspapers, which was also his job.

While combing columns of political guff, his attention was diverted by the salacious details of a call-girl's love-nest. By the time he had read the same story, but a different version, in two other newspapers, the smile had vanished from his face.

He made two calls from his secure phone and within minutes Robert Pelham had approved an 'extreme prejudice' operation.

'She says she's got a story The Sun would pay fifty thousand quid for,' Frank Dutton reported to the 10 o'clock editorial meeting.

Although The Examiner was not due to come out for five days, it had been Tessa Jordan's habit to conduct a brain-storming session early in the week to plan the inside pages. The gathering was usually confined to heads of department, chief correspondents and her news editor.

When Frank had brought up his brief phone conversation with Rebecca Ward, it had been greeted with an audible groan. The old-stagers had heard such claims many times from naive readers who thought some rumour they had heard from a friend of a friend was worth enough to a newspaper to set them up for life.

Usually, the information was inaccurate and highly-libellous and a waste of a hard-pressed reporter's precious time. So the paper's senior executives were grateful when Tessa dismissed them and they could get back to their desks. When the last had gone, Tessa motioned Frank to close the door.

'What's she got that's so hot, Frank?'

'She wouldn't tell me on the phone so I sent a taxi for her. She'll be here any minute,' Frank replied.

'OK, Frank, when she arrives we'll both see her. But it'll have to be something pretty good, because the budget's bust.'

As she spoke, Tessa's internal phone rang. After she put it down she said, 'Well, we'll soon see. She's here.' Could this be the big story that might take her off El Supremo's hit list?

Tessa wondered. Some hopes.

Rebecca was escorted from the lift through the maze of desks, computer terminals and columns in the open-plan office straight to Tessa's office.

'Please sit down Ms Ward.' Tessa indicated a chair on the other side of an oblong, sapele coffee table. She and Frank sat opposite. They both looked at the woman expectantly. She shifted nervously under their gaze and lit a king-sized cigarette.

Tessa glanced meaningfully at the No Smoking reminder notice stuck on the glass which looked onto the newsroom but Bekky either had not noticed, or did not care.

Tessa spoke. 'I read your interview in the papers this morning. I'm sorry about Linda; this must be a difficult time for you.' Bekky nodded and exhaled a jet of smoke. She stubbed out her cigarette and cleared her throat. 'I'll be honest with you. I decided to ring The Examiner because it was the first paper to carry the story about Linda and therefore you might be interested in another exclusive.'

'At a price?' Frank suggested equably.

'Well, what's wrong with that?' Rebecca replied defensively. 'It's what everyone does these days, isn't it? What's the harm? I can't bring Lindy back.'

Tessa lifted both hands, palms outwards, placatingly. 'Don't misunderstand Frank. We're not criticising. What have you got in mind.'

'Well, I found Lindy's diary and it's hot stuff and no mistake. I mean it's got names that appear in your paper every week...'

'...you mean she was having sex with public figures?' Prompted Tessa.

'Not just ordinary celebrities. Who would care tuppence if they were having it off on the side? No, I mean people who ought to know better, who should be setting an example. Who pontificate about how you and me should behave while they pretend to be squeaky clean.'

'You mean politicians?' Said Frank.

'Yeah, but not just any old MP's. I'm talking about top drawer. Cabinet ministers and such.'

Tessa and Frank exchanged glances. 'Who are these people, Rebecca?' Rebecca sat back in her chair and a smile crept across her face. 'That's why I'm here--to tell you. But not for nothing. I want some money for what I've got, or I'll go to The Sun.'

Tessa decided a bluff was worth trying. 'You realise, Miss Ward, that The Sun and most of the other national papers are owned by the same company. They come from the same stable. All editors are required by the Proprietor to exchange information on such offers as yours and agree the same price.'

Frank explained, 'It's to stop people like you from bidding the price up.' Rebecca looked uncertain. 'Oh, I see.' Then she seemed to come to a decision. 'Well, what d'you think it's worth?'

'How can we tell you that, Rebecca? Would you buy a car without looking at it first?'

'You mean, I hand over my info, you say "Ta very much" and I'm shown the door and you've got your exclusive for free?'

Frank looked Rebecca straight in the eyes. 'We wouldn't do that, I promise you. But you must understand, it's hardly reasonable for us to give you, perhaps hundreds of pounds, without seeing what we're getting for our money.'

Bekky still looked suspicious. 'Hundreds? I was thinking more in terms of thousands. OK, suggest something.'

Tessa said, 'I suggest you tell us whatever you know, we'll

record it as you speak, Frank here will type it up for you to sign as an accurate representation, and then we'll discuss a figure...'

'...IF we think it's worth anything at all, that is,' Frank stipulated.

Bekky sighed and reached down for her handbag. 'Look, I don't know why I should trust you, but I do. It's not so much what I can tell you as how I could match up what's in Lindy's little black book.' She slid it across the table. 'I found it in her bedroom. It's got dates, phone numbers, some initials and other bibs and bobs that I could help interpret.'

Frank started to leaf through the diary, while Tessa glanced over his shoulder. As he riffled, the colour rose in his neck and face.

Bekky said, 'I suppose it wouldn't take a genius to put names to those initials. But I could make it a lot easier. You see I've been thinking back to our chats and people and places started to drop into place. Given a few hours I could fill in most of the blanks for you.

'For instance, just to give you a taster, that "H.I"...' She pointed a painted nail at one particular entry '...means Howard Ingleby.'

'And who's this, then..?' Frank indicated the initials 'A.W.' which could belong to Austin Willis, the Home Secretary. Bekky's mouth quirked downwards. 'Sorry, that's all I'm saying for now.'

Frank eyed his watch. 'Look Bekky, leave the diary with us and give us half an hour to talk it over. Have you been to our neck of the woods before?' Bekky shook her head.

Frank suggested, 'Why not have a mooch around? Do some shopping. When you come back we'll give you our answer.'

Bekky looked at them both uncertainly. At length she

said, 'Alright. But, please don't destroy what little faith I've got left in human nature by photocopying it and ripping me off.'

Tessa replied, 'I promise we won't do that, Rebecca.'

Bekky said, 'And I can promise you that you'll have the scandal of the century by the time I've finished.'

When Bekky had disappeared through the double doors at the end of the office Frank exploded, 'Look at these other initials...If that young lady's to be believed and one lot belongs to Howard Ingleby, these others on this page could stand for Austin Willis and Roly Sinclair.'

He flicked rapidly through the pages. 'The fools...all so-called respectable married family men - Sinclair's even a member of the Church of England Synod.'

Tessa took the diary out of Frank's hands and scrutinised several of the pages. Then she looked up whistling under her breath. 'Frank, this is dynamite. Three members of the Cabinet, all sleeping with the same girl. Whispering goodness-knows-what sweet nothings as pillow talk. It could bring the government down.'

The two of them spent the next ten minutes going through each sheet, noting familiar initials and the sums of money that had been entered next to them. Their concentration was disturbed by a sudden flurry in the newsroom.

About 20 staff were clustered around one colleague whose face had turned the colour of skimmed milk. She had obviously just arrived in the office from the ground floor and was pointing out of the window. Then several of the group turned to stare at Tessa and Frank.

Eventually Hubert Treglown, the paper's Royalty Correspondent, broke away and headed towards his two bosses. He knocked formally at the door before coming in and closing it behind him. 'What's going on?' Tessa enquired. Treglown regarded them solemnly. 'That girl you were just talking to in here...She's been involved in a hit and run.'

They stared at him disbelievingly. 'Is she badly hurt?' Tessa asked eventually.

Treglown said lugubriously, 'From what I can gather, it's worse than that. She's probably dead.'

Twelve

It was her smile. Take it at face value and it was wide, attractive, warm. Look a little deeper, though, and there was a pallor of the spirit which could not quite be hidden from someone who had walked the same road.

Lockyer swirled the Scotch he was holding until the ice cubes tinkled. 'Christ, what am I thinking?' He asked himself. For once the emptiness of his flat had appealed to him more than the anthill of the Yard. He had made the excuse to Sergeant Bishop that he wanted to mull over, without distraction, what they had so far on the body-in-the-ditch and the hit-and-run cases.

But, if he was honest, he had retreated to the sanctuary of his home because he was beset by a jumble of confusing emotions. And he wanted to drown them at birth with the help of Mr Teacher.

And Bach's Brandenburg Concertos 1,2,4 and 6 would lull him to eventual anaesthesia. He caught himself thinking of that smile again, as the gentle, Baroque cadences washed over him.

It had started with an e-mail message from the police central computer to Claire's terminal. It informed her that one of those connected with the Linda Burchfield murder case had, herself, been killed.

Together, he and Claire had gone to Derry Street in Kensington but eye-witnesses had seen little. All spoke of a screech of tyres, the roar of an engine, a pedestrian tossed high in the air and a red-coloured car - probably a Ford Fiesta - disappearing round the corner.

The victim had died instantly from multiple injuries. Her driving licence had provided her identity - Rebecca Ward. Lockyer and his sergeant were about to return to the Yard when a journalist told them he had seen the accident victim in his newsroom a few minutes before she had been killed.

The reporter led them to The Examiner's floor in the media complex and they were quickly shown into the editor's office.

What happened next was why Lockyer was now nursing a large Teachers and feeling foolish. His old friend Frank Dutton had stood up to shake hands, but Lockyer had hardly given him a second glance. He had been mesmerised by the woman standing behind the desk.

His professional eye took in her description and filed it in one part of his brain. But, somewhere else in his being, something strange happened which made him behave utterly out of character.

From time to time over the next half an hour Claire had looked at him curiously as he stumbled through the interview asking the same questions twice. Thinking back on it Jack winced. What had been wrong with him? He had almost gone to pieces, floundering around, going over the same ground. Claire must have thought it very odd. She had even picked up the threads at one point and steered them back on track.

As the music swelled Lockyer recalled the description he had mentally salted away. Mid thirties, average height, a certain grace in her movements. Auburny hair, green eyes which seemed to twinkle with amusement when she looked at him. Or was that his imagination? Had she sensed his confusion?

Her smile.

Ah yes, back to her smile. Wide, with a hint of sadness. Fanciful claptrap. He was old enough to know better. God, how much had he drunk? A third of the bottle? Good old Mr Teacher. They had cultivated a perfect arrangement over the years, Mr Teacher and Jack Lockyer. Jack would talk and Mr Teacher would listen.

Where was he? Ah yes, no-one of his age fell in love at first sight. Love? He turned the odd-sounding word over in his mind. Then he tried another - Tessa. He grunted to himself. Bloody fool. It was ludicrous. Out of the question. A delusion. He didn't even know if she was married. And what would an attractive, sophisticated woman like her want with a clapped-out old has-been like him?

He snarled angrily and slurred out loud to the bottle near his right hand, 'I'm a stupid old fool and you're not helping matters, Teacher. Now be a good chap and steer me back to what I know something about, like the detection of crime, the cool analysis of clues, the bringing to justice of the transgressor.'

Yes, back to reality, he thought. The reality I know and feel safe with. I know what you're thinking, Mr Teacher. That my reality is loneliness and emptiness and futility. Well, that's how I want it. I shall endure. For as long as it takes.

No-one falls in love at my age.

The empty glass slipped from Jack's hand onto the carpet and the Bach fell silent. The only noise to be heard in the flat was the perpetual hum of the traffic on Putney Hill and the gentle snoring of a man who had discovered that, after all, he was still human.

Anthony Talmage

'James Sherborne.' The Speaker bawled above the cacophony which always punctuated Prime Minister's Questions.

The Right Honourable Member for Thamesdown had found it easy to catch the Speaker's eye. As Shadow Minister for European Affairs he was given priority over the back-bench rank and file. And those on the Conservative side behind him smelled blood.

Each time one of James's barbs had hit home Prime Minister Ted Lancaster's unkempt head had bowed lower over the Dispatch Box. The PM's supporters were baying and waving their order papers to give him time to rebound.

James was enjoying himself. It was a rout. The Social Democrat Front Bench were known to be divided on the subject of Europe. The Boomer's caretaker policy had been one of compliance to all the bullying demands of the EU who were following a policy of revenge ever since the divorce.

But, as events had unfolded since the Tory election disaster, the divisions in the Social Democrat Party had become unbridgeable with the one-time vociferous anti-Europe minority becoming the majority. The Boomer was falling between the two stools of appeasement and independence.

As the cat-calling subsided James noticed the expressionless face of the deputy Prime Minister, Robert Pelham. It was impossible to read his thoughts. But, it was a fair bet he was furious with the lacklustre performance his boss was putting on.

It was well known that Pelham had trenchant views on the erosion of British sovereignty. So how galling it must be for him to sit there and listen to the Opposition's spokesman making capital by espousing almost exactly the same views as his own. But views he dare not admit for fear of charges of disloyalty.

There was an expectant hush as both sides of the House waited for the coup de grace. James cleared his throat. All thoughts of last Friday evening's nightmare events were pushed to the back of his mind.

He fixed the tired figure opposite with a piercing gaze. 'Does the Prime Minister not agree that his pusillanimous fence-sitting both at home and abroad in all matters connected with Europe has almost fatally weakened this nation's independence..?

'And, further, does he not appreciate that while he is dithering, the institutions of the EU - the Commission, the Court and the Parliament have, de facto, become a United States of Europe with powers to rule over this Kingdom..?

'And that his one pathetic excuse that we dare not say "Booh" for fear of causing ruinous trade barriers, just does not hold water? Where has the Prime Minister been living while tariffs have been falling giving non-European countries like Japan and the United States better access to trade than us – now, it seems, a subjugated nation?'

Warming to his theme, James rammed his message home. 'Does the Prime Minister not realise our Mother of Parliaments is gradually being reduced to that of a local council? We might as well have stayed in the EU – at least then we would have a voice at the table. Now we are merely a voice in the wilderness...'

As James volleyed each point across the floor of the House Lancaster twitched in discomfort. He polished and re-polished the pebble lenses of his spectacles affecting insouciance. But beads of sweat were coursing down each side of his face. All around there was pandemonium. Robert

Pelham's face remained deadpan but his mouth was compressed into a grim line.

His eyes widened involuntarily and for a moment he looked startled at James's final thrust. 'Would the Prime Minister not consider, before it is too late, a disengagement with the bully boys of that supremely undemocratic bureaucracy across the Channel in favour, perhaps, of a closer relationship with our cousins across the sea, the United States of America?'

James sat down amid howls of glee from his own side and jeers of derision from the Government benches. The noise subsided instantly as Lancaster scrambled dispiritedly to his feet. He looked all about him as if gathering his ammunition for a devastating riposte. 'May I...' His voice was barely more than a croak '...refer the Right Honourable Member to the many answers I have given on this subject in this House before...'

Abruptly, he sat down amid a stunned silence. A split second later the air was pierced by shrieks of jubilation from the Opposition benches when they realised the Prime Minister had no answers to give. PMQs were over and with the catcalls still ringing in his ears the Prime Minister of England, flanked by members of his Front Bench, shuffled out of the chamber.

When James returned to his office half an hour later, he found an urgent message requesting him to come to Committee Room 3. He grunted impatiently. He was due to meet Elizabeth who had insisted they carry on as normally as possible. That was why she had continued with her plans for a shopping trip with a friend, both of whom James was due to drive home later.

Before that, he had mountains of correspondence to catch up on and had a meeting with two industrialists to discuss future trade links with China. He could ill-afford the time to fend off some ambitious new member, probably offering a tidbit in exchange for James putting in a good word higher up.

Committee room 3 was one of the smaller compartments that make up the warren that is the Palace of Westminster. When he pushed open the door James was startled to find the only other occupant was the Deputy Prime Minister himself. He was standing at the head of a gnarled, square oak table with his hands resting on a high-backed, studded chair.

'Ah James, come in and take a pew. First let me congratulate you on a devastating performance this afternoon. Quite had our dear leader on the ropes.' James's stomach tightened and a feeling of apprehension rose in his chest. He tried to keep his inner turmoil from showing on his face. Why was the Deputy Leader of the Social Democrat Party, and Deputy PM of all people, wanting to see him - his enemy?

It was unheard of. The two sides kept themselves strictly segregated in the House and rarely met on party business unless it was in committee. If a private meeting like this became known, rumours would fly around the bars and tea rooms like bush fires in a drought.

Pelham's oleaginous tones penetrated his thoughts. 'Don't look so worried, James, no-one but you and I know we are here and I'm sure it will be to both our advantages to keep it that way.' James lowered himself into a chair and Pelham sat down regarding him from under heavy brows. 'I'll come straight to the point James. I don't want you making any more rabble-rousing speeches on the subject of our European friends.'

James gaped at him in disbelief. 'Sorry, I'm not quite sure I understand. In case you hadn't noticed you're the Government and I'm the Opposition. I'm supposed to make rabble-rousing speeches.'

'Quite so, dear boy. But you will not make any more like that one. Otherwise I might be obliged to ensure that your...um...indiscretion of Friday night is brought to the attention of the proper authorities...'

James felt his face drain of blood and his heart hammered wildly in his chest. Suddenly, he was short of breath. The room began to spin. He heard a stranger's guttural voice coming out of his own mouth. 'Friday night...I...I...don't understand.'

Pelham held up his hand and said soothingly, 'James, James, I know all about Lucinda...How you kindly picked her up in the rain and then...seemingly...allowed passion to overwhelm you and, well, we both know the rest...'

'...No, no, it wasn't like that. It was an accident, you don't understand - '

' - Oh, but I do, dear James. I understand that you murdered a defenceless young woman, panicked, threw her body out of your car and then callously went home as if nothing untoward had happened...Now, how do you think that is going to look when you are arrested and the papers get hold of it?'

All James's pent-up fears burst like an over-filled dam and suddenly his head was on his hands and he was sobbing like a whipped child. Pelham said harshly, 'Stop this pathetic blubbing man. I do not intend to blow the whistle on you so long as you do as I say.' His tone softened, 'I mean, what would be the point of destroying a promising career, a marriage, the lives of your children, the respect of your peers, all because of one mad moment?'

James lifted his head and turned a face streaked with wet, to his persecutor. 'I see. Blackmail...'

'An ugly word but not as ugly as murder.'

James's face took on a tormented expression. 'But, how do you know? I told my wife and that's all. How did you find out?'

'You'd be surprised what I know. I am a veritable repository of man's fallibility. But, enough of that. Let's get back to the matter in hand. Let me make myself perfectly clear, just in case you have not fully grasped my meaning. You will cease to be the critic of all things European. In fact, you will quietly subside on the matter entirely, is that clear?'

James shook his head. He took out his handkerchief and wiped his eyes. 'No, it's not. I...I...don't understand anything. Friday...that girl...this...I'm in some horrible nightmare.'

'Now look, Sherborne, it's quite simple. You lost your head, I know about it. That makes you obliged to me to save your sorry neck. Savvy? '

'Yes, but...my speech? Why should it bother you? After all, I'm only saying what you apparently believe anyway?' James shook his head in bewilderment. 'Nothing makes sense. Your party's official policy, with which you disagree, is for re-integration with EU institutions, as far as is possble without actually re-joining. Our policy, and what I've been making speeches about, is exactly the opposite. Which is what you want to happen. So, why should you care?'

Pelham's breath came out in a deep sigh. 'Since I know your darkest secret, I feel I am safe to elaborate a little...in the interests of your peace of mind.

'Of course, should you ever reveal this conversation I shall utterly deny it. It will be your word against mine. And when your word becomes known as the ravings of a rapist and murderer...well, who do you think will be believed?' James closed his eyes as Pelham's words smacked into him like bullets.

Pelham went on evenly, 'So, the reason why I want you to button your lip is because you're stealing my lines - '

' - Sorry?'

'Your sound bites and pithy headlines on the subject of Europe are getting dangerously close to those I have in mind for myself - after I take over the leadership and launch a new Party policy.'

'Take over the leadership? You mean Lancaster's stepping down?'

'Not exactly. More an enforced retirement.'

'What, on health grounds?'

'Exactly.'

James looked at Pelham steadily. 'Everyone knows about the glaucoma but the doctors said he'd be able to carry on for a good few years yet.'

Pelham smiled thinly. 'Oh, I don't know. I have the feeling his eyes will be the death of him.'

'Wha - I'm sorry, you've lost me.'

'It matters not. What is important for now is that you do nothing to rock the boat. I have certain...plans...' James noticed Pelham raise his eyes to the ceiling, as if viewing an invisible horizon '...such plans. As the Bard would say..."There is a tide in the affairs of man..."'

He fixed James in a bright stare. 'There is a tide today, James dear boy, all round us. Can't you feel it? A tide of disillusionment with the old order, despair at the new. The people are crying out for a Messiah who can promise deliverance; a new world order; a new beginning.'

James regarded Pelham doubtfully. 'If you don't mind my

saying Pelham, you sound like a megalomaniac.'

It was as if Pelham hadn't heard him. He started to pace the floor. 'Take the EU's single currency, for instance, James. You won't know this but those…er…bully boys as you so appositely called them, are pressuring us to join the Euro, despite us not being in the EU. They see it as us tacitly admitting our departure was a terrible mistake. What a PR coup for them in the eyes of the markets. And the world.

'But let me ask you: if we sign up to the single currency, do you know the first thing we shall see?'

James felt relieved that, for the moment, Pelham seemed to have forgotten his blackmail threat. He shook his head.

'I shall tell you what we shall see. It will be a convoy of sealed and heavily-guarded vans leaving London for Frankfurt. In these vans, James, will be every penny of our £100 billion-worth of gold bullion and foreign exchange reserves used to back sterling.

'The Third Protocol of the Maastricht Treaty is quite clear about this. All our cash will end up in Europe's Central Bank and under German control. The money will be lost for ever. Effectively, the Germans will have won, at last, the Second World War.'

Pelham stopped his pacing and gazed down at James. 'Now what do you think our nation will think of that, James?' Before James could reply, Pelham went on, 'I'll tell you. They will abhor the whole idea and will rally behind anyone who is prepared to make a stand. That someone will be me, James. Not you. And certainly not The Boomer.' Pelham subsided into a chair and continued to stare across the table.

A thought occurred to James. 'All very persuasive, but…You say you'll be taking over from Lancaster. But you're not even a front-runner for the leadership. What about the

Chancellor, the Home Secretary, even Roland Sinclair? None of those are going to pass up the chance of moving into Number 10.'

Pelham smiled genially. 'Let us say they have each weighed their personal interests against those of the country and have decided to lend me their support.'

'I don't believe it. Ingleby? He's had his eye on the top job for years.' James read something in Pelham's expression. 'You've got something on them, too, haven't you? God Almighty, what's going on here?'

Pelham replied equably, 'They have been very naughty boys and I have proof positive. And, in case you think I have been discriminatory, there have been some naughty girls, too. But, that's not important now. I have a dream, James. A dream of re-launching Britain as a proud, fully independent nation again, free from the quicksands of Europe. An equal with our rightful partners. My vision is greater than the welfare of individuals, however elevated.'

Pelham ignored an expression of bafflement on James's face. 'We must transform ourselves into a society better fitted for a 21st-century, free-market economy. We must throw off the shackles of outmoded tradition - '

'Sorry, Pelham, but I still don't understand why you think my speeches will rock the boat. So far all I can see is a remarkable similarity in our views which is all to the good, surely?'

'Ah, but you see, it's all a question of timing. I have more in mind than merely taking over the Government of this country. I have plans...'

'Which are?'

'Oh, didn't I say? I intend to throw Europe overboard lock, stock and barrel and join forces with the United States in a special trading alliance. Oh, and I almost forgot, dissolve the monarchy and declare the country a republic.' James gazed at him open-mouthed. 'And I want the 100 percent support of the darling of the Opposition. Yes, James, with you behind me we can carry the country with us.'

Thirteen

Politicians pursue their ambitions with a remorseless energy. They channel this energy into ruthlessness, aggression and vanity. They conceal their lusts with talk of raising living standards, improving education, caring for the elderly.

Ambition was no different 2,000 years ago when Suetonius wrote his 'The life of the Caesars.' But then it was naked; no-one bothered to disguise it within a socially-acceptable framework. There was no talk then of issues floating around The Forum: it was power for the sake of power, conquest for the sake of conquest. 'I've won so I'm the King of the Castle.'

Suetonius would have noticed a reassuring familiarity about the motivations of Sam Harvey McGovern, President of the United States. While Britain's Deputy Prime Minister was dropping dark hints to his blackmail victim about the future of Her Majesty's First Minister, McGovern was glowering with set jaw and lowered head at his Deputy Director at the Department of Overseas Intelligence.

Tom Ginsberg knew the President's moods well. The lighthouse charm which had won him the voters' approval at the last election was rarely evident in the confines of the White House. McGovern was desperate to win a second term. But, with the next election less than 18 months away, his position in the polls was the worst any President had suffered since Jimmy

Carter and the Iranian hostage debacle in 1980.

'I need this Brit deal, Tom. But what I don't need is some piss-ant creep who can't keep his pecker in his pants, to fuck it all up.' McGovern's profanity was hardly noticed by his DD. It was well known that McGovern liked to emphasise his yeoman roots with coarse expletives.

'I'm sure you've nothing to be concerned about in that regard, Mr President. Pelham's got everything under control.' Ginsberg looked at his watch and added on five hours for the time difference. 'In fact just about now he should be lashing that particular loose cannon hard to the deck.'

Sam McGovern grunted. He stared steadily at Ginsberg. Little shit. They were all duplicitous shits at Langley - all working to thwart him. You'd think that when the President of the United States wanted to look at a secret file, they'd come running with it in five minutes flat.

But, no. It was not available, or it had been signed out elsewhere, or it was buried so deep it would take weeks to find. He knew what they were up to. It was their way of saying: you might be the President but we know the system, we invented it. If we stall long enough there'll be another President along before you know.

But he had a few tricks of his own. Every time he met Ginsberg about 'Dunkirk' he instructed his office to erase all record of the encounter. Should any nosy reporter ask, under the Freedom of Information Act, just what the President had been doing at 11.30 this Tuesday, he was 'in the Oval Office alone, attending to matters of state.' The reporter would translate that as...having a presidential crap, and leave it at that.

And, should 'Dunkirk' blow up in their faces, he would point the finger at a renegade Security Agency who had gotten out of control. And he had the doctored FBI files in his drawer to prove it. And, just to be on the safe side, he had the CIA do the same with the FBI. He was fireproof. At least if he got tipped out of 1600 Pennsylvania Avenue he'd go down with honour, not slink out the back door like Nixon.

'So Dunkirk's on schedule?'

Ginsberg leaned forward eagerly. 'It looks that way, sir. Pelham's on the home straight. He's sidelined the obvious contenders for the leadership. Now, he's all set to...er...EP...Lancaster and take over -- '

McGovern jerked up both hands with palms outwards. He lowered his voice as if someone might be listening. But he knew no-one could be. Ever since Nixon blew it with his tapes, no President ever recorded anything in the Oval Office. And the whole room was a bubble of electronic white noise so that, even if anyone had the technology to listen remotely, all they'd hear would be Niagara Falls.

His voice held a note of admiration. 'So the mother really has the balls to do it. I never thought he would, when it came to it. He's actually going to take out the Prime Minister of Great Britain..?'

Ginsberg shrugged. 'He says it's the only way, Mr President.'

'Jeez, Tom, our politics are rough enough but I can't see the vp pushing me out of Air Force One.'

Ginsberg didn't think a reply was called for so he continued, 'After assuming the reins, Pelham will announce the Queen's terminal illness and propose a referendum. Then, with the country forced to contemplate major constitutional changes, he'll fly a kite about the EU--'

'--Fly a goddamn kite. I don't want the son of a bitch to fly anything. I want him to whip his people into line and get the Hell out of that European straightjacket which they dress up as a so-called Deep and Special Partnership.'

'--with respect, Mr President,' Ginsberg soothed, '...flying a kite is just an expression. When he wants to be, Pelham can play the crowd like an old-time Hell-fire preacher. Add in the fact that he's one of the most duplicitous bastards I've known and he's backed by the world's biggest media tycoon and I'd say you and he are set to stake your claim to a place in history, sir.'

McGovern looked slightly mollified. 'Well, I guess you're right,' he grumbled. 'But, as the Iron Lady once said, it's a funny old world. You're sure he doesn't know what the real agenda is? Get the Brits to burn their boats and then squeeze 'em into line. I know it'll be a long haul, Tom, but when they're finally part of the Union, history'll remember it all started with me.'

Ginsberg kept his face impassive. It was best not to respond, or he'd be another hour listening to McGovern's game plan for the 20th time. McGovern might or might not pull it off, thought Ginsberg. But, before that, there was a minefield to negotiate. And, not the least part of that minefield was Pelham himself, who was as slippery as a snake. If he had guessed at the President's real motives for supporting him, it would be a question of who was taking whom for a ride.

McGovern must have read something in Ginsberg's expression because he said, 'Call me a goddamned pessimist but I'd sorta like to be prepared if Dunkirk goes apeshit. So, come on Tom, play me the Jeremiah.'

'Well, sir, as I said, I think Pelham's on course...' McGovern flicked him a warning look '...but, OK, let's look at some negatives.' He began ticking off on his fingers, 'One, Pelham's three main rivals in the Cabinet could blow the whistle--'

'--Unlikely. They've all got too much to lose. They're more likely to keep their piss-ant mouths shut no matter what.'

'Exactly our assessment, sir. Two, the guy who killed the hooker could get a rush of blood to the head and turn himself in--'

--'Again, unlikely.'

'Three, our honey-trap hookers sell their information to the Press. But, that's no longer a possibility.'

'Oh?'

'We carried out another...er...Extreme Prejudice operation to eliminate the last risk.'

'Goddamn it, Ginsberg, it's England not fucking Chicago.'

'I know, Mr President, but it was necessary. The first girl's picture appeared in the papers and we suspect the second one was about to sell her story. We couldn't afford some nosy cop or reporter sniffing around now.'

McGovern's breath exploded in disgust. 'It's getting messy, Ginsberg. Are you sure you've covered all the exits? What about the cops? I suppose they're just sitting there with their thumbs up their asses while the corpses pile up around them?'

'No sir, they have one cop working on the case but his chief just happens to be in Pelham's pocket--'

'--Christ, that Pelham sounds like some kind of Svengali.'

Ginsberg grinned. 'You could say that, sir. As I've said before, Pelham's a true patriot. And he feels he's engaged in an epic struggle for the soul of his country. But he believes the only way he'll achieve his ends is by grabbing power and exercising it ruthlessly...'

'...The ends justifying the means..?'

'Just so, sir. Before Pelham became Deputy Leader of the Social Democrats he was Chief Whip. As you know, Mr

President, that's a kind of party manager's job. As such, every piece of dirt - you know, who's screwing who, who likes little boys, who's got money problems, who's had their hand in some till - crosses the Chief Whip's desk and he gets to know where all the bodies are buried.'

The President's face cleared. 'So, with an eye to the future, he keeps all this dirt close to his vest until it's needed. And, I guess, that's how the DOI got the lowdown on his main political rivals?'

'Exactly, Mr President. Which we then embroidered, just to add veracity.'

Sam McGovern blew out his cheeks. 'If the Press corps could hear this conversation - their President conniving in the elimination of a sovereign country's Prime Minister - they'd have my pecker in the mincer...' He nodded at the tranquil scene outside the green, bulletproof windows '...and they'd scatter the bits to mulch the White House rose garden.'

Ginsberg said hastily, 'As you know, sir, there's nothing at all to connect you with Dunkirk. And, quite honestly, I can't see what can go wrong with the operation at this time. We've given Pelham the stuff. All he has to do is drop it in Lancaster's coffee and...boom...exit a tired old guy whose ticker gave out under the pressures of office. And nothing to show up at an autopsy.'

McGovern's mouth turned up in the ghost of a smile. 'There are a few round here I'd like to drop dead in the service of their country.'

Ginsberg chortled dutifully. 'So, sir, as you see there really seems to be little that can stop Dunkirk now.'

McGovern's face shone with fervour. 'By God, Tom, I can't wait for it to start. Just imagine: I go on tv for one of my state-of-the-union addresses and knock 'em dead with my announcement: that instead of drowning in the quagmire of Europe, the Brits--the new Commonwealth of Great Britain--are to join their kinsmen here, in a new "associated" status.

'The Republic of Great Britain and the United States of America, in a new Atlantic Alliance. Under a treaty to be approved by both governments, they give us a base from which to trade with 500 million people in Greater Europe. In return we give them a guaranteed market, plus a defence umbrella to shelter them from an increasingly unstable world.

'They ditch their monarchy and we embrace each other like brothers. A lovers' clinch as the sun sets in the west. There won't be a dry eye in the house, Tom.'

'And worth at least 20 percentage points in the polls, Mr President.'

Fourteen

Over the months that Det Sgt Claire Bishop had worked with Jack Lockyer she had learned not to ambush him as soon as he arrived at the office. He liked time to settle in behind his desk and take stock. She placed a plastic cup of machine-brewed coffee in front of him and silently noted the bloodshot eyes and dark smudges beneath. Another bender. So that's where he had been yesterday afternoon.

He was always grumpy after one of his solitary boozing sessions. She was surprised, then, when he smiled at her and said cheerfully, 'Well, sergeant, out with it.'

'Sorry?'

I can tell by your face you have some intelligence to impart so let's have it?'

She replied tentatively, 'There are a couple of messages.' His face took on a wary look at her tone.

'Don't tell me - my boss would like the pleasure of my company at my earliest convenience?'

'Something like that. Mr Forsyth popped by yesterday afternoon. Apparently we were supposed to provide a daily report of our progress on the Linda Burchfield case. To be honest, sir, he wasn't best pleased that you hadn't told him about the hit-and-run development...'

'...Or, no doubt, that he was having to glean this

information from a mere sergeant.'

Claire grinned. 'And, especially a mere woman.' Jack chuckled. 'And who was the other message from?'

'Tessa Jordan, the editor we interviewed yesterday. When I told her you weren't here she said would you contact her as soon as possible. She wouldn't tell me what it was about but she gave me the impression it was important. She left her direct-line number.'

Claire covertly watched Lockyer's expression as she mentioned Tessa Jordan's name. He had acted very peculiarly yesterday at The Examiner's offices, bumbling and stuttering. It seemed to afflict him as soon as he was introduced to that editor woman. Perhaps she'd got through his defences somehow, Claire thought.

Apart from an involuntary widening of the eyes, Lockyer's face remained impassive. 'Thanks, Claire. Now,' he said looking at her amusedly, 'contrary to what you might imagine, I took yesterday afternoon off to mull over, without the blessed phone going every five minutes, some puzzling aspects of this case that I can't pin down.'

He waved her to a mottled, metal chair with the stuffing coming out of its cushion. 'Let me summarise the situation so far and then I'd like to hear what you think.'

Claire got out her notebook. Jack leaned back and stared at the ceiling collecting his thoughts. Abruptly he hunched forward, his expression grave. 'From now on I want you to keep strictly between us everything about this case. There's something very odd going on. So, no briefings to Commanders, and no gossiping with colleagues.'

Claire hesitated. 'Of course, sir. But what if Mr Forsyth makes one of his unannounced visits while you're out?'

'Tell him I'm keeping everything to myself and therefore

if he wants any info he'll have to get it from me.' Claire smiled wryly. 'He's going to love that.'

Lockyer said, 'Now, let's look at what we've got. First, a bog-standard homicide which, on the face of it, only requires the local plod to track down a jealous boyfriend, or maybe a known rapist. Pretty routine. And yet, in less than an hour from the discovery of the body, the Yard's called in. So question one is: Why?

'Second, the victim's been strangled and sexually-assaulted. Nothing unusual there. But, in her handbag there's a small fortune in used notes which, we might conclude, came from a mysterious American who, according to her flatmate, acted as some kind of go-between. Question two: Who was she seeing and what service was she offering for that kind of money?'

While Jack spoke, Claire was taking careful notes. Lockyer continued, 'Third, her flatmate talks to The Press about running some kind of dubious escort service and then, after offering to sell more salacious details, she's killed in a mysterious hit-and-run. The car's later found torched so no possibiity of DNA evidence.'

'Which suggests a professional job, not a random accident,' Claire interjected.

'Precisely. And, if we make the assumption that the two girls' murders are not co-incidental, then we no longer have a bog standard anything. There's a link which must have something to do with their escort service and who they were providing a service for. Or, perhaps, what information they picked up through it. So, question three is: If they were killed to silence them, what did they know that was so dangerous? And who was it dangerous to?'

Claire looked puzzled. 'But, according to Miss Jordan and

her news editor yesterday, Rebecca hadn't offered them anything worth paying for.'

'Hmmm. Never trust a journalist, young Claire. Which brings us back to why she wants to speak to me. Perhaps she's thought back on their conversation with Rebecca and has remembered something significant. I'll give her a call when we've finished here.

'Meanwhile, if there is a link with the killings, and what the girls knew, it means this is much more than a routine case. And I smell politics somewhere along the line. So, is that why the Yard's been brought in and why Mr Forsyth keeps hopping up and down like a demented frog?'

Claire sucked the end of her pen thoughtfully, 'With respect, sir, that implies some sort of conspiracy. Don't you think that's a bit fanciful? There could be a hundred other reasons why the Commander wants to keep his finger on this particular pulse.'

Jack rubbed his tired eyes with the heel of both hands. 'I might be maligning my superior unfairly, and if it turns out I'm wrong, I'll be taking involuntary early retirement. But, corruption at the Met's not unheard of you know. If, and it's a big if, Forsyth is mixed up in some kind of cover-up, it would explain a lot.'

Claire nodded. 'Certainly it would make sense of us being called in so quickly. And why he's taking such an unusually close interest. But, surely he hasn't the authority to take the investigation away from Wiltshire? Wouldn't that kind of clout have to come from higher up?'

Jack said, 'I'd guess it would have to be a political decision enforced by some mandarin at the Home Office.'

'So, now we've got political corruption as well?'

'Lockyer coughed. 'One step at a time, eh?'

Claire persisted, 'But, sir. Suppose it was? Doesn't that suggest blackmail somewhere in the frame? Suppose these girls had stumbled across some juicy stuff in the course of their...er...activities and decided to put the arm on someone...'

Lockyer stared at his assistant meditatively '...who happens to be powerful enough to have them killed just to shut them up? You know, you may just have something. It does add up. But, as I said, let's take one step at a time. All this is mere speculation. We've got to get some evidence and I think the starting place for that is Linda and Rebecca.'

Lockyer hummed to himself for a moment and then made up his mind. 'Look, go back to their flat and search every inch. What you're looking for is names, contacts, meeting places, club memberships, anything that might give us a better idea of their routines...who they met, who their friends were, where they spent their time. Even where they did their weekly shop; you know the kind of thing.'

'And bank accounts? Do you want me to check those?'

'Especially bank accounts. See if there's any pattern. Money going in and flowing out. I suppose it's too much to hope our American friend paid them by cheque.'

'Wrong time of the year for Santa,' Claire replied drily. 'Any more clues about that mystery message? You know, PA 4PM.' Lockyer shook his head slowly. 'I've racked my brains. How about you.?'

'Well sir, on the face of it, it must be an appointment of some kind. Linda was due to meet someone with the initials PA somewhere at 4PM. But, since no-one so far connected with the case seems to have those initials, it could be something else.'

'Like?'

'Like, might the initials stand for Press Association?'

'You mean she might have been meeting someone from the Press Association at 4pm? Right check into it. What else?'

'Does the 4pm have to be a time? Could it mean something like four per month..?'

Lockyer absent mindedly drummed his fingers on the metal desktop. 'Hmmm. PA four per month? Payment Arranged - four per month? Payment Average - four per month?' He thumped his fist down in frustration. 'God, we could go on guessing for ever like this. Look, you check on this Press Association thing and I'll contact Miss Jordan.'

'Don't forget Mr Forsyth.'

'When I have something positive to tell him, I'll beard the lion...Until then, he'll have to contain his impatience. You never know, if he gets frustrated enough he might let slip the real reason the Yard's involved.'

When Claire had left, Lockyer dialled The Examiner editor's direct line number. He noticed with alarm that his palm had begun to feel sticky as he held the phone. And his heart was thumping rebelliously as he waited for Tessa to answer.

What the heck was going on? He refused to admit to the alien and utterly ridiculous notion of...falling in love. After Jennie, he was past all that nonsense. But, how else could he explain the damp hands, the racing heart and the slight visceral clutch of fear?

It was only a phone call. And to a stranger he had met for the first time yesterday and for about half an hour. Maybe the sweats and the gut-ache were symptoms of the booze. Or was he cracking up and didn't know it? He shuddered as he recalled his gauche performance yesterday.

By this morning, when he had sobered up, the feeling of uneasiness mixed with exhilaration was still there. He couldn't get away from it: the moment he had set eyes on Tessa Jordan something peculiar had taken him over. Some long frozen component of his inner being had begun to stir.

The unfamiliar feeling had taken him totally by surprise and made a mockery of his normal, detached professionalism.

Yesterday- he had struggled to assemble his questions but they kept flying out of his head. He must have looked such a fool. He recalled part of himself watching in bemusement as he had floundered through the interview, helped manfully by Claire stepping in when he had dried up. Whatever she must have thought, she hadn't let it show just now.

'Tessa Jordan.'

Lockyer cleared his throat and noted with relief that his voice sounded confident and steady as he announced himself. 'Miss Jordan, Det Insp Jack Lockyer. You wanted to speak to me I believe?'

'Ah yes, Inspector. I have a confession to make.'

Jack noted a hesitancy in her voice as if what she was about to say was going to put her at a disadvantage. He said levelly, 'Confession?'

'Yes. Look Inspector, I'd prefer not to talk about this on the phone.'

'Very well, I'll come to your office again. Or perhaps you'd prefer to come to the Yard?'

'As far as the office goes, I'm tied up in meetings until this evening and, as for Scotland Yard, not an attractive prospect after a hard day.'

Lockyer had encountered reluctant witnesses a thousand times and found himself slipping into an automatic response. He said testily, 'Miss Jordan, if you have evidence material to a murder investigation, might I suggest it takes precedence over the processes involved in producing a newspaper, however exalted, and your preferences for ambiance.'

There was silence on the line. Then Tessa spoke. 'You're right of course. And I'm not the only busy person. How about a compromise?'

Jack found himself regretting his churlishness. What was the matter with him? Why were his reactions so extreme every time he encountered this woman? His attempt to sound conciliatory translated itself into an inept double entendre. 'I'm open to suggestions.'

Tessa did not seem to notice. 'Since we've both got to eat, how about a sandwich and, even in these abstemious times, possibly a glass of wine at lunchtime? Falstaff's in Arundel Street, which is about half way for us both, is generally quite quiet on a Wednesday. Would 12.30 suit?'

'I think I can manage that. All right, I'll see you then.'

When Jack hung up he noticed to his disgust that his hands were shaking uncontrollably.

Fifteen

Jack often spent his lunch breaks walking along the Thames Embankment retracing the route he and Jennie used to take when they could both grab a few hours off. Today, for once, he was thinking of someone else as he hunched against the stiff breeze and, under lowering skies, made his way past Cleopatra's Needle towards Waterloo Bridge.

When he entered the gloom of Falstaff's, he felt a surge of pleasure at seeing Tessa Jordan waving discreetly to him from a gingham-covered table on the far side of the bar.

She stood up and they shook hands. Her grip was firm and her green eyes looked directly into his. The awkwardness he felt must be showing on his face, he thought. Silently, he thanked the interior designer who had decided on a nocturnal ambience.

They ordered a glass of chablis and a chicken and salad sandwich each. And, as Tessa exchanged pleasantries with the waiter, Jack looked closely for the first time at the woman who seemed to be having an alarming effect on his equilibrium.

He noted she was about average height, slim, with a good figure and wavy hair. The direct way she had of looking at you was offset by a friendly manner. Not a bit like a stereotypical, Fleet Street harridan, he thought.

She wore a white blouse, done up at the neck, under a light-brown, two-piece suit which combined formality with elegance.

For Tessa's part she was weighing Jack up out of the corner of her eye. What she saw was a big, bulky, battered man, in his late forties, with crinkly hair and a strong face. Ever since he had turned up at the paper after that dreadful accident yesterday, she had found to her puzzlement that he kept intruding on her thoughts.

And yet he was nothing like her idea of the ideal partner. She had always been attracted to the tall, slim, confident go-getters who peopled her world. That was why she had been perplexed at her reaction in the presence of this stranger.

As a reporter she had met scores of coppers and she had learned over the years to categorise them into two basic types - earnest but dull or bright and brash.

However, Jack Lockyer had been neither. As he had questioned both Frank and herself, he had seemed diffident and, at times, confused. And there was something else about him, she thought. A loneliness? A certain vulnerability? A soul in despair but who had no choice but to labour on? Like the Flying Dutchman?

She mutely remonstrated with herself. Fanciful codswallop. What was the matter with her? She was thinking like some gushing schoolgirl. He was probably happily married with children, a mortgage and a lawn he cut on Saturdays and a car he washed on Sundays.

She turned to him and said, 'I rather got off on the wrong foot this morning, didn't I?' Jack shrugged noncommittally. 'Forget it,' he replied. 'What was it you wanted to see me about?' The wine arrived and she took a tentative sip before saying, 'That confession I mentioned. Frank and I didn't tell you everything yesterday.'

'Oh?'

'In fact we deliberately gave you a lot of guff as a smokescreen because we knew we were probably sitting on the best story of our lives.' Jack gazed at his companion levelly. Tessa went on, 'Just before she left, Rebecca handed over Linda Burchfield's diary which we said we had to examine before we could start negotiating a price. Rebecca left it with us--'

--'very trusting of her,' Jack said drily.

Tessa inclined her head. 'I gave her my word we wouldn't rip her off and she seemed to accept that. Anyway, I think she was probably scared when she knew what she had. In her mind, if she could make a quick sale, she could drop out somewhere until things had blown over.'

Jack prompted, 'So she didn't want to hang around for a cat and mouse negotiation?'

'No, she was desperate for a deal. Anyway, Frank and I were horrified when we heard she'd been killed just outside the building. It occurred to us that her "accident" might possibly have something to do with what she was going to tell us.

'So, by the time you arrived we had studied the diary more closely and realised it was dynamite.'

Tessa said intensely, 'I don't suppose you will understand this Inspector, but when a journalist stumbles on a scoop the instinct is to run with it. So, we agreed to fob you off to give us more time to assess what we had.'

'And?'

'We pretty quickly realised we couldn't justify withholding material evidence.' Tessa reached down to rummage in her handbag on the floor. She slid a pocket book across the table to him. 'However, we would like to do a deal with you. Frank's story boosted last Sunday's circulation by about 20,000.

'We reckon we've got enough usable stuff from what's in there for a follow-up exclusive...' Jack was about to protest when Tessa cut him off '...But, we'd be willing to hold off in exchange for first dibs at the whole story once it all comes out.'

Jack shook his head. 'Sorry, Miss Jordan, you know I can't do that. I'd be accused by your media colleagues of blatant favouritism.' He added warningly, 'And, if you use any material which might divert or obstruct the course of an investigation, you would be committing an offence.'

He opened the diary and riffled through the leaves. The light was too dim to make anything out. But, it was obvious there were entries for every page. He frowned across at Tessa. 'So what's so explosive?'

Her expression toughened. 'Sorry, Inspector, but I haven't finished negotiating our exclusive yet. Our lawyers have told us how far we can go with the information we've got. But, quite honestly, I'd rather have the whole story than half of it so why can't we come to a sensible arrangement?'

'I've already told you. If I start feeding titbits to one journalist but not another it'd cause all kinds of resentment. Don't forget, after this case is over I have to work with your lot on the next one. And the one after that. Putting their backs up isn't worth it for short-term expediency.'

Tessa grinned. 'Frank said you have a tendency to pomposity when you're pushed into a corner.'

Pompous? He didn't think he was being pompous, thought Jack. 'I don't regard myself as in a corner.'

'There you go again. Sorry. Look, Frank suggested I used the "fair play" card. He said I should point out that Rebecca did come to The Examiner in the first place and if it hadn't been for that, you might not have anything.'

Jack beetled his brows. 'And she might be alive today, Miss Jordan.' There was a long silence, during which Tessa looked chastened. Eventually, Jack grumbled, 'I suppose you have got a point. Look, I can't stop you from writing your story next week. But, as for an exclusive if, and when, we get to the bottom of it all, I'll see what I can do, but I won't promise anything.' He slipped the diary into his pocket. Now what's so explosive about it?'

Tessa regarded Jack silently for a moment and then shrugged. 'OK, it's a deal.' For the next 10 minutes Tessa gave Jack a run-down of the diary's contents and her and Frank's conclusions. Finally, she said, 'I expect one thing will jump off the page at you when you see it. Apparently, on the day Lucinda died, she was due to meet someone with the initials PA. The appointment was down for four in the afternoon. We reckon whoever PA is killed her.'

Jack, who had been unnerved by Tessa's jibe at his pomposity, jutted his head forward. 'Sorry? Say that last bit again.' Tessa repeated what she had seen pencilled in Linda's diary for Friday, May 19th, 2023.

'By the look on your face Inspector, the initials are significant.'

Jack looked at her uncertainly. 'Miss Jordan...' He began.

'...Inspector, can't we stop this "Miss Jordan" stuff. I feel like a suspect. Why not call me Tessa?'

'Alright...Tessa. I'm going to take you into my confidence. And, bearing in mind you're a journalist, some of my colleagues would regard that as a certifiable decision. However, since you and Frank have obviously studied the diary from cover to cover, and probably scanned every page into your computers--'

Tessa had, of course, copied the diary. But to avoid

leaving an electronic imprint anywhere that might be uncovered later, she had painstakingly written every detail by hand herself. And in a diary an exact facsimile of Linda's. A handwriting expert would immediately have detected the forgery. But otherwise, to all intents and purposes, it was Linda's diary.

Tessa opened her mouth to say something but Jack held up his hand to stop her '--what I'm about to tell you comes under the same heading of confidentiality as the rest of this discussion. One of the things I didn't tell Frank Dutton before he wrote his story last week was about the crumpled piece of paper we found in Linda's handbag.'

Tessa looked at him balefully. 'Don't tell me. It had a phone number on it, you traced it and you've arrested the murderer and you've come here to tell me not to waste any more of your time?'

He replied soberly, 'Waste my time? No, nothing like that. The point is that crumpled piece of paper had the same initials on it as those you say are in Linda's diary.'

They both regarded each other thoughtfully. At length Tessa said, 'But, if it was an appointment of some sort, why have it scribbled down on a piece of paper as well?'

'A very good point. My sergeant believes in what she calls "lateral thinking"--that is not always being seduced by the obvious...'

'...I think I know what lateral thinking means, Inspector.' A broad grin took any sting out of the words. Jack smiled apologetically. 'Sorry. Anyway, we brainstormed all kinds of possibilities but are still clueless.'

Tessa said, 'Apparently, she didn't take her diary out with her, prefering to leave it in her apartment. So, perhaps she scribbled the entry down on a bit of scrap paper to make sure she didn't forget the time or the place.'

'But, that doesn't make sense. You'd have to have a pretty poor memory if you couldn't remember you had to meet someone called PA at four o' clock.'

'But, suppose your sergeant's right and it isn't the obvious. Suppose its the order of the letters and digit that are important so that, to be on the safe side, you jot them down to check against the original.'

Jack furrowed his brow. 'Like a winning ticket number..?'

'Or some sort of code sequence..?' They sat there for a few moments not speaking. Jack was enjoying the presence of this attractive, intelligent woman who pricked his pomposity so gently. Suddenly he wanted to know more about her.

'Why are you looking at me like that, Inspector?'

'Wha...Sorry. I was just wondering...um...how long you've been a national newspaper editor. I mean...er...well...it's still fairly unusual even in these days of the sexual revolution.'

She eyed him uncertainly. 'So we've concluded our discussion on Linda and her diary, have we? Yes, I can see from your face that we have. How long have I been an editor? About a year now.'

'And you obviously enjoy it.'

'What makes you say that?'

Jack, who was saying the first thing that came into his head to justify his staring at Tessa, found himself wallowing deeper in the conversational quicksands. 'Well...I...I mean...It must be exciting. Being at the top of your profession, meeting powerful people, being feted by politicians and captains of industry...' Jack faded into silence.

Tessa sighed heavily. 'To tell you the truth, Inspector...Look, since I'm baring my soul, I can't keep calling you Inspector. May I call you Jack..?' Jack nodded. Hearing his name come out of her mouth gave him an odd surge of pleasure. 'To tell you the truth, Jack, it's not nearly so glamorous as you might imagine - especially if, like me, you're one of Ben Hobart's functionaries.

'These days its less lunching with cabinet ministers and shaping a nation's destiny and more maximising profit potential, downsizing, core re-emphasis and all the rest of the Harvard Business School jargon. I'm not so much an editor as a business manager.

'My success is judged more by how much money the paper makes than the quality of the journalism. That's why, when a story like this one comes up, the reporter in me gets excited and the adrenalin starts to pump. For a few delicious moments it transports me away from finance plans, performance indicators and target evaluations and back to a world I feel in harmony with.'

Jack gazed at her in wonder. Her eyes were dancing and her face was alive with pleasure as she talked of the thrill of the chase and being first with the big story. 'But these days,' Tessa said regretfully, 'there's little room for individual distinction.

'All Hobart's editors are required to toe the same editorial lines and achieve the same percentage profits. This means most of the time you're bogged down in bureaucracy churning out widgets. They may be different shapes and sizes but they're Hobart widgets just the same.'

Jack said sympathetically, 'I know exactly what you mean. In fact it's no different at the Yard. I swear I spend more time filling in forms, compiling statistics and producing crime surveys than chasing villains. Where's it all going to end?'

Tessa laughed. 'Listen to us. We're like a couple of "disgusteds of Tunbridge Wells." Tell me about yourself? How long have you been a policeman?'

For the next quarter of an hour Jack opened up more than he had in years. It was easy to talk to this kindred spirit. And Tessa enjoyed their conversation, too. She learned that Jack Lockyer joined the police force as a cadet thirty-odd years previously. He loved his work and when he had fallen in love and married, his life was complete.

'So, what does your wife do now? Or is she a full-time house-person, looking after her family?'

For the first time, a shadow crossed Jack's face. 'She died. She was killed in a car crash.'

Tessa found herself overwhelmed with mixed emotions. All she could say was, 'I'm so sorry. How awful for you.'

Jack looked at her sombrely. 'Yes, it was pretty bloody. But that was six years ago and...well...life goes on.'

'Do you have any children?'

Jack shook his head. 'No, we never did. In a way it was a good job we didn't. I don't know how I could have coped with the responsibilities on my own.'

'And you've never re-married?'

'Never felt the need. My job takes up most of my time and...I enjoy my own company...up to a point, anyway.' He grinned crookedly. 'I've learned to keep the ghosts at bay.' Abruptly, he changed the subject. 'What about you. Are you married?'

Tessa compressed her lips into a regretful line. 'I was, once. But, it didn't work out. Now I live with a lovely, kind man called Josh.'

'And you're happy.' Jack saw her hesitate before answering. 'Happy? There's no reason why I shouldn't be. Josh is considerate, caring and good company...'

'But..?'

Tessa replied, 'Did I say there was a but?' She looked at

her watch and gasped, 'Oh Lord, look at the time. I've got a meeting in 10 minutes.'

As she stood up to go, she leaned across the table and held out her hand formally. Jack took it reluctantly. 'Nice to have met you, Inspector...Jack. I hope the diary helps. Frank'll be in touch about whether we might use anything this week to keep the pot boiling.'

She added with a smile, 'And, so long as you don't regard it as at attempt to bribe a police officer, the sandwiches and the wine are on me.'

She strode through the swing doors of the bar into the sunshine. When she had gone Jack felt an inexplicable sadness settle over him.

Sixteen

The Prime Minister felt a surge of relief as his routine, Thursday morning Cabinet meeting at Number 10 finally ended. It had been an ill-tempered affair with the splits among his ministers over Europe now becoming chasms.

The last person closed the door leaving him alone in the room. Thank God, he thought, the squabblers' instinct for survival meant they were still just about presenting a united front to the media. But for how long?

He sighed. And, as if he hadn't enough problems, his eyes were playing him up again. Despite enjoying the services of one of the finest ophthalmic consultants in the country, Ted Lancaster acknowledged to himself that his sight was getting worse, as was the pain. He had followed instructions and now carried his eye-drops with him everywhere he went. He had put some in to ease the grittiness before his meeting started.

But, about an hour afterwards the soreness was back and the blurring vision turned his quarrelling colleagues into cabbages with arms. But, he had stuck it out. It wouldn't do to show any weakness. Not now. Not when the biggest bastard of all the bastards in his Cabinet, Robert Pelham, was so obviously after his job. But, it would be over my dead body, he resolved.

He had only appointed Pelham to the symbolic position of Deputy Prime Minister in the first place to take away the power-base of an actual department. And so that he could keep an eye on the man's manoeuverings. Rather a smart move, The Boomer thought. Leaving the way clear for Ingleby, Willis and Sinclair to jockey for the heir-apparent's mantle. Which marginalised Pelham while consolidating his own position as PM.

A neat little gavotte, that. United they might possibly stand, but divided they will certainly fall, making him the indisputable leader. So long as he could maintain his role as healer of Social Democrat wounds. And, provided his bloody eyesight didn't get any worse. Who ever heard of a blind Prime Minister?

A discreet cough interrupted his introspection. Bugger it, he had forgotten Pelham had asked for a private word after the meeting. Had he been sitting there all this time, watching him ruminating?

He swivelled his head in the direction of a fuzzy image half way down the Cabinet table on the left. 'Robert? So sorry. I was just thinking what the media might make of it, if they could see how we argy-bargy among ourselves.'

He shook his head. 'And as for the Tories - how they would love it. Think of the political capital people like Sherborne could make of it.' Lancaster shrugged, 'But, it was ever thus. I don't suppose any PM ever had unanimity over everything?'

'Oh, I don't know,' Pelham smiled thinly, 'I doubt if Margaret Thatcher would admit that. She seemed to achieve unanimity whether the Cabinet liked it or not. Now, there was a strong leader.'

Lancaster chose to ignore the implied criticism. Instead, he expelled his breath in a long sigh. 'I dare say. But those days are long over, last century's goings-on are firmly in the past.

Consensus politics is now the thing. We may disagree privately but as long as we show a united front in public the hacks won't be down on our necks claiming the Social Democrat Party's too split to govern.'

'If you don't mind my saying, Ted, that's rather typical of your instinct for appeasement. What the Party, and the country, needs right now is the smack of firm leadership.'

Lancaster scowled at his colleague. 'Whether you approve of my style or not, Robert, so long as I'm Prime Minister there will be no open warfare. My Cabinet members will be free to speak their minds provided they abide by the majority decision when it comes to the vote.'

Pelham replied acidly, 'The majority decision being your fence-sitting on Europe endorsed by your poodles. Can't you see that by clutching at the shirt-tails of Germany and France you're selling our country down the river..?'

'Bollocks! Without European institutions behind us Britain would wither and die. Whether you like it or not, Pelham, the arguments of 2016 have moved on. Our successful future depends on a fair wind from Europe. We couldn't survive without the trade, we'd lose inward investment, the benefits of a single market, we'd risk trade barriers and our viability as an independent nation. We'd be isolated and vulnerable. It's so obvious, I can't understand why an intelligent man like you cannot see it.'

Pelham leaned forward, 'What I see is an old fumbler prating absurdities. Britain will wither and die, indeed. Here are a few facts: One, our future depends on Europe? Well what about China, the tiger economies of the Far East, India, the Americas? A bigger market available there, and without us having to bow and scrape to Euro nonentities who're just loving the feel of their boots on our necks.

'Two: Inward Investment? If we opted back out of the Social Chapter and our work-force was cheap again and our exchange rate flexible, the Japs, Koreans, Chinese would go on building factories here, just because we're a handy jumping off point for the Continent.

'Three: Trade barriers? Do you think Brussels would risk flouting the rules of the World Trade Organisation? They'd huff and puff for a while, but in the end they'd do nothing. And we'd be just as free as Switzerland or Norway to buy and sell in Europe.

'Four: Our influence? We don't need to be at the EU Top Table. We have our place on the UN Security Council because of our nuclear weapons. If we ever give these up it won't be because of whinges from the EU. So, you see, PM, none of your parroted arguments stand up to scrutiny.'

The Prime Minister shifted uncomfortably. 'Alright then, what kind of Brave New World would we all have if Robert Pelham were running things?'

'Since you ask, PM, I'll tell you. We would not be haemorrhaging multi-billions a year to support indolent Continental farmers, we'd regain all of our fishing grounds, not just what Europe will allow us. So much for the brave new world or our so-called independent status. I'd re-negotiate world-wide trading agreements and we'd restore public confidence in the accountability of their elected representatives. And that's just for starters.'

'Oh, what a visionary you are, Robert. And, no doubt, you have even more ambitious plans which, I take it, you are not going to vouchsafe to me?'

'Correct. But, in order to achieve these plans, I need you to hand over the baton, as it were.'

The PM's smile slipped from his face. 'Hand over..? You

are jesting?'

'No, Prime Minister. I am serious.'

Lancaster gazed uncertainly in Pelham's direction. 'I do believe you are. What...exactly are you getting at?'

'It's simple. I'm suggesting you should hand over to someone with a firm hand, who can whip the rabble into line behind a united Cabinet intent on extricating us from the farce of a European so-called friendship pact.'

Lancaster replied bleakly, 'And, I suppose you have just such a person in mind?'

Pelham pushed his chair away and stood up. He advanced towards the PM's seat at the head of the table and leaned downwards. He said ominously, 'You know damn well I have. I want it and you're going to ensure I get it.'

Lancaster stared at him. 'I'm sorry, Robert, is this a joke? If it is, I have to say it's in poor taste. If it isn't, you are obviously suffering from delusions of grandeur.'

Pelham said calmly, 'I'll spell it out: I want you to resign through ill health and I shall assume command. Since I'm already Deputy PM that will seem perfectly in order. Then, when it comes to a vote, you will endorse me as your chosen successor...' As Pelham spoke, Lancaster gawped at him with mounting incredulity.

Finally, he could not contain a snort of derision. He said, 'Endorse you? You're the last person I'd want to take over. I've never heard such unmitigated arrogance. And I can't believe I'm hearing this. I have absolutely no intention of resigning. And, as for backing you as my heir apparent...there are at least three others better qualified and more suited to succeed me than you.'

For several seconds their eyes locked in silence. Then Pelham turned away and stood with his hands behind his back.

He gazed out through the bomb-proof window to the tiny courtyard beyond. Lancaster felt a tide of unease sweep through him. Eventually, Pelham said casually, 'Nevertheless, that is what will happen.'

'I absolutely refuse to listen to this...this...fantasising any longer. I suggest, Robert, you consult a psychiatrist because I do believe you've lost your sanity.' Pelham tossed three brown folders in front of the Prime Minister who looked at them irritably. 'Now what? I really haven't time for these games.'

'Just cast your eyes - if your waning visual powers will allow, that is - over their contents if you would. By the way, these are the hard copies. I have stored their contents electronically in a safe place that only I know.'

Impatiently, Lancaster hooked his thick glasses round his ears, extracted the papers and peered closely at the documents and photographs. As he read, his hands began to shake; so much that eventually he had to lay the sheets flat on the table and lower his head to continue his examination.

When he had finished, his face had turned the colour of yeast. He took his spectacles off and raised a defeated visage to his companion. 'They're not..not...genuine?'

Pelham collected the contents up and bounced their edges on the surface of the walnut table. 'Let's put it this way, PM, there's enough truth in each of those dossiers to bring the government down if they fell into the hands of the tabloids.'

'But...senior members of the government...Cabinet ministers...getting involved in such...such...squalor.'

'I have to say, Prime Minister, it never ceases to amaze me how apparently intelligent men can bring themselves to risk all - just for the sake of a sexual gratification.'

'But...Howard, Austin, Roland...with the same girl...doing those...disgusting things.'

'To be strictly accurate, their performances were as individuals on separate occasions. I mean, none knew about the others...'

'...But how?'

'The oldest trick in the book. An apparent chance meeting, a little flattery, an invitation back to the young lady's boudoir, a hidden video-recorder and microphone. Result: a folder full of compromising pictures and enough government secrets to keep the Russians and Chinese happily preoccupied for the next five years.'

Abruptly, Lancaster jumped to his feet. 'By God, Pelham, I'll...I'll...' Pelham leaned forward until their eyes were just inches apart. '...You'll do exactly as you are told. Unless you want an early election, that is. Mind, it would be one you won't win, not after the voters find out about their elected representatives' darker sides. You know how prudish the British voter can be.'

Pelham ticked off a litany of former political scandals: 'Remember Profumo? And David Mellor and the toe-sucking actress? Alan Clark and his "Coven"? Edwina Curry and John Major? David Cameron and a late-lamented pig? The poor, unfortunate Chief of Defence Staff entrapped by a scheming vixen and sacked for being a security risk?

'With three government ministers caught simultaneously with their pants down, so to speak, it would be a bonanza for the more prurient Press. After reading about it avidly, the great unwashed would register their stern disapproval in the time-honoured way. And the Social Democrat government would remain out of office for a decade.'

Lancaster sagged back into his chair and stared blankly ahead. Eventually he said tonelessly, 'Do they know you've got all this...this...information?'

Pelham inclined his head. 'Indeed they do, Prime Minister. They have each graciously agreed to co-operate fully.'

Lancaster looked up as a thought suddenly occurred to him. 'Just a minute. That girl in those files? She's the one that's been murdered. And...her friend, the one she lived with, also dead? By God, Pelham, don't tell me you had anything to do with that?'

'I certainly won't tell you, PM. I suggest you forget you ever made the connection.'

'But...But...murder. As well as blackmail.'

'Don't make assumptions Prime Minister. All I will say is that sometimes it is necessary to take certain...actions...for the greater good. Now, I trust you intend to co-operate?'

Lancaster shook his head in bewilderment. 'Murder? Is it possible..? What...what is it you want me to do?'

'Spoken like a true pragmatist, Prime Minister. Now, as I indicated. You let it be known that, regretfully, the burdens of office have been too much for your health. Sadly, you are being forced to hand over the mantle. But, happily, that mantle was tailor-made for your deputy PM who has indicated that, if fate has so decreed, he will do his humble best to continue the unifying traditions of his erstwhile leader.'

Lancaster's reply had an ironic note. 'And I suppose your three main rivals will inexplicably forgo their own ambitions to rally behind my choice?'

'Precisely. So when it comes to an election to ratify my position, it'll be a one-horse race.'

Lancaster said bitterly, 'So that's all you want?'

Pelham rocked on his heels. 'Not quite. There must be no announcement about Her Majesty's...er...illness--'

'--But I was intending to make it public this afternoon.'

'Well, now you will not. I wish to do that as one of my

first...um...reluctant duties.'

Realisation dawned on Lancaster's face. 'My God, Pelham, you're a devious bastard. As soon as you make that announcement everyone will forget about everything else and the country will unite in its grief - behind you.'

Pelham retorted, 'And I suppose that idea's only just occurred to you this minute? Come off your high horse Prime Minister .'

Seventeen

Ever since his meeting with Pelham on Tuesday, James had been in turmoil. Somehow he had got through the next few days fending off enquiries about his fretful demeanour with excuses of a persistent migraine.

Now it was Saturday and at last he had a chance to talk things over properly with Elizabeth. The kids had been brilliant. Once again they had accepted his irritability was part of the winding-down process after a pressured week. Daniel had taken refuge in his room and was playing with his X-box and Sarah was out riding.

As James and Elizabeth ambled round the garden he scarcely noticed the splashes of brilliant early summer hues made by the scarlet tulips, purple pansies and lily of the valley in the borders, which took up so much of his wife's spare time during the week.

He slouched along, head down and hands in his pockets, with Elizabeth's arm tucked through his. Suddenly James stamped his right foot viciously. 'The man's a megalomaniac. But he's got me over a barrel, Lizzie. I'm at his mercy and there's not a damned thing I can do about it.'

Taking a deep breath to calm himself he eventually said to his wife, 'Behind his ambition to take over the world there's something extremely sinister going on. We've now got two deaths, what with that hit-and-run as well as my...accident.

'And, the only way he could have known about last Friday

is if someone followed me, saw everything, and reported back. And why? Was I supposed to pick the girl up? Was it all part of some rotten plan?'

Elizabeth watched a wood pigeon flapping joyfully into the sky, allowing itself to glide down again into the field beyond their boundary. She replied hesitantly, 'James, I'm frightened. What have we become mixed up in?'

They both stopped and looked at each other. James compressed his lips. 'This whole nightmare started when someone arranged for that Lucinda girl to be there in the rain when they knew I'd be along.'

Elizabeth nodded. 'Obviously, it was a trap. They wanted to manoeuvre you into a compromising situation --'

'--And the "they" has got to be Robert Pelham,' said her husband.

Elizabeth stopped abruptly. 'Darling, I've just thought of something. You know you said that when you first saw the girl, she appeared to be ill? Bent over I think you said.'

'Yes, I thought at first she was doubled up in pain.'

'Suppose she wasn't ill at all. Suppose she was crouching down to read your registration number - to make sure she'd got the right car?'

James looked at Elizabeth in astonishment. 'By God, you're right. Because I had my headlights on, she couldn't have been certain who was driving along that lane. No! She wasn't ill at all. She was peering at my number plate.'

Elizabeth said, 'And as soon as she knew it was your car she switched on her performance.'

'And all to get me where they want me. It all adds up.' James started to pace up and down the lawn, punching his hand as he made each point. 'First, Pelham says I have to keep my mouth shut over Europe. Next, he says he's all set to take over the leadership of his Party, and therefore become PM by default.

'Then he blithely announces he wants my backing for his ideas on the monarchy, turning our backs on Europe and cosying up to the United States.'

Elizabeth said, 'And, if he gets it, that would almost guarantee a smooth passage through the Commons. Yes, first he must have seen you as some kind of threat to his plans. And then he realised he could kill two birds with the same stone. If he had you under his thumb, he could get the Tories behind his schemes.'

She continued, 'A girl cries rape and you're blackmailed into toeing the line. But by a ghastly accident the poor creature dies which, for Pelham, actually works out as a bonus.'

James said resignedly, 'The man's a bloody Machiavelli.'

'The question now is, James, what are you going to do about it?'

'What can I do, darling? He's got me where he wants me. If I damn him I end up by damning myself even more.'

'There must be something we can do. What about going straight to Lancaster and telling him?'

'That wouldn't work. Why should he believe me, a member of the Opposition, against his own deputy? He'd think I'd flipped. Anyway, what could I say? That his Number Two is probably an accessory to murder and has hatched some plot to oust him from the top job and change the Party's policy?'

'No,' his wife agreed, 'and he certainly wouldn't believe some story about a girl's accidental asphyxiation. He'd have you arrested on the spot.'

'So you see, my darling, I'm on my own. Pelham's got me by the short and curlies and I can do F-all about it.'

As they moved back towards the house, Elizabeth was

deep in thought. At length she said, 'James, do you really think Pelham had anything to do with that hit-and-run? It's just too much of a co-incidence that two girls, living in the same apartment, end up dead within days of each other.

'If he was behind a plot to blackmail you, there's no knowing what he might be capable of. If he did have something to do with the second killing, and you could prove it, it would turn the tables.'

'Lizzie, this is all too fantastic. We're talking here about a public figure, a household name, a future Prime Minister if he gets his way, being involved in blackmail and murder. Anyway, even if Pelham doesn't draw the line at a spot of coercion, why should he resort to murder? He seems to be doing very nicely manipulating people to his requirements without taking unnecessary risks.'

'But just suppose he is somehow pulling the strings. Why? What's so important that it's worth killing for?'

James absent-mindedly kicked a pebble into the shrubbery. 'Plenty of people have murdered for less. He said he intended to take over the leadership of his party. Nothing unusual about that kind of ambition, of course.' He shook his head in exasperation. 'But, I can't see where the two females with dubious reputations come in.'

'It strikes me, James, that if Pelham's capable of blackmailing you, he's equally capable of doing the same with anyone else who stands in his way. What if those girls were used to coerce certain people, exactly as you were?'

James looked at his wife as enlightenment dawned. 'Of course. I've been so stupid! Ingleby, Willis and Sinclair. Pelham said they had been - what did he say - ? Naughty boys, or something. And that he had positive proof. Yes, he must be blackmailing them. And that's where those girls come in. By

God, the man's positively Satanic.'

Elizabeth said steadily, 'Tell me again what he said about The Boomer giving up office?'

James thought for a moment. 'He said it would be through ill-health. Which struck me as a bit strange because apart from his eyes, which everyone knows about, Lancaster's averagely fit for his age.'

James peered abstractedly into the middle-distance. 'Come to think of it, there was something distinctly odd about the way Pelham talked of The Boomer's retirement - as though it would more likely be...permanent. You know, like he was dying or something.'

'Dying?'

'Yes, you know. He said something about the PM's eyes killing him...or some such. No, I know, he said the PM's eyes would be the end of him. That's right. No, I've got it. Pelham said...I have a feeling his eyes will be the death of him.'

Elizabeth looked at her husband quizzically. 'Is the man enough of a fiend to contemplate actually...I can hardly bring myself to say it...actually murdering Britain's Prime Minister?

In one of his more wry moments, Ted Lancaster had joked about it being handy 'living above the shop.' The truth was his wife, Maud, did not like Chequers, the country residence available to the serving Prime Minister.

She preferred the cosiness of the apartment above Number 10. That's why they spent most of their weekends there and that is where they were now discussing Pelham's extraordinary ultimatum.

'The man's a barbarian. You can't possibly give in to him, Edward.'

Ted Lancaster sighed as he watched his wife busily drying the breakfast dishes. She was always on the move, was Maud. Hyperactive is what they called it these days. It was 'nervous energy' when he was a lad. And all their married lives Maud had been the dominant partner. It was she who had pushed him from the back benches through the ranks to Shadow Cabinet status.

Before the last election, when the Conservatives had been thrown out neck and crop, he had been happy as Shadow Minister for Trade and Industry. He had been content with his lot, touring factories and making encouraging speeches. And promising closer links with Europe where politicians fell on his neck gratefully after the isolationist policies of the Tories.

Then, when his beloved Labour Party had gone into meltdown after a Neo-Marxist grass-roots takeover, Ted had found himself thrust into the most high-profile role in Opposition. He had no illusions. It wasn't due to his charisma. It was more because he was seen as the one neutral member of the Front Bench who would not offend. His job had been to stop the Labour movement from tearing itself apart before winning the election. Well, that he had done. But only after a cataclysmic schism which had led to the formation of the Social Democratic Party.

After forming the government, he had been asked to stay on but, to make it more acceptable to the country, and reassuring to the majority in his Party who now opposed bowing the knee to Europe, the spin doctors had advised him to appoint Robert Pelham, a known sceptic, as his deputy.

Lancaster had hated the idea but he reasoned to himself that, in truth, it would be for the best. Being deputy leader was actually a non-job, except for the limited portfolio on trade and industry which Ted had handed over on Pelham's appointment.

The positive advantage to Ted had been that he could keep a close eye on whatever his deputy was getting up to. Which he had done, except for the short period Pelham had been in the United States on a trade mission.

Altogether, he had kept the egregious man on a tight rein. But, to outsiders, it looked like a close partnership and a balanced ticket to take the Party through to 2026 and the next election.

He and Pelham had nothing in common, Lancaster reflected. Whilst he was a traditionalist, opting for the status quo, but edging softly towards Europe, Pelham was a radical, wanting withdrawal of co-operation.

In his modesty, Ted had been genuinely surprised at his election as the caretaker PM. But, he knew Robert Pelham had always believed that Robert Pelham had a destiny. However, somehow, the two unlikely opposites had achieved a sort of equilibrium for the Party.

Ted hadn't been fooled for a moment by Pelham's patina of civility towards him. He'd sensed that, underneath the urbanity, was an impatient, ruthless politician who saw his leader as a temporary necessary evil.

With Maud's advice, though, Ted had taken steps to stymie Pelham's aspirations by insinuating other levels of power between him and the top job. This, he knew, had added to his deputy's hatred of him and his policies.

And now it would appear Pelham was set to achieve his revenge. He was amoral and unprincipled. And, recalling their conversation in the Cabinet office, it was not beyond the realms of possibility that Pelham was also implicated in murder as well as blackmail.

Ted cursed his failing eyes. If only they would stop

playing him up, he thought. Then, perhaps, he might take Pelham on and beat him at his own game. But, what could he do? The pain was so bad at times he couldn't think straight. As far as he could make out, Pelham held all the cards.

As Maud put the last dish away and dried her hands on her pinafore, she shot a startled look at her husband sitting at the table in the tiny kitchen. His face was contorted in agony.

'Darling, what's the matter? Is it your poor eyes again?'

Lancaster nodded groping in his pocket for the plastic container with its droplet dispenser. The grittiness he had felt on waking had turned from soreness into a searing sensation. He had put off for as long as he could resorting to the Pilocarpine but now he had no choice. His hands shook as he unscrewed the top and tilted his head back.

As the cooling liquid flooded each eye, the sharpness began to recede and Maud's fuzzy outline cleared. His wife stood over him and gently cuddled his head to her abdomen. 'My poor darling, it's all getting too much for you, isn't it? Damn that bloody man.'

Ted said flatly, 'I can't let him get away with it, Maud, but what can I do? He's not the kind to bluff. If I shop him, he'll bring us all down with him. And I owe it to the Party, and to the country, to avoid that.'

'But, on the other hand, my dear, should such a man go unpunished?'

'Maud, Maud, this is the real world we're talking about. The Pelhams seem to have a nasty habit of winning. If I try to stop him, I punish three of my colleagues who, I admit, have behaved stupidly and irresponsibly--'

'--not to mention immorally.'

'Quite. But neither they, nor their families, deserve to be destroyed. And that's what would happen if Pelham releases his...ah...dossiers to the media.'

'So, he's going to get away with it? And, possibly, murder as well?'

Lancaster shook his head helplessly. 'I don't know. I can't think of any way at present to stop him.'

'But stop him you must,' said his wife.

Eighteen

After Lockyer's meeting with Tessa Jordan earlier in the week, Frank Dutton had pulled together some usable facts, spiced it with a bit of speculation, added in some snippets he had picked up from his contacts and had written a follow-up to last week's exclusive.

And in the early hours of Sunday morning digital versions of The Examiner were downloaded into computerised print rooms in various locations in the country, while bundles of printed copies were physically loaded into vans for distribution to the Home Counties. Thus the story became available to all-night garages, cafes, clubs, supermarkets and government Press Offices. Consequently, a scan of the front page was emailed to Robert Pelham at home. Within minutes he was dialling Dresner's number.

'I thought everything was under control,' Pelham said coldly down his secure line to a Grosvenor Square embassy apartment.

'Jesus, Bob, do you know what time it is? I've only been in bed an hour.'

'Never mind that. You obviously haven't seen The Examiner yet.'

'The Examiner?' Dresner replied thickly. He had treated himself to a rare Saturday night out and had over-indulged on cheap champagne at a Soho club. Well, a man's got to let his hair down sometimes or he'd go nuts. Not everyone was a calculating machine like Pelham.

He forced himself into wakefulness and adopted a respectful tone. 'What about The Examiner, Robert?'

'Let me quote an extract,' Pelham said with controlled calm. 'First the headline: "SLEAZE COVER-UP LINKED TO KILLING No 2"'. Dresner jerked into wakefulness. 'How the Hell..?'

Pelham continued remorselessly, 'The story goes on to hint that the female victim of a hit-and-run outside their offices this week was murdered because she knew too much.'

Dresner groaned.

'...There's more. And I quote..."Rebecca Ward offered to tell this newspaper of facts which, she alleged, would implicate senior government figures in scandals that could, she claimed, bring about the downfall of this administration. As a reputable newspaper, not given to retailing unsubstantiated accusations, we asked Miss Ward to bring us proof of her allegations.

'"She was on her way to collect this proof when she was struck down and killed by the driver of a stolen red Fiesta whom police are still seeking."'

Pelham continued quoting the story held in a quivering hand, '"In a statement late last night from Number 10 Downing Street Ted Lancaster, the Prime Minister, dismissed Miss Ward's allegations as 'outrageous.' He said there was not a shred of proof linking the women's deaths to his Government, or his ministers."'

Pelham read on, '"The whole idea was no more than 'journalistic wishful thinking and a scandalous calumny,' a shocked Mr Lancaster told us. He added that it was inconceivable that any member of his government, many of whom he counted as personal friends, could ever be involved in anything as heinous as the murder of two innocent people.

"'The Prime Minister pledged to The Examiner that, were we able to offer any concrete proof of guilt, he would leave no stone unturned to root out and expose the culprit or culprits to the full rigours of the law. 'As long as I am Prime Minister, there will be no cover-up,' he promised.'"

Dresner felt bile rise in his throat and the prickle of the sweatglands in his armpits as Pelham quoted, "'Despite the Prime Minister's protestations, it seems to this newspaper that the number of co-incidences coming to light in this case point to a political time-bomb of Watergate proportions.

"'Here is our reasoning: Linda Burchfield and her flatmate, Rebecca Ward, ran an escort agency offering companionship and sex to celebrities, some of whom were almost certainly politicians. This made the girls privy to pillow-talk indiscretions. Just over a week ago one of the two woman, Linda Burchfield, was murdered within hours of meeting one of those clients, as evidenced by the £1,000 in used notes in her handbag.

"'Four days later, and within minutes of threatening to reveal details of the agency's clientele, Rebecca Ward is also killed. An extrapolation of these facts would suggest that Linda and Rebecca got to know more than was good for them. Perhaps they were tempted to blackmail one or more of their clients? But, whatever the truth is, both are now dead and the endangered reputations are now secure. Or are they?

"'My Editor, Tessa Jordan, and I took careful notes of all the allegations, and the names linked to these allegations, and have passed them on to Chief Inspector Jack Lockyer, who is leading the investigation into both deaths.'"

By the time Pelham had finished, two pools of sweat had stained the sheets either side of Dresner's naked torso. His mind raced back over what he had just heard and matched it with what he knew. The reporter was just guessing. He had got it all wrong about Lucinda, or surely James Sherborne would have been fingered.

And, as for the other girl, Bekky or whatever she had called herself, no-one could know for sure that her death was linked to what she knew. Unless...the Ward woman really had spilled her guts to The Examiner. If she had, then the game was up. But, it was his bet that the reporter was bluffing, just to string the story along.

The journalist had nothing to lose. He could speculate all he wanted and neither girl was in a position to deny it. And the reporter had been careful not to mention any other names. Which meant they hadn't gotten any, because if they had you could bet your life they'd be splashed across the front page in 144-point bold. No, Dresner reasoned, they knew nothing.

Except, had the Ward woman really been on her way to collect evidence? And, if so, what was it? Photographs? Tapes? Nah, he'd kept his eye on Linda when she 'entertained' the DOI's 'clients.' She'd done exactly what she'd been told. Nothing more. The only evidence in existence was what his operatives had so painstakingly compiled, with the help of hidden cameras.

And if one of the girls had kept a diary, it hadn't been anywhere in their flat. Because, after his man had torched the Fiesta, he'd gone straight to his victim's apartment and searched it, room by room, and had come up with nothing.

So, all in all, it seemed The Examiner was just kite-flying - hoping that they might panic someone into making a stupid move. But, just supposing the Ward girl had given them names, and these names were now in the hands of the cop in charge of the case, Lockyer? Maybe that was the one weak link.

'I'm waiting, Dresner, for some reassurance that the entire edifice is not about to come crashing down.' Pelham's voice cut into his thoughts.

'It's not going to be a problem, Bob--'

'--I don't think you quite understand the implications, Dresner. It's not just what this rag says. It's what the rest of the Press are going to make of it. They'll be indulging in their usual mindless frenzy, opening every cupboard in the Palace of Westminster to see what skeletons might fall out--'

'Listen Robert, I busted my ass to keep this operation in a vacuum and nothing's leaked, I promise. All any reporter can do is string a lot of guesswork together and make a big, fat nothing of it...'

Pelham replied sharply, 'Shots in the dark, yes. But they might be too close for comfort all the same. And what if that Scotland Yard man really has got something? What if he, or the hacks, start pressuring Ingleby, Willis or Sinclair?'

'Yeah, and what're they going to say..? We've been naughty boys and now we've got our balls caught in the mangle? No, they want to survive just the same as the rest of us. They'll deny everything and there's no proof because you've got all the dirt that exists.'

'What if the Ward woman were going to fetch some kind of evidence, like a diary for instance?'

'We're pretty sure there is no diary. We checked out the girls' apartment and found nothing. But, if one turns up, I guess you'll just have to get your tame top gun at the Yard to make it disappear. If necessary, get him to take the cop Lockyer off the case and then make sure any evidence that's been turned up goes missing.'

Pelham was slightly mollified. 'That shouldn't be too much of a problem.' He added doubtfully, 'But I don't like it, though. It's getting messy. I suggest, Harry, that you acquaint Tom Ginsberg with all this. I'll be easier in my mind when I know the President's on top of developments, if you see what I mean.'

There was a click in Dresner's ear as Pelham put the phone down. Dresner cursed silently. There was no way Ginsberg would swallow the same bullshit he had just fed Pelham. He was not certain that Pelham had swallowed it. You could never be sure about Pelham - an unfathomable s.o.b.

He looked at his watch. It would be nine at night in Washington DC. Which meant he had about three hours to find out just how much three Right Honourable Members might have confided, off camera, to their late bedmate. And therefore precisely what state secrets might be floating about in some hooker's little black book.

He'd bet it was as he said: a reporter's bluff. But, he couldn't take any chances. He sighed and turned the phone's dialling pad towards him. There were going to be some very curious wives when he called.

As Dresner was punching out the Home Secretary's private number, Pelham was putting a call through to a London penthouse, currently occupied by the one person who had the power to make or break the next President of Great Britain, Media tycoon Benjamin Morgan Hobart.

Nineteen

They didn't know it, but the battle lines had been drawn. On the one side was a ruthless politician, aided by the most powerful country in the world, a malleable British Establishment and a multi-billion pound media empire. On the other side was one honest copper and the first woman to put a spring in his heels for six years.

It was nearly lunchtime and they were sitting in the sunshine on the towpath of the Thames at Chiswick outside the Bull Inn. Jack was half way through a pint of bitter and Tessa was toying with a dry cider. Also at the table was Det Sgt Claire Bishop and Josh Hamilton, Tessa's live-in partner.

Josh was surprised to find he was enjoying the company of the man he now knew was his rival for Tessa's affections. He had sensed it immediately in Tessa's change of attitude to him. Ironically, she was being more even-tempered and less critical.

After their talk a week ago, Josh had faced the fact that their days as a couple were numbered. He admitted to himself that Tessa needed something from a relationship that he was incapable of giving. Instead of raging against the inevitable, he had decided to let Tessa make the running.

When she knew what she wanted he would go along with it. That way they would at least preserve their friendship. In the meantime, it was a relief from the undercurrents to come out here by the river and enjoy a Sunday pint. He looked across the table at Claire. Quite a looker. Not really his type, though. But pleasant enough company.

And she obviously liked and respected her boss. You could tell by the way she nodded in agreement with his quiet logic and smiled at his self-deprecation. Lockyer seemed a decent bloke. A bit of a stick-in-the-mud, maybe.

Had a rough time of it, apparently. According to Tessa, who'd heard it from Frank Dutton, Jack Lockyer was a lonely man. He had gone into his shell after his wife had been killed by some would-be suicide and had never re-emerged.

Was that why Tess had suggested this invite to a Sunday drink? A thoughtful gesture to ease a lonely soul's isolation? Who are you trying to kid? Josh chided himself inwardly. You could tell by the way she talked about him, that there was something in Lockyer's curious mix of stolid determination and vulnerability that appealed to Tess. No, she was falling for the man.

Lockyer had readily agreed to meet them. But, Josh smiled to himself, he had obviously needed a bit of moral support. That must have been why he had turned up with his sergeant.

So, here they all were, with Tess and Lockyer chatting amiably together as though they had known each other for years. Come to think of it, Josh had never seen Tess so animated. As he took a gulp from his glass, he caught Claire's eye and they both quirked a smile in recognition that four had obviously become a crowd.

'Penny for them, Josh.'

Josh swivelled his gaze back to Tessa. 'Sorry, Tess, what?'

'You seemed a long way away.'

Suddenly, Lockyer noticed he had been monopolising

Tessa and grinned diffidently at their companions. 'Sorry. I can be a crashing bore when I get going about a case. I was just saying to Miss Jor...er...Tessa that today's story in The Examiner should set the cat among the pigeons.'

'What, you mean dark hints that certain household names are known to the police. Who are they? Or shouldn't I ask,' said Josh.

Lockyer looked at him steadily. 'Sorry Josh, that'll have to remain confidential.' Josh shrugged his shoulders and Lockyer hurried on, 'God, that sounds pompous, doesn't it? Look, I really can't reveal names as such but I would appreciate your input on what we've got so far. I don't mind telling you Claire and I need all the brain-power we can bring to bear on this damned investigation.'

Josh drained his glass and stood up. 'My round, I think. I'll get them in now and then I can concentrate on my role as Dr Watson.'

As he disappeared inside the bar, Claire turned to Lockyer. 'Mr Forsyth caught me in the office again this morning, sir.'

'Oh, Lord. Another third degree?'

'Well, not really sir. Luckily, it was just on the phone this time. It was ringing in your office and I picked it up and there he was. He wanted to know who these names were and whether we had found a diary. He seemed...well...agitated.'

Lockyer turned to Tessa. 'Commander Forsyth's my boss. He's taking a keen interest in this case and wants an hour-by-hour report. I'm being...um...somewhat evasive and poor Sergeant Bishop here finds herself fending him off, for which I apologise again, Claire.'

Claire said, 'I managed to fudge the diary bit. I'm afraid I had to say you were playing things very close to your chest and weren't confiding in me. I'm sorry, sir.'

Lockyer grinned. 'As I recall, that's how I instructed you to play it so I can hardly blame you for carrying out my orders.'

Claire relaxed and replied, 'To be perfectly honest, fudging hasn't been that difficult because there genuinely hasn't been much to tell him. I mean we haven't got very far, have we sir?'

Jack made a wry face. 'To all appearances, no. But, I'm quietly confident.' Claire shot him a quizzical look. 'Is there something you're not telling me, sir?'

Tessa leaned forward and lowered her voice. 'Would you like me to take a stroll?'

Before Lockyer had a chance to answer, Josh returned and handed round the drinks before drawing his chair up to the table. 'Right, Holmes, how can we help?'

Lockyer looked at him steadily. 'I'd like to assume that everything we discuss will remain confidential. It could jeopardise the case if certain things became generally known.'

Josh raised his right hand in a three-fingered salute. 'I won't tell a soul, scout's honour.' Ignoring the schoolboy humour Lockyer nodded. 'Right let's look at the facts we've got so far.'

Jack ticked off the main points starting with the discovery of Linda's body. He went on to mention his appointment to the case after a political decision to remove it from local jurisdiction.

Then he mentioned the offer to The Examiner by Rebecca of Linda's diary, Rebecca's subsequent murder, and the discovery by Claire that the women's flat had been searched. He concluded with the large, regular payments into Linda's bank account, which tied in with appointments in her diary.

'The dates, times, places and names in Linda's little black book would make your hair stand on end,' said Lockyer soberly. 'But, unfortunately they're not identified as names, just initials. Oh, you can make an educated guess, alright, but they're nothing that would stand up in a court of law.'

'You mean,' said Josh, 'that all that stuff in The Examiner today about a cover-up and political corruption, was just journalistic licence?'

Jack looked at Tessa and nodded. 'Complete bluffery. But it might just flush something out of the woodwork.'

Tessa said, 'Jack rumbled Frank and me straight away. He knew we'd made a copy of Linda's diary. In the end it seemed sensible to work together. We're 99 per cent sure we know who the initials belong to.'

She turned to Jack. 'How about just calling on them and confronting them? Build on the bluff. They'll have read our lead story by now and will probably be expecting a knock on the door at any moment.'

Claire said gloomily, 'If only it was as simple as that. We can't go confronting government ministers on the strength of some entries in some tart's diary. Unless we can get something a lot more substantial we've absolutely nothing that will tie these deaths in with a political cover-up--.'

Jack interrupted, '--But, circumstantially, we know some very powerful people have a lot to lose if it's true that they were...ah...seeing Lucinda on the side.'

Tessa said, 'Enough to lose to commit murder? I mean...a minister caught with his pants down might get chucked out in disgrace, but that wouldn't be motive enough for killing someone, would it?'

Jack tugged the lobe of his ear thoughtfully. 'On the face of it, no. But, what if the revelations were enough to bring the entire government down? It wouldn't be the first time. Then there would be a hell of a lot riding on keeping it secret.'

'Hmmm. Motive enough for murder, then, I suppose,' said Josh.

Claire looked doubtful. 'Theoretically, yes. But I still think it's unlikely. I just can't see this as a government conspiracy.'

Josh snorted, 'I can. Politicians are in it for the power. If something threatens that power most of them would litter the streets with bodies to hang on to it.'

Jack said, 'If you're right, it leads us straight back to the names in the diary. They're the ones with the motive. But, at the moment, our hands are tied.'

They all stared at each other in silence. Claire said, 'Anyone had any ideas about PA 4PM?'

Jack said, 'I'm convinced it's the key to this whole thing but neither Claire nor I can crack it. I mentioned it to Tessa last Wednesday and she tells me she and Frank have also brainstormed but...nothing.'

Josh thought for a moment and said, 'I hope you don't mind, Inspector, but Tess tried it out on me, too.' He gazed round the table and smirked. 'I think I might have the answer.'

Lockyer and Claire looked at him incredulously and Tessa stared in disbelief. The edges of Josh's mouth twitched downwards. 'I could be wrong of course...' Jack exploded impatiently, 'Get on with it man. If you can solve the clue I...I...I'll...get them to tear up all your parking tickets for the next 10 years.'

Josh held up his hand in a show of modesty. 'No need for that...But, if you could see your way clear to getting the six points removed from my licence--'

'Josh!'

'Sorry love. Well, as you probably know Chief Inspector

and Sergeant, I am employed in the sales department of a Mercedes distributors. And this really is what put me on to it.'

'What, man, What?'

'Car numbers.'

'Car numbers, car numbers? What are you blathering about?'

'Sorry, Inspector, I'll get to the point. I think PA 4PM is not an appointment to meet anyone. I think it may be a special car registration. You know, elite numbers. For instance, a racehorse trainer might buy himself something like "GG I". Or Richard Branson might go for something like "FL1 ME", that sort of thing.'

Claire said drolly, 'And the Commissioner might go for MET 1?'

Josh grinned. 'He might, if he was an extrovert, I suppose. But, seriously, anyone can buy them. They're advertised in the trade Press and national papers. I bet PA 4PM is an elite registration.'

Lockyer thumped his fist on the table. 'By God, you could be right. PA 4PM? Whoever PA is, he is for PM whoever he, or she is.'

Tessa wrinkled her nose. 'That's frightfully convoluted. What about PA being a potential something, not someone - you know, like: "Press Association?"'

Jack shook his head. 'We thought of that and Claire looked into it. As far as we can make out the Press Association aren't involved.'

Josh said, 'Or could PA be a company. You could have: "Prudential Assurance 4...er...Pension Management.'

Tessa said unconvinced, 'Bit too obscure that. It's got to be something more obvious.'

Claire said excitedly, 'You're right. I think I've got it.

Apart from PM meaning the afternoon, what else do the initials make you think of? And I don't mean Post Mortem...' Before anyone could answer, Claire plunged on...'Prime Minister. We've already talked about politicians being involved. So what about PA 4 Prime Minister?'

There was a silence round the table as they all looked in Claire's direction. Eventually, Lockyer said calmly, 'Well done, Sergeant Bishop. A brilliant piece of deduction. If PA 4PM is a car registration, that would make sense. Some MP with the initials PA fancying his chances.'

Claire said, 'An NPR check will soon tell us.'

Lockyer inhaled deeply. 'And if you're right we'll have the name and address of our murderer.'

Twenty

Ginsberg grunted occasionally in response to his driver's monologue, delivered while the DOI pool car stopped and started through London's late Sunday evening traffic. London! It was the last place he expected to be. But, after Dresner had phoned yesterday - no Goddamn it, this morning - all his other duties had been put on hold.

When President McGovern roared, you didn't hook and jab on the phone, you jumped. Ginsberg went over events in his mind again. He'd been woken in the wee, small hours by Dresner to be told that some newspaper, which turned out later to be one of Hobart's, was linking the whores' deaths with political corruption.

Dresner had tried to feed him some crap about flimsy speculation and it all dying down. Their blackmailees were scared shitless but had accepted Dresner's assurance that it was only a reporter's bluff. They had been told that their dossiers were safely under wraps and it was in everyone's interest to keep it that way.

But the warning bells in Ginsberg's head pretty near blew the top of his skull off.

That's why he had risked a seismic eruption by ringing the President at three in the morning. And that was how a DOI helicopter had been laid on at dawn to ferry Ginsberg to New York. From where he had boarded the 0745 American Airlines flight which had arrived, on schedule, at London's Heathrow Airport at 1935 local time.

Even with diplomatic clearance by the time he had gotten through immigration they had hit heavy traffic. Weekenders on their way home, he thought. He consulted his watch. But still, he should be in Kensington by nine-thirty for a council of war scheduled for ten. Jesus, what a way to spend a Sunday.

His driver's cockney vowels penetrated his musings...'No offence, guv, but everyfing in America's supposed to be bigger and better than the rest of the world. But us Brits are catchin' up. London's Shard is over 1,000 feet high and the tallest buildin' in Britain and the fourth-'ighest in Europe...'

Ginsberg grunted, 'You don't say..?'

Instead of taking the hint the man, who said his name was Don, took Ginsberg's response as a sign of interest and launched enthusiastically into an impromptu travelogue. Ginsberg sighed and gazed blankly out of the window as they faltered through Hammersmith towards Kensington.

Although the traffic was thinning there were still plenty of people about. Ginsberg noticed that Britain's capital had finally succumbed to the American custom of armed police. But not the usual .375 Smith and Wesson magnums. These boys really meant business, walking in pairs ostentatiously shouldering Heckler and Koch sub-machine guns.

Although the US was experiencing its fair share of terrorism, Ginsberg mused, the odd shooting spree by home-grown terrorists had left 99.9 per cent of the population untouched. But, jeez, these Brits were something else. The IRA and Islamist fanatics vying with each other as to who could cause the most mayhem with stabbings, lorry attacks, bombs in shopping centres, the whole shooting match (literally) but life just carried on as normal. The Dunkirk spirit, Ginsberg grinned to himself.

Don's voice penetrated his consciousness '...Yeah, despite Brexit bein' a damp squib the City of London's still the biggest financial centre in the world...Even bigger than New York...'

What was it the President had said..? Ginsberg tried to recollect, shutting out Don's droning...We were almost at home base and he wasn't about to see his re-election hopes and his place in history, tossed into the shredder by some jerk reporter and a lush cop.

If necessary, we should bring 'Dunkirk' forward. And that, reflected Ginsberg, was why he was here. To get everyone on side for an earlier start. They had chosen Ben Hobart's penthouse suite for the meeting because it was discreet and convenient. They could all use his private entrance and elevator at the rear of the building and be seen by no-one.

Hobart's private parking space would also conceal Pelham's ubiquitous driver and bodyguard. Perfect.

'...Firty-two lifts and 40 seconds to get to the top floor...1.2 million square feet of office space...Home to several national newspapers...' Don was unstoppable. He continued mournfully, 'They all left Fleet Street after Murdoch took on the unions. Pity that. The name "Fleet Street" had a sort 'o ring to it. Canary Wharf don't sound the same some'ow...'course Mr 'obart was ahead of the game as usual, setting up his London papers in Kensin'ton – better location for the staff and better ambience for the business...I guess finking' ahtside the box is how you get to be a multi billionaire...'

Ginsberg was relieved when the car finally pulled up. The trip from the airport had taken longer than expected. But he was here. With half an hour to spare.

Anthony Talmage

You could smell the money. Afghan rugs on the floor; a Gauguin portrait and a Pissaro townscape of Dieppe on the walls. Underneath them, in small alcoves, a bank of computers showing Stock Market prices in London, Tokyo and New York.

There were also television screens for video-conferencing or watching the CNN news. When the technology wasn't needed it could be swivelled back to be hidden behind carved, wooden panels.

El Supremo's penthouse suite offered a spectacular night-time view over London, but none of the four men present tonight was in a mood to enjoy it. And, in any case, the windows were shrouded in heavy damask curtains. It was unlikely anyone could have seen in, but there was no point in taking chances.

Ginsberg looked about him. Under a brilliantly-lit tropical fish-tank sat an elegant chaise-longue. A restful spot to wait for inspiration, he reflected. Or to cook up your next multi-billion takeover.

Under the largest window which, during the day would have looked onto the snaking blue highway of the Thames, was a magnificent, William and Mary walnut desk.

Earlier its owner, Ben Hobart, had abandoned it still covered in papers, to greet his first visitor- Ginsberg - as he had stepped out of the personal elevator. As Tom had shaken Hobart's hand he noted the tycoon was just as he appeared in his own papers and on tv: bald and bearded, with a bouncy step and piercing eyes.

Amazingly, the remnants of an accent picked up during his boyhood in Australia, were still evident.

He looked younger than his 46 years, especially when he switched on his deceptive smile.

158

Within minutes the others had arrived and they were all now settled around an oblong, glass-topped coffee table. To Hobart's left sat Pelham, ascetic, eyes hooded, watchful. Like an American eagle, thought Ginsberg. Opposite, and next to himself, sat Dresner, his conduit.

Ginsberg glanced sideways at him and detected an uncharacteristic nervousness. So, Harry wasn't as confident as he had sounded on the phone this morning.

Ginsberg cleared his throat. 'First guys, the President of the United States wants me to thank you for meeting with me at such short notice. As you can guess, he was a mite jittery when I interrupted his beauty sleep this morning.'

The others grinned at the euphemism. McGovern had probably been apoplectic, thought Pelham. Which was all to the good, if Dunkirk was to stay on schedule.

Ginsberg went on, 'He asked me to come here as his personal representative. First, he wishes you to know that he's right behind Dunkirk. But, at this moment in time, he still cannot be seen to be involved in any way.

'So, before we begin I must remind you that, should anything go wrong and our plans are blown, he will disavow any knowledge. We will just be a renegade bunch of plotters who deserve to spend the rest of our lives behind bars.' This was greeted by sober murmurs around the table.

'But, if - when - we pull it off, he will give us his personal support every way he can to help Great Britain forge a new alliance.' His three listeners nodded in agreement. 'Having said that, people, the Great Man wants to bring Dunkirk forward.'

Ginsberg pointed downwards to the 49 floors below among which resided Hobart's flagship broadsheet, The Examiner. 'The President thinks some reporter in this very building might get lucky, so the sooner we...um...start the ball rolling, the better.'

All eyes swivelled to Pelham, who had made a steeple of his fingers. 'I agree. In fact I have been thinking along the same lines myself. There's no reason why we...I...can't deal with Lancaster this week. Everything's in place. If you all agree, I shall do it on Tuesday.'

Hobart interjected, 'Hold on, fellers. Are we absolutely sure there's no alternative? It's not that I'm squeamish or anything but...well...not putting too fine a point on it, we are talking about assassination here.'

Pelham looked at him sardonically. 'Cold feet, Benjamin?'

'Look, I don't give a wallaby's tit for Lancaster. I'm talking about calculated risks. Once that old guy hits the floor all Hell's gonna break loose.'

Ginsberg said emphatically, 'We've got to do it, Ben. The best brains in the business have worked out the whole Dunkirk scenario and the key to it is Lancaster's elimination. That's the only way we can get Robert in place. And without Robert Dunkirk's dead in the water.'

Hobart said doubtfully, 'He couldn't be persuaded to just jack it in - if someone offered him the chance to live out the rest of his days in luxury in a sun-drenched paradise of his choice?'

Pelham shook his head slowly. 'Sadly no. He pretended to go along with my...er...persuasive arguments to feign failing health. But I don't believe he'll actually go through with it. Apart from anything else, that interfering wife of his will persuade him otherwise. So there's only one way to be certain. And the longer we leave it, the greater the risk that Dunkirk will unravel.'

Hobart said resignedly, 'So be it. Dammit, to think it's one of my own papers throwing a stick in the spokes. Frankly, I didn't think Tessa Jordan had it in her.' He grinned round at everyone. 'I'll kick the rest of my editors into line though. Plus, I'll make sure Jordan's story gets rubbished. That should cool things off for just about long enough for Robert to do his stuff.'

Dresner said, 'Yeah, but as the President says, the sooner we start Dunkirk the better. However watertight you think your papers might be on this, some maverick journalist trying to be a Woodward or Bernstein could still be ferreting away.'

'And this Jordan woman seems to be getting her rocks off on this scoop of hers. She's dangerous. What if she really has turned up some evidence?'

Ginsberg said sharply, 'But I thought you said you'd searched the hookers' apartment and found nothing?'

'We did, but that doesn't mean there couldn't be something, somewhere. A diary, say.'

Hobart said. 'Now come on fellers, we're spooking ourselves with guesswork. But if it'll put Dresner's mind at rest I'll check Jordan's safe later tonight. If she has got something I'll...ah...confiscate it. That'll stop Woodward dead in her tracks.'

Ginsberg warned, 'Talking of dead, Sam McGovern's getting nervous about these killings. Unless Dunkirk itself is in jeopardy, they're to stop.'

Hobart said, 'Apart from the Big One, Eh?'

'Apart from the Big One,' agreed Ginsberg.

'No problem, Tom,' replied Hobart. 'No need for any rough stuff with Jordan.' He laughed humourlessly, 'If she gets too much of a pain in the nether regions I'll downsize her. She won't be surprised. She knows my policy on failure and The Examiner's circulation's been slipping for months.'

Ginsberg swivelled towards Dresner. 'If all else fails,

Dresner here's gonna get us off the hook, aren't you Harry?'

Dresner gazed back balefully. 'Yeah. I'm the fall guy.'

Pelham chortled, 'I must say I salute whoever thought up that particular chicanery. Let's hope we never have to resort to it, Eh Dresner?'

'It's unlikely. And the heat'll be off pretty soon anyway,' Ginsberg pointed out. 'This will all be chickenshit compared to what'll be hitting the headlines in a couple of days.'

Pelham said sombrely. 'The tragic demise of the nation's leader through selfless devotion to duty...Followed by the elevation of myself and the devastating news about our dear Sovereign which I shall feel duty-bound to disclose.'

The tightness in Ginsberg's stomach which had refused to go away since he woke up, began to un-knot. He said flatly, 'Yeah, phantom government cover-ups'll be forgotten in one crazy orgy of national mourning.'

He looked at Hobart. 'And all your media outlets'll give Robert all the backing he needs?'

Hobart replied, 'Sure. Bob's going to get saturation coverage. By the time I've finished he'll be a cross between Abraham Lincoln and Jesus Christ. There won't be another politician in the running.'

'Good.' Then Ginsberg remembered the President's other concern. 'Robert, what're you going to do about this cop the paper mentioned?'

Pelham smiled thinly. 'He's become something of a nuisance, I admit. But I have that in hand.'

Ginsberg looked at him uncertainly, then shrugged. Looking round at the others he said, 'OK, let's go over Dunkirk one last time so I can assure the Chief that nothing - absolutely nothing - is being left to chance.'

Twenty-one

'You've got to hand it to Tessa's boyfriend, sir. It was a brilliant piece of lateral thinking.' Claire had picked up her boss from his flat and they were now heading down the M4 in the direction of Hinton Magna.

As soon as they had left the pub yesterday, Lockyer had despatched Claire back to the Yard where a computer trace on the car registration PA 4PM had revealed it to be a Mercedes belonging to one James Sherborne, of Priory House, Hinton Magna, Wiltshire.

Lockyer had been tempted to drive down to see the MP there and then. In the end he decided to take his time and examine his new piece of evidence from every angle. There was that oddity in the pathologist's report which hadn't fitted in with the earlier theories of a dead body being dumped in a ditch.

He and Claire had discussed it thoroughly and had now got clear in their minds how Sherborne might fit into the case.

He was glad Claire enjoyed driving. It gave him chance to ponder just one last time in case they had missed anything.

To avoid forewarning his suspect, but to make sure he would be at home on a Monday morning and not on his way to the Commons, Lockyer had enlisted the help of Keith Passmore at Wiltshire CID.

Keith had agreed to ring Sherborne to warn him that a

copper would be calling round later for a routine check of his shotgun licence. Sherborne said he would be in until midday. It was now 10 o'clock.

As they passed Heathrow Airport, Jack idly watched the planes lining up for their approaches while others were landing and taking off. 'Do you still think, sir, that Sherborne was being blackmailed by Lucinda so he strangled her?'

'It's the most obvious explanation as I see it. But, if that was the case, how do you explain that note in Hamish's file on Linda's body? Something still doesn't add up.'

Jack added thoughtfully, 'Look, before we confront the suspect, let's go over things again. Only this time you play Devil's Advocate. Argue against my logic. OK?'

'Right sir, go ahead.'

'Lucinda was dumped in a ditch within a suspicious distance of Sherborne's house. She was left there on a Friday night and that's when Sherborne would have been driving home for the weekend.'

'Very circumstantial connection, sir. Thousands of people live within suspicious distance of the murder scene.'

'Alright, point taken. But, since her murder, we have uncovered a connection between Linda and scandalous goings-on involving MP's, as evidenced by the initials in her little black book.'

'But no evidence of the initials "JS".'

'True, but there were initials and a number written in it for the very day she was murdered. This turns out to be no less than the registration number of a vehicle registered to our man, who lives within suspicious distance of where Linda died.'

Claire persisted, 'Still circumstantial, sir.'

'You're a hard taskmaster, Claire Bishop. But, members of the jury, I haven't finished yet. Linda's flatmate, Rebecca, who shared Linda's knowledge of disreputable and reprehensible behaviour on the part of our elected representatives, is also murdered. This would suggest to any reasonable-minded person that, somehow, the two murders are connected.'

Claire indicated left as she approached the Hungerford junction before interrupting. 'May the jury ask what evidence there is to connect our suspect to Rebecca's death?'

'Ahem. As yet, there is no evidence.'

'Then, since you have already suggested the two deaths are connected, why is it you suspect the accused of being implicated in one murder but not the other?'

'Blimey sergeant, you should have been a barrister...To get back to the investigation in hand: Besides PA 4PM being written in the dead girl's diary, the suspect's vehicle number was also found on the body, which indicates that she had the need to identify his car for some reason. Perhaps, they were to meet back at his car in some car park somewhere and she'd scribbled the registration down--'

'--What? And in her diary back at the flat?'

'Well, suppose she actually did have a poor memory?'

Claire shot Jack an old-fashioned look.

Jack said exasperatedly, 'OK, OK. What we do know is that she had the number in advance with the intention of rendezvousing with him on the night – an assignation. Perhaps he'd given her his number over the phone so she could recognise his car when it drove up.'

'But, why should it have been him who gave her the number, sir? Someone else could have supplied it.'

'For what reason?'

'I really don't know, sir. What I'm getting at is: what we have proves nothing at all. Sherborne could be completely ignorant of any of this. He doesn't need to explain how his car number came to be in the possession of a murdered girl. There could be a thousand innocent reasons.'

Lockyer sighed heavily. 'You're right, of course. I'll tread carefully. But I want you to watch his reactions, especially when I produce the glove.'

They were shown into an impressive drawing room which was dominated by a French-crystal chandelier. On the floor directly beneath it was a handwoven Baktiari rug. A fireplace made of granite would, when lit, have provided the focal point for the family. As it was, it was empty and covered by a Chinese-lacquer fire-screen.

Certainly cosmopolitan, Jack thought.

A tall man with a boyish lock of undisciplined hair and a televisual face, which Lockyer recognised instantly, entered the room. As soon as he saw them a puzzled look chased across his features. 'My wife told me she thought it was a bit extravagant of the police to send two police officers to check one document. Anyway, here it is. I think you'll find it in order.'

He held out his shotgun certificate which Lockyer glanced casually at before handing it back. 'I'm sorry, sir, I think there must have been a mistake. I'm Inspector Jack Lockyer and this is Sergeant Claire Bishop. We're from Scotland Yard and we're investigating the murder of a young woman whose body was found not far from here. I expect you read about it?'

As he spoke, Lockyer watched Sherborne's expression. It froze and his eyes widened. 'A terrible thing, Inspector. Indeed, I not only read about it but I have had letters from my constituents on the subject. And I've made a speech in the House. It's an indictment of the times we live in, and this

Government's abject failure to tackle crime, and the causes of crime, that this sort of tragedy is allowed to happen.'

'Quite, sir. But my job is to apprehend the murderer and that's why I'm here.' As Lockyer finished speaking the door opened again and Mrs Sherborne put her head round. 'I'm about to get my husband a coffee, would either of you like one?'

Sherborne called out, 'Don't bother about that now, darling. Come in.' As Elizabeth Sherborne closed the door and looked at all three the smile vanished from her face. Her husband said, 'There was a bit of a mix-up, darling. This is Inspector Lockyer and this lady is Sergeant Bishop - the Inspector's here to talk about that terrible murder.'

Elizabeth Sherborne looked at Lockyer sharply. 'I see. Won't you please sit down.' Jack and Claire lowered themselves onto a long, six-seater sofa while their suspect sat on the edge of an easy chair with his wife perching on an arm. James said, 'Now, how may we help, Inspector?'

Claire said, 'Firstly, Mr Sherborne, we were wondering if there's anything you want to tell us.'

James Sherborne was rocking back and forth, both hands clasped round his knee. 'Want to tell you? That's a strange way of putting it. What could there be? All we know is what we've read in the papers and what we've heard on TV.'

Lockyer asked casually, 'Which route, and at what time, did you drive home on the night the young woman was killed? That was a week ago last Friday?'

Sherborne's face took on a look of concentration. 'Let me see now, there was nothing out of the ordinary that night as far as my routine goes. I took the M4, the A338 and the A4. But, I left the House a bit earlier than usual that day and was home by about - what was it darling, six?'

His wife furrowed her brow. 'I think it was a little before six, because I remember thinking we would be able to watch the TV news together, for a change.'

Lockyer persisted, 'But you would virtually have passed the spot where Linda Burchfield was murdered?'

'True, Inspector. But, correct me if I'm wrong, didn't I read somewhere that the poor girl died about nine in the evening?'

'It could have been earlier.'

'You're not suggesting, Inspector, that my husband might have...actually...had something to do with this girl's death?'

'I'm not suggesting anything, Mrs Sherborne. I am anxious to locate anyone who might have been in the vicinity when the murder took place.'

Abruptly, Sherborne stood up. 'I'm sorry we can't help, Inspector...Now, if you'll excuse me I have a great deal of constituency business to attend to.'

'Of course, sir. Before we go, I wonder if you could explain how your car's registration came to be in the murdered girl's possession.' James looked shocked but quickly recovered.

'Registration? You mean PA 4PM? There could be any number of explanations, Inspector. You see that plate's pretty legendary about Westminster.'

Elizabeth Sherwood interrupted. 'You see, Inspector, it was a present a few years ago from the children. In fact it was an inspired idea by our son, Daniel. We were always talking at mealtimes about politics and on one occasion Daniel said..."one day my dad's going to be Prime Minister". You know how it is, Inspector? Children have such blind faith at that age.'

James Sherborne chipped in, 'Anyway, because it became something of a family joke, Daniel came up with the idea of an elite number plate telling the world how confident he and his sister were that dad was going to be PM one day.'

Elizabeth noted Jack's mystified look. 'We couldn't find one on the list available with James's initials so we had to settle for Pa...you know, dad...'

James said, 'Hence Pa for Prime Minister - PA 4PM.'

Lockyer exchanged glances with Claire. 'I see, sir. Very droll.'

'And when I started turning up at the House with it on the car, everyone thought I'd got delusions of grandeur. Until they heard the story behind it. Then it sort of went into the Westminster folk lore.'

'So you see, Inspector, my husband's car registration was public property. There's no telling why some stranger might have it.'

'I see. Well, thank you both for your time.' As Lockyer made to leave he said, 'One last thing.' He groped in his pocket and pulled out a man's leather, left-hand glove. 'Have you seen this before, sir?'

Sherborne looked at it and swayed on his heels. His face drained of blood but when he spoke his voice was steady. 'I must say, it looks like one of a pair of gloves I used to have.'

'Used to have, sir?' Claire prompted.

Elizabeth Sherborne stood by her husband and linked her arm through his. 'Yes, sergeant. I gave my husband a pair of gloves not unlike that but the silly man left them in a restaurant somewhere and we never got them back.'

'Can you remember the name of this restaurant, sir?'

'Sherborne shook his head. 'It was ages ago and I was on some parliamentary business up north. I went in for a quick bite on my own and left them there. By the time I missed them I was home again. And, as I didn't have a receipt for the meal,

I didn't have the name of the restaurant. Stupid of me, I know. But hardly worth a drive of a couple of hundred miles.'

Lockyer looked steadily at them both. 'I see. Well thank you for your time, Mr and Mrs Sherborne. We'll be on our way.

Claire waited until they were on the A4 before she spoke. 'They were both lying sir, I'm sure of it.'

'So am I young Claire. But, taking a leaf from your book, the fact that they were lying doesn't mean Sherborne murdered Linda. But, if he did, he knows we're on to him. At last, things are beginning to go our way.'

Twenty-two

Lockyer and Claire did not arrive back at Scotland Yard until after lunch. Claire went off to the canteen and Jack bought himself a cheese sandwich out of the machine. When he walked into his office intending to have a munch and a quiet think, he was startled to find Commander Forsyth sitting behind his desk.

Forsyth's face was thunderous and Lockyer's pulse quickened.

'Sir?'

'Sit down, Lockyer.'

Jack realised his boss had no intention of vacating his seat so he glanced around and pulled up the visitors' chair with the stuffing hanging out.

'Lockyer, I don't understand why you've deliberately disobeyed my express wish to be kept informed over the Wiltshire murder case. I asked for daily reports but all I've received is what I have managed to glean from your sergeant, and that's been precious little.'

'Well, sir, I...'

Forsyth held up his hand to stop him. 'Frankly, Lockyer, I'm not interested in whatever excuse you may have. You give me no other choice than to remove you from the investigation.'

Lockyer stared, disbelievingly.

Anthony Talmage

Forsyth said bleakly, 'Before you say anything, just let me acquaint you with a few facts of life. All in all, what with the newspaper coverage etc, this is a sensitive case. While you might find it irksome to report your progress to me, believe me I find it a lot more discommoding to be unable to keep my superiors abreast of what's going on.

'They ask me if I have no control over my subordinates, whether this is a sign that I'm not up to fulfilling my responsibilities as a Commander. In short, Lockyer, I'm buggered if I'm going to allow one maverick old reactionary copper to blight my career.'

'I'm sorry sir, but...'

'It's too late, Lockyer. I'm here out of courtesy. Because I believe I should explain to you personally my reasons. I've already instructed Superintendent Gorringe to take over. He'll work with your sergeant. Please hand over all your paperwork. I'm sure there are other matters requiring your energies.'

Lockyer looked searchingly at Forsyth for several seconds and then shook his head. He could feel the anger rising within him. He said hoarsely, 'I protest in the strongest terms, sir. This case is complex and there's been little I could have told you up to now. However, just as I'm beginning to unravel it, you remove me.'

Forsyth's eyes narrowed. 'Unravel it? How exactly Lockyer?'

Jack ignored his superior's question. Instead, he found his frustration pouring out in a torrent of resentment. 'It's curious that the closer I get, the more interest you've shown. And, now that I'm...' He held out his thumb and forefinger '...that far away from finding out what's going on, suddenly I'm off the case.'

'I don't know what you're getting at Lockyer, but have a

care.' Forsyth stood up and leaned across the desk on his knuckles. 'I'll tell you exactly what decided me. Not only are you embarrassing me with my superiors, but you're a dangerous, loose cannon. You've been cosying up to the papers with unfounded allegations of political corruption.

'And, if that wasn't enough, you've actually had the brass nerve to interview James Sherborne...'

So that was it, thought Jack. Sherborne had not wasted much time.

'Sir, I was just doing my job. I interviewed Mr Sherborne because his car's registration number was found among the first dead girl's possessions. Plus, her body was discovered close to the route Sherborne normally takes home. And, he admits he passed that way on the night in question.'

Forsyth walked out from behind the desk and stood, eyeball to eyeball with his subordinate. 'You're not seriously suggesting that a member of the Opposition Front Bench, a man probably destined to be Foreign Secretary or even Prime Minister, strangled some tart and dumped her in a ditch near his own home?'

Lockyer replied evenly, 'I'm saying it was perfectly proper for me to interview Sherborne to eliminate him from our enquiries.'

Forsyth turned away and started pacing the floor. 'Don't give me that bullshit, Lockyer. It might wash with the public but don't insult me with your TV cop show jargon. I'm not arguing the toss with you any more.'

He tapped a finger on top of Lockyer's desk drawer. 'I've found your files and I've given the lot to Gorringe. Please, hand over any notes you might have relating to this morning's interview and then back off.' Abruptly he strode through the door, slamming it behind him.

Almost immediately there was a knock and Jack called out harshly. 'Yes, what is it?' Claire poked her head round the jamb. 'What's up with the Commander?'

Jack smiled ruefully, 'He's just taken me off the case.'

'What?'

'It appears I've rattled someone's cage.'

'Sherborne?'

'Possibly. Anyway, Vic Gorringe is now in charge and you'll work with him.'

'Gorringe! That's as good as sweeping it all under the carpet. You know what a sycophant he is.' She saw Jack's admonishing look and added apologetically. 'I know, sir, I should have more respect for my superiors but Vic Gorringe?' She added, 'I didn't go along with your earlier theories, sir, but it is starting to look awfully like a cover-up.'

Lockyer sank wearily into his chair, still warm from its previous occupant. He fiddled with a pencil as he pondered. Eventually he looked up. 'It's a damned conspiracy. It's got to be. Two murders, sleazy shenanigans, MP's implicated. It stands out a mile. We start to get close, we interview a high-profile politician and the next thing we know, I'm off the case.' He thumped his fist on the desk. 'It's so damned frustrating.'

Claire looked at him sympathetically. 'If you're right, sir. What can we do? '

'Bugger all.' His expression softened. 'Thanks for your support, Claire, and sorry if I've queered your pitch with Forsyth. Now, off you go and report to Vic.'

'But what are you going to do, sir?'

'Oh, I shall be at the cutting edge of crime-fighting performing useful tasks like catching up on appraisals, the monthly crime statistics, making sure none of my staff have overspent their stationery budgets, that sort of thing.

'But, before all that I intend to go home and put myself on the outside of a very large Scotch.'

'Gone, Frank. Everything. All the notes I'd written and my copy of Linda's diary. Someone's taken the lot.' Tessa had made her discovery on a rare Monday afternoon visit to the office to catch up with the endless paperwork.

On opening the editor's office safe she had noticed immediately that the Linda/Rebecca material had disappeared. Her first reaction had been to call the police. But when she realised nothing else was missing she rang Frank at home instead and he'd arrived in minutes and was now peering at the numbered dial. He said, perplexed, 'But, who had the combination apart from you and me?'

'No-one. No-one at all. I treat it like my own pin number. But is it true that professionals can open safes using stethoscopes, like you see on TV?'

Frank shrugged. 'Search me. I always put that down to artistic licence.' He was suddenly struck by a thought. 'But, there is a man who could tell us for sure.'

An hour later Frank and Tessa were slumped on the office settee watching Lockyer moodily sipping a coffee from a plastic cup.

'You say it is possible, Jack, to use a stethoscope to open a safe?' Lockyer noted Tessa was now calling him Jack and not Inspector which was a small consolation for the depression which had descended on him. He nodded. 'Quite possible. The pros just listen for the tumblers dropping into place.'

Frank said, 'So, it was a professional job?'

Tessa said, 'It must have been, because whoever did it was

professional enough to avoid the security men in reception, come all the way to the eighth floor without being seen, get into my locked office and then calmly sit here twiddling until he cracked the combination.'

'Unless, of course,' suggested Lockyer, 'he already had the combination and was well-known enough round the building not to raise any eyebrows if he was seen.'

Tessa said, 'But there isn't anyone else...unless...you can't mean El Supremo?'

Frank said excitedly, 'It would certainly explain how someone can just waltz in here, lift the stuff and waltz out like the Invisible Man.'

Tessa said incredulously, 'Hobart has got the combination, I admit. He insists on it. That's because if he suddenly sacked one of his editors, he wouldn't want the embarrassment of having to call in a safe-cracker to retrieve any vital documents.'

Frank said, 'But why would Hobart want to nick the Linda/Rebecca stuff? It doesn't make sense.'

Jack said bitterly, 'It makes as much sense as me being taken off the case by my boss on the flimsy pretext of not keeping him in touch.' Tessa and Frank gaped at him. 'I was just about to go home for a bit of liquid consolation when Frank rang.'

Tessa said slowly, 'We're all being stitched up. I haven't mentioned this yet, but I had a call at home from Hobart today. He started by congratulating me on a lively front page yesterday.'

'And then..?' Frowned Frank.

'And then he just casually slipped in the suggestion that I ease off on the political corruption angle. It was intelligent speculation, he admitted, but...now let me see what were his precise words..? Yes I know...he said...but, unless there was hard proof to take the story on, then it would be counter-productive in the wider context of his own political philosophy.'

'Claptrap!' Exclaimed Frank. There's something else going on, I know it.' Lockyer nodded soberly and Tessa found her heart going out to this reclusive bear of a man.

She turned to him, 'What do you think, Jack? You must have a theory.'

'Something stinks alright, but I don't know what. Another call I had just before leaving the office this afternoon was from my opposite number in Wiltshire, a chap called Passmore.'

Frank said, 'I know Keith Passmore. He's straight enough.'

'Well Keith helped me out with a bit of harmless deception so I could get an interview with James Sherborne without him being forewarned. Apparently, Sherborne was furious. And because he knows Keith personally, he rang him to say he didn't like being deliberately lied to.'

'Can't blame him for that, I suppose,' Frank said.

'I suppose not. Anyway, Sherborne went berserk down the phone and Keith just sat there and listened to it all pour out...'

'So..?' Tessa prompted.

'Keith said he'd never heard the man so...uncontrolled. He reckons Sherborne must be under incredible strain. Anyway, in the course of his tirade he let slip something about the Met needing to look a bit closer to home for villains.

'That the law was being flouted under our noses. And that the very fabric of government was under attack.'

Frank said, 'Sounds like the ravings of a lunatic.'

'And very un-Sherborne-like,' said Tessa. 'Did he say

anything else?'

'Only some cryptic comment about not even the highest echelons of government being safe.'

Frank stroked his chin thoughtfully. 'I don't suppose he means that literally. More in the sense of being in the political firing line. I mean, the Cabinet are having a rough ride at present what with party splits over Europe, interests rates going up, public spending out of control and increased costs because of the minimum national wage. They're ruddy well under siege.'

Tessa agreed. 'Sounds more likely than some sinister plot or other.'

Jack said, 'But, just for the exercise, let's take a leaf out of Sergeant Bishop's book and think laterally. Just suppose Sherborne is mixed up in something. And just suppose he does know something's afoot. What could he mean by...the law being flouted under our noses and looking for villains closer to home?'

'Maybe it's something to do with Linda's little black book,' Tessa suggested. 'Closer to home could mean the Palace of Westminster. After all, it's only...what...quarter of a mile from here?'

Jack said, 'Look, let's assume the worst. There's something rotten going on at the very top in government. And, bearing in mind my suspicions about why I've been taken off the Burchfield and Ward cases, someone in the Met's also involved. What does all this add up to?'

Frank said, succinctly, 'Two murdered prostitutes, political sleaze, a cover-up at the highest level? A blockbusting exclusive I'd say.'

Jack said, 'No, seriously. The Social Democratic Party is fighting for its political life. Somehow, two killings and possible blackmail against at least three Cabinet ministers are connected. Sherborne hints that treachery's afoot. What did he say? The fabric of government under attack? Now, if it wasn't meant just figuratively, could he mean the actual suborning of Ministers of State?'

Frank said pensively, 'If this was some country in South America and not England, and it wasn't the outpourings of a man on the edge of cracking up, I suppose we'd think in terms of a coup. You know, the foundations of democracy crumbling etc?'

Tessa said dubiously, 'But, not here in the Mother of Parliaments. We're straying into the realms of fantasy.'

Frank cut in, 'No, wait a minute. Not a coup, maybe. But what about a change at the top? According to our daily newspaper colleagues, old Lancaster's becoming more of a lame duck every day. The one name that keeps coming up as the crown prince is Robert Pelham.'

'So, why doesn't Lancaster step down gracefully and let his deputy take over? Nothing undemocratic about that,' said Tessa.

A look of realisation flooded Jack's face. 'But, what if he doesn't want to step down? And, don't you find it a strange co-incidence that the three main contenders for PM's job, just happen to be all three names in Linda's diary.

'And not one of them is being touted as a future Party leader although you could argue their credentials are weightier than Pelham's.

'Putting my sergeant's lateral thinking on overtime a minute: how about this for a theory - all three are being blackmailed into keeping a low profile, leaving the way clear to Pelham.'

Tessa shook her head. 'Just one snag, Jack. Lancaster's

shown no inclination so far of stepping down. And, as long as he wants to hang on at Number 10, and he has the support of his parliamentary party, there's nothing Pelham or anyone can do about it.'

All three subsided into silence with their own thoughts. Eventually, Frank said, 'Call it an old hack's wishful thinking for the scoop of a lifetime, but what if Pelham intends to...um...get rid of Lancaster somehow?'

Tessa laughed disbelievingly. 'You mean push him off the Commons Terrace into the Thames?'

Frank's look wiped the smile from Tessa's face.

'I'm serious Tessa. Maybe Lancaster's being blackmailed, too? Or even worse...Pelham could be planning some kind of "accident" to happen to the PM which won't look suspicious but will leave the way clear for him to take over.'

Jack stared at Frank contemplatively. 'Do you know, it does all add up. Think of it. The three main contenders neutralised by blackmail. The two witnesses to that blackmail silenced permanently, a growing groundswell in the papers in favour of Pelham. All it needs is Lancaster's removal.'

Frank clicked his fingers in a loud crack. 'Hey, I've just remembered something. I was talking to Treglown and he swears he saw Pelham getting into the private lift to Hobart's apartment on Sunday night.

'Hubert said he'd just dropped into the office to collect some notes. He came by bike - you know what an environment freak he is - and had left it locked to the railings at the back of the building because it's more secure there.

'He was collecting it when he spotted the government limo. He watched Pelham get out and walk into the penthouse elevator. Hubert thought I might like to know in case it was a story.'

Tessa said, 'So, if our famous lateral thinking proposition is right, then Pelham and Hobart are cooking something up – perhaps putting together some strategy for backing Pelham when he makes his move.'

Jack said meditatively, 'It's a fantastic theory I know, but if Pelham's already an accessory to blackmail and murder, what's to stop him having a go at Lancaster?'

Tessa smiled thinly. 'Shall we get back to reality, now? We're all winding each other up. There's no way the Deputy Prime Minister of England is scheming to assassinate his boss.'

Jack said gloomily, 'And, even if he was, what the Hell could we do about it? We can hardly ring up Lancaster and say..."Please Mr Prime Minister, sir, we think someone's plotting to murder you..."'

Frank sighed heavily. 'Tessa's right. We've allowed ourselves to get carried away, stitching some theory together on the flimsiest of evidence. If we tried to approach anyone with our suspicions they'd think we'd gone round the bend.'

Jack said, 'Yes, but what if we're right?'

Twenty-three

At 1130 hours Washington DC time a freshly-bathed, shaved but exhausted Ginsberg was shown into the Oval Office by the President's appointments secretary. Once again, there would be no record of the meeting. The airline passenger lists recorded no-one by the name of Ginsberg had travelled to and from London in the past week.

If it ever came to an enquiry, any future investigator would find that Tom Ginsberg, Deputy Director of the DOI, had signed in at Langley at eight o'clock the day before and was still there come midnight.

Those kind of hours were not unusual, which is why the DD's office contained an ante-room with its own bed, shower and john.

For the Monday morning meeting that never took place, Sam McGovern sat with his feet up on the presidential desk. He beamed at Ginsberg as he approached deferentially. The Chief Executive boomed, 'Good to see ya, my boy. Pull up a chair. I hear Dunkirk's looking good.'

Ginsberg cleared his throat. Yessir, Mr President. The schedule's brought forward as you suggested. It starts tomorrow.' A delighted rumble emitted from somewhere in McGovern's barrel chest. 'I'll pencil the funeral in for next Monday or Tuesday.'

He took a deep breath, 'So, we're on our way...And me for

a second term. I can't wait to see their faces when those piss-ants on The Hill realise my rating in the polls has just soared like a Patriot missile.'

Abruptly his face froze and he looked at his Deputy Director gravely. 'Nothing must be allowed to go wrong. This is history we're talking about. And if things pan out the 51st State of the Union. So, are you sure you've taken care of the newspapers and the nosy cop?'

'Absolutely, Mr President. All the holes have been plugged and we're ready to roll. And once it starts, it'll be carried forward by its own momentum. Nothing can stop it.'

'Yah, well, I guess it's sounding OK. And, if the shit hits the fan, we've always got our fall-back plan. It'll mean Dresner'll take some heat, but it'll get us off the hook.'

Ginsberg replied drily, 'Yes, Mr President.'

President McGovern gazed over Ginsberg's shoulder to the picture of Abraham Lincoln hanging above the fireplace. 'Maybe Old 'Abe wouldn't've approved. But times have changed. These days it's out-duck and out-weave the others, or you're dead.'

He swung his feet to the ground and grinned across the desk. 'And the bonus to this little operation is, when I personally attend the funeral I can go over the final details of Dunkirk with Pelham without having to give out some sort of goddamned communique on what we discussed.

'No-one'll raise an eyebrow at me passing my condolences in private to Lancaster's successor.'

His face creased with worry again, 'Pelham doesn't suspect anything, does he Tom? You know, corralling Britain into the Union.'

'I believe not, sir.'

The president's tone hardened. 'And, he will keep his

nerve with Lancaster won't he, Tom?'

'I don't see why not, Mr President. As I've said before he's a cold-hearted s.o.b.'

Those who worked in Ted Lancaster's private office at 10 Downing Street, noticed the Prime Minister had been irritable all morning. They put it down to the discomfort he obviously suffered these days from his eyes.

They weren't surprised when he told them to cancel all his appointments from 11am that Tuesday morning. They concluded that he wanted to swat up on his briefing notes. He did not want Prime Minister's Question Time to be a repeat of last week's debacle.

But, the truth was, Ted wanted to rehearse until he was word-perfect the arguments he intended to put forward to his deputy to explain why he was refusing to bend to his blackmail. At Pelham's request, Ted had arranged a private lunch in his rooms at The Commons to be attended by the two of them alone. There would be plain speaking with no fear of being overheard.

Afterwards, he would go straight into PMQs and make his tragic announcement that Her Majesty, God bless her, was not long for this world.

As he thought of his coming confrontation, his back stiffened automatically. Maud was right. He couldn't give in to Pelham. It was a matter of principle. For a start Pelham might be an accessory to murder. If that were the case, the threat of exposure might dissuade him from going ahead with his plan.

If it did not and Pelham chose to reveal the peccadilloes of his colleagues, so be it. They should have thought of the consequences before they indulged their pathetic appetites.

And, if the government fell...Well it was better even to have a Tory administration than a Social Democrat one with a moral cancer at its core.

As for himself, he would not lie about failing health. He would either see the job through to beyond the next election or go down with his head held high. And his announcement about the Queen should take the media's mind off government sleaze. You never knew, he might even get away with it. So, he would face Pelham and challenge him to do his worst.

'Another coffee, Prime Minister?' Lancaster looked suspiciously across the dining table at his sole luncheon companion. Though the House was a termite's nest of activity, as it always was when parliament was sitting, no extraneous sounds penetrated the PM's private rooms.

As soon as the two waiters had withdrawn, the Prime Minister had come straight to the point. He had told Pelham: no deal. He could do his worst but he was not going to give in to a squalid attempt at blackmail.

To The Boomer's surprise, Pelham had remained impassive. He had even smiled occasionally. Perhaps, thought Lancaster, it was all some sort of joke. No, it couldn't be that. Maybe Pelham had had second thoughts, realising it was all too risky.

He looked at his watch. 1.45pm. Time for one more coffee then for his announcement. No, not another coffee. The stuff had tasted ghastly. Really bitter. God, it was hot in this damned room. Surely, they didn't still have the central heating going? He would have to have a word with someone.

He surveyed his co-diner. He was outwardly perfectly calm. Too calm for someone whose plans had just been consigned to the bin. He really was an extraordinary character, Pelham. Like an indiarubber ball; he bounced back into shape whatever the setback.

The PM took out a handkerchief and fastidiously wiped each eye. They were streaming now. It really was too hot in here. Why were his eyes watering like this? He took a deep breath. As he exhaled he noticed the air came out in long wheezes, making a noise like a damaged accordion.

'Are you feeling unwell, Prime Minister?'

'Wha...I...yes...Hot in here...can't catch my breath.'

Pelham raised one eyebrow higher than the other. 'Mouth watering, perspiring heavily, eyes streaming? Classic symptoms.'

Lancaster screwed up his eyes and peered breathlessly across the table. Symptoms...symptoms...I...I don't understand.'

Pelham leaned across the table. 'Pilocarpine poisoning.'

'Poisoning? I...Pilo..?'

'Pilocarpine, Prime Minister. Your eye drops.'

Lancaster felt his heart thumping wildly. He was burning with fever. He couldn't focus. He tried to stand but his limbs wouldn't move. He was going to faint and fall off his chair. What an indignity, in front of Pelham of all people.

If only he could reach the button by the mantelpiece. That would bring them running. But the 15-foot gap might just as well be a mile. He felt light-headed now and there was a rushing noise in his head.

Out of a long tunnel somewhere there was this familiar voice. He would use every ounce of strength he had got to concentrate on that voice. As long as he focused, he would not go under...

'You see, PM, I suspected you might reject my proposition so I took certain precautions. You might have noticed, your coffee wasn't the usual flavoursome beverage. That would have been the eye drops. Yes, one of life's paradoxes those little sight-savers. Perfectly harmless so long as you use them externally.'

Pelham shook his head sadly. 'But, if somehow you came to swallow enough of them, then...alas it would be fatal, I'm afraid.'

Lancaster was struggling to stop his head nodding forward onto his chest. His breathing was coming in short gasps now and a mist was beginning to fall over his mind. Pelham reached over the table and slapped the Prime Minister hard.

The shock momentarily cleared Lancaster's mind. He croaked defiantly, 'You'll never...get away with it...prime minister...assassination...Police will suspect...'

Pelham laughed harshly. 'I fear not Prime Minister. You see I have an insurance policy there which I am going to claim on. The police will, of course, investigate your sad demise thoroughly. But, alas, they will conclude that it was the Grim Reaper knocking at your door and inviting you to join him...'

Lancaster's mouth opened and shut, as he tried to say something. Pelham cut him off. 'Yes, a tragedy but nature taking its course. There will be a most diligent investigation but, in the end, all they will find is a heart that gave out in the service of the nation.'

Lancaster's eyelids were being pulled down by heavy weights. As Pelham's voice began to fade, a dying Boomer just caught his killer's last words...'You see, PM, Pilocarpine cannot be detected in the blood and its presence in the urine will simply be put down to your use of the eye-drops. The fact that they also stopped your heart will be our little secret...'

Abruptly, the poisoned man's head rolled onto his chest.

The sudden movement upset the equilibrium of his body. Slowly it slipped sideways and crumpled into an untidy pile on the floor.

Deliberately, Pelham walked round the table and felt for a pulse. When he was satisfied there wasn't one, he distorted his face into a mask of anxiety and screamed, 'Help, someone, quickly, I think the Prime Minister's had a heart attack.'

All Parliamentary business was cancelled for the rest of the week, out of respect for the late Prime Minister. Heads of State around the world made hasty arrangements to attend the funeral, which was set for the following Monday.

Suddenly it seemed that a nation was at one in its sorrow. While there had been many in the country who had not agreed with Ted Lancaster's politics, most held him in respect as an elder statesman and man of integrity. And they were genuinely shocked at the sudden-ness of his passing.

After the first rash of headlines mourning the loss, to politics and the country, of such distinguished a politician, thoughts rapidly began to turn to who his successor would be.

It seemed to be generally agreed that Robert Pelham, the deputy PM, was ideally suited to take over the reins temporarily. Then the idea began to catch on. And many of the tabloids and broadsheets, led by those in Ben Hobart's stable, openly began promoting him as the only sensible candidate for the permanent post.

'Dunkirk' was proceeding to plan.

Twenty-four

However stressed out James Sherborne got during a week of political cut and thrust, a few hours at home amid the tranquility of a Designated Area of Outstanding Natural Beauty rarely failed to restore his sense of perspective.

But today was an exception. As he surveyed Friday's papers scattered across his study desk, he felt a rising sense of outrage and disgust. Outrage that Pelham seemed to be unstoppable and disgust at himself, for his silence.

Ben Hobart's publications had swung four-square behind their man with headlines like 'BOB FOR THE JOB', 'BOB BEST FOR BRITAIN', 'PELHAM-A NEW MAN FOR A NEW WORLD' and 'I'LL PUT THE "GREAT" BACK INTO BRITAIN - PELHAM'.

Despite James's progress up the Palace of Westminster ladder he had never been seduced by the fools' gold of political ambition. He had never allowed himself to forget what was really important in life. He valued above all else the love of his wife and family.

But, ever since that horrific Friday exactly three weeks ago, those pure and good things he had always kept inviolate, had been under threat. The decision by him and Elizabeth that first night, to pretend it had never happened, had led him into a maze of lies and duplicity. And the final straw was Pelham's hold on him.

He gazed out of the leaded-light windows across the lawn and yew hedges. He did not know he would feel unclean like this. Every lie, each hypocritical gesture, was a betrayal of Elizabeth and the children. That poor girl's death was not going to fade in his mind. Instead, there was a real danger that it would corrupt everything he believed in, like a cancer.

He was startled by a gentle tap at the door followed by Elizabeth carrying a small tin tray of tea and an opened packet of chocolate digestives.

'I thought you could do with a cuppa,' his wife said. As she put the tray down on the desk, she noticed his expression. She put an arm round his shoulder. 'Our agreement isn't working, is it darling?'

He shook his head miserably. 'I...I...didn't know I'd feel like this.' He gestured at the headlines. 'That bastard's going to get everything he wants. I don't know how he did it but, somehow, he managed to contrive poor old Lancaster's death. And I'm part of it. Every move I make gets me deeper into something utterly...alien. Something I can't control.'

His eyes brimmed as he took his wife in his arms. 'I really don't care for myself; it's you and the kids I'm scared about. I don't want to lose you. The more I go on with the lies and the deception the more I feel cut off from you.' He choked back the tears. 'It's as though a curtain's coming down and separating us. I can feel you drifting further and further away.'

Suddenly he was racked with sobs. Elizabeth clutched him to her and together they stood as he wept away three weeks of wretchedness.

For the first time in three days, Jack was not agonising over what he might have done to prevent Ted Lancaster's death. When he had first heard the news, he was incredulous. Had they been right, after all? Him and Frank and Tessa? Or was the Prime Minister's sudden collapse a pure co-incidence? He had rung the others up immediately to find them in the same inner turmoil.

They had all decided there was little they could do at this stage but watch and await developments. But he still couldn't get out of his mind a feeling of guilt that, somehow, he should have done something. They had all guessed that the unthinkable might happen and it had. But he had done nothing to stop it. But, what action could he have taken?

He was already in conflict with Forsyth. How could he have got anyone to take seriously a wild theory that maybe, just maybe, the Prime Minister's life was in danger? No, they would have laughed him off the force and put his ravings down to the booze. And after the PM's collapse he had double checked the Post Mortem results which had clearly shown death by natural causes.

As the thoughts started chasing around his head again, Jack pushed them away. This evening he had something else to think about. Something much more pleasant. And to him, personally, probably something more important.

He had not felt as nervous as this since he had first started dating Jennie. For the umpteenth time he checked himself in the mirror. He grunted at his reflection, 'A face only a mother could love. But, it's the best one I've got, so it'll have to do,' he told himself.

He dabbed on some long-forgotten aftershave he had found in one corner of the bathroom cabinet. He winced. God, he smelled like a ponce.

They were only going to a Greek bistro place in Holland Park but he had dressed in blazer, white shirt, grey trousers and black shoes. When Jennie had died, he had lost all interest in his appearance. He had worn his usual nondescript suit for work and every time he needed to replace his casual wear he had simply copied what he had already.

He now realised he probably resembled something that had stepped out of a time capsule. But, he didn't care. All he could think about was Tessa. It had taken him days to pluck up the courage to ask her out.

And even then, it had only been because dear old Frank had assured him that Tessa's relationship with Josh was heading for an amicable parting of the ways.

Jack took one more look at himself. What was he playing at? At his age? And how did one court a woman these days. Court? That dated him for a start. But, who'd have thought it? There he was, heading for a crusty bachelor-dom, when a woman called Tessa Jordan sends all his resolutions flying out the window.

He grinned at himself in the mirror and shook his head in wonderment. From the first moment he had seen her, something about Tessa had managed to burrow its way through several thicknesses of assiduously-cultivated skins. And here he was, going out on his first date in years.

'So it wasn't anyone's fault really. We came to realise that for one reason or another our relationship wasn't getting anywhere.'

They had both ordered and Tessa was explaining why Josh didn't mind about her spending an evening with another man. She looked at Jack across the top of her glass of white Burgundy. She said awkwardly, 'Frank filled me in on the details of what happened to your wife; I'm sorry.'

Jack was surprised he didn't experience the usual dull ache at the mention of Jennie's death. He stared back at Tess solemnly. 'It was Hell at the time. But it's now in the past.'

Tessa said, 'Perhaps I shouldn't have brought it up. But it just seemed sort of...dishonest...to skate round such a significant part of your life.'

Jack fiddled with his glass absent-mindedly. 'To tell you the truth I felt I'd died, too, at the time.'

'It must have been terrible. What some people go through in life. I sometimes feel ashamed that there's so much suffering and I've been spared. I've been so lucky.'

'In my experience, Tessa, its all relative. I've seen some people who's so-called loved ones have been killed - even murdered - and they haven't turned a hair. Probably glad to be rid of them if the truth were known. Others have suffered a thousand agonies when they've split up with their partners. Don't tell me that's never happened to you?'

Tessa smiled at him sorrowfully. 'Guilty, m'lud. I'm afraid in that way my life's been a bit of a mess.'

'How so?'

'I'm heading for middle age, divorced, with another failed relationship about to be notched onto my bedpost.'

'Divorced? Oh yes, I remember you mentioned it in Falstaff's...'

'We were both young. We married against our parents wishes in the first flush of sexual passion and when we woke up we found we had nothing in common.

'He started beating me up and 18 months later we were divorced. He's now married again with three children and, presumably, a wife who's prepared to put up with being smacked about.'

'Now, it's my turn to say sorry. What happened after that?'

'After that I decided if I couldn't make it emotionally, I'd succeed in other ways. That's when I set my mind on becoming an editor...'

'And finally you made it?'

'After a fashion, yes. And, along the way I satisfied my physical needs with a series of casual encounters. Until I met Josh, that is. He was supposed to be the icing on my cake. I'd made it professionally, now I was completing the equation with a steady relationship. Everything in the garden was lovely.'

'But..?

'But...In the good old snakes and ladders of life, I'm about to slip right back down the snake again.'

Lockyer reached out and covered Tessa's hand with his. It felt small and cool. 'Maybe we can both jump onto a ladder somewhere in the game.' Tessa grinned and squeezed one of his fingers. 'That's a nice thought.'

Throughout the rest of the meal they talked like old friends, revealing their hopes and disappointments, successes and failures. When coffee arrived Lockyer reluctantly changed the subject to his other obsession. He lowered his voice. 'So, what do you think now about Lancaster's death?'

Tessa shook her head sombrely. 'I don't know what to think. It's been going round and round in my head...' Suddenly her countenance cleared and she added with a glimmer of amusement in her eyes, 'D'you know, I haven't once this evening thought about you as a policeman...'

'...For which, dear lady, I am most grateful...'

'...But now you've put your Inspector Lockyer hat on, Eh?'

Jack smiled back. 'After our previous joint deductions we can hardly avoid talking about it now can we?'

Tessa's face became grave again. 'I still can't believe that what we talked about wasn't just a lucky shot in the dark.'

Jack shrugged. 'Oh, I don't know. Remember, we used logic as the basis of our theorising. Now, if the truth were known, we were probably spot on.'

'But, that's just the point, Jack...If the truth were known, you say. How are we ever likely to get to the truth? Did the Prime Minister die from heart failure or not? According to the autopsy report it was natural causes. Don't tell me your own pathologist's been got at?'

Jack thought for a moment. 'No, there's no way the autopsy could have been rigged. If Hamish Jackson says it was heart failure then heart failure it was.'

Tessa said, 'There you are then.' She eyed Jack quizzically. 'But, all the same, Lancaster's collapse was mightily convenient, wasn't it? And in the sole presence of Pelham, too. Which wouldn't be the first occurrence of its kind, either. That's another thing that keeps nagging at me.'

'Sorry, Tessa, I'm not with you.'

'Well, cast your mind back a minute. What do you remember about the death of John Pargetter?'

'Pargetter? The man tipped for high political office? He fell out of a train. Faulty door mechanism, wasn't it?'

'Yes, and who was the only witness at the time?'

'Witness..?' Lockyer thought back and then said meditatively, 'None other than Robert Pelham I do believe.'

'Exactly. And who was the only witness as our late, lamented PM was struck down by an alleged heart attack?'

'Robert Pelham.' Jack blew out his breath in exasperation. 'But as I said, the scientific evidence completely rules out foul play. As you can imagine, Lancaster's death was subject to the most rigorous forensic tests.'

Jack continued, 'And I happen to know personally the

pathologist who carried out examination of the body. He's one of the most conscientious and experienced forensic scientists in the business. His conclusion was that Lancaster's heart just gave out on him. Nothing more nothing less.'

Tessa whispered. 'Last Monday we were convinced that Pelham had used blackmail and murder to set himself up to take over the top job. Now, he's done just that and seems to be in the clear.'

Jack said, 'I'm convinced the one person with a key to all this is James Sherborne.'

'But as we've discovered he's taken cover and nothing's going to winkle him out.'

Twenty-five

Unusually, Jack was looking forward to his weekend at home. As he set about cleaning his flat he caught a glimpse of his face in the hall mirror and he was grinning to himself.

He kept thinking back to his evening with Tessa. How easy it had been to talk. He felt cleansed; renewed. He had a new spring in his step. It must be love, he thought jokingly. He could even face the crime stats on Monday.

His musings were interrupted by a ring at the door. He frowned. He wasn't expecting anyone. It was Claire on the step. She shouldn't be here, he realised. She was working for Vic Gorringe now. Jack noticed she seemed uneasy.

'I'm really sorry to drop in on you like this sir, but something important's come up.'

He showed her into his small living room and they sat down opposite each other. He waited for her to speak. Eventually she said, 'I hope I've done the right thing, sir. I wasn't sure how I should play it at first.'

'Well you're here now Claire, out with it.'

'Well sir, James Sherborne's on his way to see you...'

'Sherborne? But I'm off the case, Claire. Didn't you tell him that.'

Claire eyed him artfully. 'No, I had a sudden memory lapse, I'm afraid.'

'Sergeant. What's all this about?'

Claire told Jack about a call she had taken at the Yard which had turned out to be Sherborne. She said he seemed nervous, insisting on speaking to Inspector Lockyer. 'In the end, I told him it was one of your rare Saturdays off. He sounded so...so...crushed when I told him, that I said you'd probably see him if he agreed to meet you off duty. He jumped at the chance and...well...he's on his way here.'

'Here? Claire you know it's strictly against the rules to give out private addresses to the public.'

She looked at Lockyer resolutely. 'Sir, I've broken protocol already by diverting him to you. One more transgression won't make much difference. I have a feeling this is important. I mean, why would he take the initiative to ring up having got you off his back? It doesn't make sense. It's got to be something significant and I didn't want him telling Mr Gorringe if I could help it. I couldn't think of anything else to do. Sorry.'

Jack eyed her for several seconds. Then he seemed to make up his mind. He said, 'Might as well be hung for a sheep and all that. Mr Forsyth'd suspend me on the spot if he knew what I was doing. But I think you're right, Claire. And if Sherborne has anything significant to say, to Hell with protocol. Let's just hope we can crack this case before either Forsyth or Gorringe rumble what we're doing.'

Jack looked at his watch. 'What time did you arrange for Sherborne to be here.'

'I knew he had to drive up from Wiltshire and that would take him about two hours, so I made it midday.'

'Which means he'll be arriving in about an hour.' Lockyer suddenly slapped his forehead with the palm of his hand. 'My God, Tessa Jordan'll be here then.' Claire looked at Lockyer with a twinkle of amusement. 'Really, sir?'

Lockyer harrumped, 'Yes, we...er...have been comparing notes on this case--unofficially, of course. I said I would take her to lunch as a...sort of thank you.'

Claire kept a straight face. 'I see, sir. It does make it a bit awkward.'

'I agree, sergeant. There's only one thing for it.'

'And that is, sir?'

'Grab yourself a duster, we don't want them thinking I'm a slob about the house do we?'

It was a different James Sherborne who sat hesitantly down in Lockyer's front room. His bluster of the previous Monday had been replaced by a red-eyed exhaustion. Tessa was already there and after Jack had introduced her she volunteered to make herself scarce.

Sherborne dismally shook his head. 'Don't bother. I might as well get used to everyone knowing what I'm about to say.'

All four sat round and James began to speak. He told of the strange girl who had stepped out of the rain in front of his car, how she had gone berserk, how he had panicked and somehow accidentally killed her.

As he talked, his pent-up thoughts flooded out in a torrent. James mentioned Pelham's blackmail hold over his main rivals and himself, Lancaster's suspicious death and his successor's ambitions to secure a place in history.

Claire said wryly, 'Pelham doesn't believe in doing things by halves, does he? Could he really carry it off? Turn our backs on Europe, join hands with the US and ditch the monarchy? He's either completely mad or a genius.'

Jack said, 'Probably a bit of both. Pity he's had to resort to breaking the law. That's going to be his big mistake.'

Tessa said, 'But is it? We might all know what he's up to but we can't prove a thing.'

James said bitterly, 'He certainly stitched me up neatly. Probably the last thing he expected was for me to come clean with the authorities. Even then it's his word against mine.'

He jumped to his feet and thrust his hands deep into his pockets. 'I know he was behind Lancaster's death but I can't prove a thing.'

'Yes, we had the same thought. Plus we think he's implicated in that hit and run,' said Tessa.

James said, 'I know. It's all so unbelievable. I talked it through with my wife, and tried to explain why I was becoming more and more cut off from her and the children, because of all this deceit. In the end we realised there was only one thing for me to do. I had to give myself up to the police and tell them everything.'

He looked at Lockyer. 'That's why I rang Scotland Yard this morning and insisted on speaking to you immediately. I thought if I didn't do it straight away I might lose my nerve.'

Jack, who had been staring intently at James throughout his monologue, poured a generous measure of whisky into a glass and handed it to him. 'That couldn't have been easy. Here, drink this.'

James took it gratefully and sank down into his chair again. He downed the drink in one gulp and shuddered slightly as he put the empty glass on a table next to his chair. 'So, what happens now. Do you get the handcuffs out?'

Jack smiled grimly. 'No, but I know someone who ought to have them on. Would you be prepared to swear in court everything you've told us?'

James nodded, 'But, let's be realistic. It's my word against Pelham's. As he said, who're people going to believe, the new

Prime Minister of England or some Opposition MP with a murder charge hanging over him?'

Claire said, 'He's right, sir. We still haven't got any real proof. This could all just be a story made up to discredit the man struggling to get the country on an even keel after its leader's tragic death.'

Tessa said, 'Hmmm, and Lucinda was strangled, whatever Mr Sherborne might tell a jury. The police have still not found the person who ran down Rebecca and the blackmail victims are hardly likely to come forward while the dossiers against them remain with Pelham. And Lancaster's death was judged to be natural causes, so there's nothing to pin on anyone - except Mr Sherborne here.'

James said savagely, 'Meanwhile, with Hobart's help, Robert Pelham goes from strength to strength with not a blot against him. The hero of the hour, in fact, sharing the country's grief and promising to lead us to a new sense of nationhood.'

Jack gazed round at all of them. 'I think there might be a way to beat the man,' he said. 'But, first things first.' He rose and poured another stiff whisky. He handed it to James who looked up at him quizzically. 'Don't worry about driving, Mr Sherborne, we'll get you home somehow. But I think you may need this after you hear what I have to say.'

They all looked at Jack questioningly. 'For a start, Mr Sherborne, you've just confessed to the wrong person. Claire didn't tell you when you spoke to her this morning, but I am no longer working on the Burchfield and Ward murder cases.' James frowned.

'And for a second thing, you didn't kill Lucinda.'

Tessa gazed at Jack in astonishment and James gaped at him. 'But...I...her eyes...her tongue.' Lockyer nodded briskly. 'A catatonic state brought on by severe restriction of the blood to the brain. It's quite common. Linda might well have been close to death, but it wasn't you who killed her.'

Jack explained, 'There was something that struck me immediately as odd in the forensic report, so I had it double checked. The pathologist is adamant that Lucinda died after she had been thrown out of your car. You see, he found water in her lungs which means that Lucinda, or Linda or whatever you want to call her, was still breathing when she ended up in the ditch.'

James stuttered, 'You mean...I didn't kill her?'

Jack shook his head. 'Forensics say the severe crushing of the larynx and the windpipe would not have permitted the inhalation of water, and therefore those injuries must have occurred after your struggle with her. She had probably lost consciousness then, but she wasn't dead.'

Claire said, 'We think someone came along after you left, Mr Sherborne, and finished the poor girl off. This would account for the ditchwater in her lungs despite her strangulation.'

Jack added, 'In any case, now you have come forward it will be a simple matter to prove because the laboratory has a 3-D photocopy of the bruising on Linda's throat. The fingers and thumb-prints were those of a left-handed man. Are you left-handed Mr Sherborne?'

James shook his head slowly.

'I thought not, despite the glove we found at the scene which did belong to you, didn't it?'

James mutely nodded.

Jack said, 'And it should be a simple matter to eliminate you from any allegations of sexual assault by the simple expediency of DNA testing.'

James's hands shook as he raised the whisky to his lips.

He took a long swallow and stared sightlessly at the floor. 'You mean, I'm not a murderer?'

Claire said gently, 'If what you've just told us is true, you probably would have faced a charge of manslaughter, not murder, as you had no intent to kill.'

'As it is,' added Jack, 'if we can catch the real killer, we might be able to get any charges against you reduced to obstructing the course of justice or even dropped altogether.'

A look of pure delight chased across James's face. 'I...I...just can't believe it. Wait till I tell Elizabeth that it's all over. ' Another thought occurred to him. 'And I'll even have Pelham off my back.'

Lockyer said, 'Whoah...Not so fast. I said we've got to catch the real murderer first. Someone must have followed you when you were driving home that night. Whoever it was must be our man.'

James said, 'I'm afraid I didn't notice anyone. It was a foul night and visibility was pretty bad.'

Jack said disappointedly, 'Oh well, it was worth a try.'

'So what happens now, Inspector?'

'As I said, Mr Sherborne, I'm off the case. And, I have to say my colleague, Superintendent Gorringe, might not be so keen to examine the forensic evidence as minutely.

'Whoever's pulling his strings might now decide that hauling you in as a suspect would be preferable to you rocking the boat.'

James face fell and he was plunged into despair again. 'Oh, God. For one minute I thought the nightmare was over.' He looked at Jack miserably.' So what do I do now?'

'Nothing. Nothing at all--'

'--But I...I...don't think I can go on like this much longer.'

Claire leaned forward in her chair. 'We know what you

must be going through, Mr Sherborne. But I think the Inspector's right. Once we can find the real murderer, the whole plot will start unravelling. If you go to Superintendent Gorringe now and tell him what you've told us, you could still end up on a murder charge.'

James looked from one to the other of them. 'Alright, apart from doing nothing is there anything positive I can contribute?'

'I think there may be. But, for a start,' said Lockyer, 'do you know anything about a mysterious American who seems to be a sinister figure somewhere in all this?'

James arched an eyebrow. 'You don't mean Harry Dresner?' He laughed mirthlessly. 'He certainly fits your description. He seems to have a Svengali-like attachment to Pelham.'

Lockyer shifted forward in his seat. 'Does he now. Tell us more.'

'I don't know that I can, really. He's on one of these "swop attachments" that seem to be all the rage these days. He suddenly turned up from the US as a so-called Special Adviser for Pelham about six months ago.'

Claire asked, 'Why "so-called?"'

'Well, it's Westminster-speak for a person-Friday. Dresner is supposed to be a senatorial aide in Washington and was attached to Pelham's office to widen his experience of British politics. But while here he does seem to have upset a lot of people.'

'Tessa said, 'Why? What's he been doing?'

'Well, nothing you can exactly put your finger on. It's more his typical American brashness coupled with...I don't know...a sort of...coldness...an implacability. Ruthlessness I suppose. At one time rumours were going around that he was really CIA.'

James gave a wintry smile. 'But no-one took it seriously. And he carried on wearing his hob-nailed boots and, as long as he had Pelham's ear, no-one dared complain.'

Lockyer said musingly, 'A person-Friday, you say? I wonder...'

Twenty-six

His Royal Highness The Prince of Wales KG, KT, GCB, Great Master of the Order of the Bath and Duke of Cornwall, stared at Robert Pelham with rising incredulity. The man was raving. Hardly had he got poor old Lancaster's baton in his grasp than he was rattling on in the most...disrespectful manner.

It had been bad enough, Charles thought, when the new acting PM had insisted on an audience when Camilla had particularly asked him to keep their weekend at Highgrove free from matters of state. And he had agreed. He had wanted to enjoy a rare chance for companionship with his wife, away from the glare of the media spotlight, just as much as she with him.

And now here he was listening to this...this...political parvenu lecturing him on the Constitution and certain changes he intended to make. Well, he'd see about that.

His Royal Highness said icily, 'I can only assume, Mr Pelham, that its been the strain of the late Prime Minister's passing that must be...ah...distorting your usual unerring good judgment.'

The two men were alone in the Audience Room at Highgrove House, the Prince's country home in Gloucestershire. Charles was spending more and more of his time there since his sons William and Harry seemed to be taking on an ever-rising list of royal duties. It was almost as if, he thought, they were trying to ease him out of the public's consciousness. Whenever he was given to moody introspection he found the tranquility of the house and grounds afforded a balm to his frayed sensibilities.

He'd had to endure the usual disrespectful barrage from the media when Prince Harry had announced the end of his marriage. But his mother, The Queen, had been all for the dissolving of the relationship. She said things had moved on from the days of his own engagement, and later marriage to Camilla, of which she had disapproved.

But, he reflected, since mummy had made that dreadful announcement about her terminal illness to a discreetly-arranged family gathering, her tone had softened. She'd confessed to him that the happiness of her children and grandchildren was the only thing she cared about now. The fact that Harry and Meghan were splitting up had not seemed to faze her at all. It was almost as if she now accepted that people had to work out what was best for their lives in their own way.

And she had told him that her original opinion of Camilla had changed. She realised her son might be a Royal Prince, and heir to the throne, but he was also a man. A sensitive one at that. He needed a woman who understood him. And Camilla had been exactly the right one.

With Camilla, he thought, there had been a meeting of minds as well as the sex. Over the years they had ridden out the various tabloid storms and she had always consoled him with the reminder that, one day, he would be king. Nothing could take that away.

Now, this...political opportunist...this johnnie-come-lately...was actually suggesting...no threatening...to block his succession to the throne. In fact, if he understood the upstart correctly, he intended to...to...bring down the House of Windsor. Over his dead body, thought Charles. This man Pelham had no idea what national outrage would greet such a treasonous suggestion.

Pelham gazed at the prince coolly, seemingly undeterred by his royal displeasure. Damn the man, thought Charles, he really was the limit. 'If you have not temporarily taken leave of your senses then I regard your intrusion here, two days before Mr Lancaster's funeral and while my mother is terminally ill, as grossly offensive.'

'Ah, regretfully Your Royal Highness, there are some matters that take precedence over personal sensitivities - even royal ones. I am here out of courtesy to inform you that on Tuesday I intend to break the tragic news of your dear mother's grievous condition.'

'I had already approved Mr Lancaster's intention to do the same...'

'...I shall then pay tribute to her lifelong devotion to duty and her unsurpassed contribution to the standing of our nation in the eyes of the world...'

The prince nodded curtly in agreement.

'...and the dignity which she has always bestowed on the office of Sovereign and Head of State...'

Pelham paused and glanced over Charles's shoulder at the portrait above the mantelpiece of King George V1 '...following a tradition that, sadly, now seems to have passed into history.'

He turned back to the prince and held his eyes in a determined gaze. 'A dignity that seems to have been abandoned by the descendants of those...' He pointed back at the picture '...illustrious ancestors thus making our royal heritage increasingly irrelevant to these changing times.'

Charles's face turned an angry crimson. 'May I remind you, Mr Pelham, who you are talking to? And I do not relish being lectured in my own home.'

Pelham replied smoothly, 'Sir, perish the thought. I am merely doing you the courtesy of outlining the shape of my announcement next week. After mourning the impending loss of so dazzling an eminence as your mother I shall point out the simple fact that the irreplaceable...well...simply cannot be replaced. Therefore, perhaps we should not attempt to do so. The Monarchy should end on a high note, as it were...'

Charles sank onto a red velvet Louis Quinze chair. 'You're really serious.'

Pelham inclined his head. 'Surprisingly, Your Royal Highness, it will be a relatively simple matter to...ah...bring the reign of the House of Windsor to a...natural conclusion. One simple Act of Parliament, no more.'

'But you...you'll never be allowed...the people..?'

'Sir, I regret to have to point this out but one of the very criticisms made against your good self has been that you are no longer "of the people." You are out of touch. If you weren't, you would realise that the days of unquestioning reverence for the Monarchy are gone.

'The antics of your...um...turbulent family have, I'm afraid, cooked your goose. And the royal dysfunctional chickens are coming home to roost.'

'Don't be so bloody smug and impertinent.'

Pelham's expression hardened. 'Do you really think when I make my announcement that your subjects will be manning the barricades? Let me tell you something, sir. Your mother has been held in almost universal esteem, even by republicans.

'But her children have attracted nothing but contempt for their stupidity, vulgarity and insane compulsion to hitch up their robes at every opportunity to display their feet of clay.'

Charles began to feel alarmed. 'But, even if all that is true, the people know what value we are to this country, not the least in public relations terms. If they lose us, they'll lose billions in tourist revenues alone.'

Pelham shook his head sorrowfully, 'Not so, sir. The Americans and Japanese will still come here to see Buckingham Palace, even if there isn't a king living there.

'And, in terms of public relations, I believe all the bad publicity surrounding the royal shenanigans, has more than likely harmed this country. However, I can repair some of the damage with the money I shall get from selling off the royal estates and hiring out, or even selling, the crown jewels.'

Charles choked back the torrent of rage rising in his throat. 'That's the nation's heritage, man. Have you no sense of history?'

'Oh, I have a sense of history all right. In fact I intend to be part of it in years to come. Ask yourself this: What would the metaphorical man on the Clapham omnibus prefer - some baubles locked away and toffs living in country seats, or more hospitals, lower taxes, and a higher standard of living?'

Charles said, 'But what assets the Royal Family has got is a drop in the ocean compared with the sort of money you'd need for that.'

'A drop in the ocean? My advisers tell me your mother's jewels and art collection are worth a conservative £20 billion. Then there's the odd palace at Kensington, St James, Clarence House, Hampton Court. Not to mention your estates in the Duchies of Cornwall and Lancaster. Hardly small change.'

Pelham said emphatically, 'All the conditions are right, economically and psychologically, to make the break and for Britain to forge ahead as a republic.'

Kingdom And The Glory

The prince shook his head slowly from side to side. 'You're stark, staring mad. You'll never persuade the country to throw over 1000 years of tradition, just like that.'

'When they understand about better schools, hospitals, public services and lower taxes there'll be a stampede to put their crosses in favour, believe me.'

Crosses? So you intend going to the country on this?'

'I intend to hold a referendum, yes. We cannot make such a change to our constitution without consulting the electorate. Especially when there are other factors to consider.'

'Oh?'

'Well, sir I might as well vouchsafe the information to you since your mother has already agreed to sign the Royal Assent, making her Elizabeth the Last as it were.'

Charles's face turned the colour of parchment. 'You mean the Queen, my own mother, is prepared to go along with this and...and... keep me off the throne?'

'Regrettably, sir, she judges you an unfit heir. And as your son, William, has indicated that he doesn't want the job, and the young Prince George of Cambridge is not yet a teenager and cannot have an opinion, the way is clear.'

Charles said savagely, 'I just cannot believe all this has been going on and I knew nothing about it. Of course I shall fight you all the way. With every means in my power.'

Pelham smiled thinly. 'You will not win. I believe the country will have more weighty matters on its mind.' He drew in a long breath. 'What I have told you is only half the equation. I have such plans. I intend to go for the grand slam.'

'All this is so fantastic nothing would surprise me. What is this grand slam?'

'Withdrawal from all those European Union institutions we're still shackled to, and paying for, despite Brexit - to be

211

exchanged for closer, formal ties with the United States. The new "Commonwealth of Great Britain and Northern Ireland" will be offered "Free Association" with the US.'

Charles's lip curled contemptuously. 'Free Association? Exactly what is that?'

'Britain will be treated rather along the lines of Puerto Rico. We will, of course, maintain full independence. But we will have a special, legal, relationship with our American cousins. We will have representation in their Congress and they will have a certain allocations of seats at Westminster.

'All in all it should prove a mutually beneficial arrangement. And, since we have no written constitution, it will be a relatively simple matter to draw one up dis-establishing our Constitutional Monarchy and substituting one for a republic with special links to the United States of America.'

Charles slumped deeper into his chair. 'I...I...just cannot comprehend what you're intending. It's all so...unthinkable.'

'Not at all Your Royal Highness. It's all eminently feasible. For our part we will shake off the straightjacket of a Federal Europe and fully regain our independence. We will enjoy yet closer trade links with our kin across the Atlantic while they will take over all our defence responsibilities, thus freeing up 20 percent of GDP for lowering taxes.

'We will also save vast sums in contributions to inefficient Continental farmers which can immediately be ploughed back into making life better for our own citizens.'

'And what do the American's get out of it?'

'Psychologically, a more sympatico relationship with the "old country" who've decided to follow their lead after 200-odd years.'

Charles snorted and Pelham raised his hand. 'But, more important, they will have a ready entry into the European

Economic Area, through us. While we may not be in the EU, we still retain full access to Europe's economic area which they will have by default. It will be an enormous boost to their export market and jobs. So, we all gain. Like all brilliant ideas, this one is so simple.'

Charles narrowed his eyes. 'Have you actually had discussions with the United States about all this?'

Pelham bounced on his heels. 'Let us say, sir, that we have taken...um...soundings - unofficially at present. But I am confident that President McGovern will swing right behind me when I announce my intentions. Incidentally, I also have the support of Ben Hobart's media empire I honestly don't think I have left a thing to chance.'

Charles said tartly, 'I suppose you even have a plan for myself and my wife?'

'Indeed, sir. I do not intend to deprive you of Balmoral or Sandringham so you may continue to live in the United Kingdom, if you so wish. However, you may prefer to start a new life in, say, Canada, where I am assured you will be given a very warm welcome.'

Pelham continued, 'In fact, it would be perfectly feasible for you to remain sovereign of Canada and those countries of the Commonwealth who desire to maintain you as their Head of State, and...er...rule from there.'

'By God, Pelham, you're an absolute swine.'

Pelham inclined his head. 'I do believe I am, sir.'

Twenty-seven

When Tessa got back to The Examiner from having lunch with Jack she found an excited Frank Dutton pacing the floor in her office. Before she could say anything, Frank forestalled her. 'I've got tomorrow's lead and it's seismic. It'll blow your socks off.'

Tessa grinned as she settled herself behind her desk and logged into her computer terminal. 'What a co-incidence. I was about to say exactly the same to you.'

Frank said, 'I had a call from a contact in the Palace Press Office this morning. He gave me chapter and verse of a conversation Charles was supposed to have had earlier today with Pelham.'

Tessa said, 'Oh, you mean..."the end of the royal line for the Windsors"...and all that?'

Frank's breath exploded in exasperation. 'How the heck did you know?' He eyed her suspiciously. 'Where were you this morning?'

For the next 10 minutes, Tessa told Frank of James's 'confession' and Pelham's dream of being the first President of the Republic of Great Britain and Northern Ireland. She also mentioned the other half of the equation: Pelham's plan to pull away from Europe, underwritten by the United States.

Frank abstractedly sank into a chair. 'Wow! I said seismic

just now. This is Chernobyl. The fallout will be global.'

'And as we've had the same story from two different sources, I'd say we're on to a pretty safe bet to run it tomorrow.'

Frank agreed. 'Obviously, the lawyers'll crawl all over it but, even so, "PELHAM TO SACK MONARCH SENSATION" should guarantee us a few more readers.'

Tessa could feel the surge of adrenaline she always got when she was on the trail of a big story. But this one was different. When it came out it would not only electrify the country but it would also wreck the corrupt new Prime Minister's grand design.

Which was a pity, because the scheme had a lot of merits, she thought. But, if the country should decide to back such a plan, it couldn't be led through it by a murderer and blackmailer. Perhaps someone else might take on the challenge? James Sherborne? Maybe when things had died down.

Meantime, she determined, she had a job to do. If The Examiner's exclusive tomorrow tied Pelham's scheme in with hints of sleaze and corruption, the man would lose all credibility.

There would be a tide of righteous outrage in support of the Queen and her family when it was announced that she is terminally-ill and the United States would deny all knowledge of any 'closer links' initiative.

Then, when other journalists started digging for their own nuggets the murders, blackmail and sinister manoeuverings would begin to emerge. With any luck Pelham would end up behind bars for a very long time.

Thinking back to this morning's scene at Jack's place, they had all felt so impotent. She recalled how Jack had said he had the glimmerings of an idea, but that it would take time to work out. Although Jack hadn't elaborated, she had the feeling it involved Sherborne himself. But, whatever it was, it was not going to have the immediate, and explosive, impact of her plan.

It was while she was driving back to Kensington Tessa realised the answer was staring her in the face. Blow the whole thing wide open in tomorrow's Examiner.

Suddenly a thought occurred to her. She looked at Frank suspiciously. 'I don't suppose this tipster of yours at the Palace is also ringing every reporter in his contacts book?'

Frank shook his head adamantly. 'No way. Apparently, after his cosy chat with Pelham, Charles was apoplectic. He swore he'd use every means at his disposal to scupper the man. Because of the whole Princess Diana saga, Charles learned a few valuable lessons about manipulating the media. His idea is for one paper, us as it happens, to fly a kite tomorrow.

'Since all the nationals will be obsessed with Lancaster's funeral on Monday, they'll unleash their investigative reporters with a brief to either confirm or rubbish our story by Tuesday...'

Tessa's face cleared. 'But, HRH knows that if it's true the non-Hobart media will go berserk. Tuesday's papers will be full of it, pulling the rug from under Pelham's planned statement to The House. He'll have to switch to the defensive as the hacks ferret around looking for dirt.

She plunged on, 'And even if the Hobart journalists are muzzled, Pelham will still sink under the weight of the outcry from the rest of the media.' She added with satisfaction, 'It couldn't happen to a nicer man.'

Tessa said decisively, 'OK, Frank, write me an exclusive and throw everything you've got into it. The riddle of the murdered call girls, the possible blackmailing of various – unnamed - political luminaries, the cover-up, Pelham's mad scheme to take over the world...'

'What about the suspicions that Lancaster's death wasn't natural causes?'

Tessa winced. 'Sorry, can't touch it. We've got no proof. As far as the Post Mortem goes, his heart just gave out. We can't even hint that Pelham might be implicated. That's the one innuendo he could deny, which would undermine the credibility of the rest of the story.'

Frank grinned, 'I thought it was worth a try.'

'I'll follow what you're writing on my screen. Then when I clear it, we'll get the lawyers in to check it over again. There'll be a few ruined breakfasts tomorrow morning.'

Frank frowned. "Course you know you're taking a big risk with this don't you? You talk about El Supremo muzzling his editors but you're one of them. He's already very twitchy over the splashes we've been running. When he sees this one, he'll go into orbit.'

Tessa replied equably, 'By the time he reads it over his kedgeree, it'll be too late. Besides, he wants The Examiner's circulation boosted so he can hardly complain if we succeed, can he?'

The Metropolitan Police Forensic Science Laboratory forms part of Scotland Yard's Criminal Investigations Department. It employs 250 scientists. One fifth of those have doctorate degrees.

The longest-serving member of staff, who can recall when the entire department comprised 20 people, is Hamish Jackson. He was not a fan of what he sometimes referred to as 'gimmicky gizmos' but, nevertheless, a combination of his experience and the latest in forensic technology, made him almost mistake-proof as well as a formidable aid to crime-solving.

And that was why he had been given the job of carrying out a post mortem analysis of Ted Lancaster's death. And it was also why he was irritated by Jack Lockyer's insistence on going over all the ground again.

He said testily, 'If you don't mind my asking, Jack, what's Lancaster's death got to do with you?'

Jack smiled placatingly at his old friend. 'It's a long story, Hamish. I just need to check a few things that's all.'

Hamish gave him a considering look. 'Well...OK. But I don't know what I can tell you that didn't go down in my official report. You wouldn't believe it, Jack. I had a queue of spooks waiting for my findings. First there was Special Branch, then MI6, even the National Crime Agency got in on the act. I suppose they were only making doubly sure the poor old boy hadn't been knocked off. But even so...'

'And you're certain he hadn't been?'

Hamish stared at Jack, aghast. 'Of course I bloody-well am. Do you think I would have given the all clear with half the country's security services breathing down my neck?'

'So he died of heart failure, brought on by the stress of the job?'

Hamish nodded. 'That's about the size of it. I found no irregularity in his system, no narcotics, no poisons. He was typical for a man of his age. I dare say if he had been a retired schoolteacher, or bank manager, and the only worries he had were the greenfly on his roses, he'd still be with us today.'

Jack stroked his chin. 'No narcotics in his system, you say.'

'None. Except, of course, Pilocarpine.'

'Pilocarpine? What's that?'

'Eye drops to you and me. I found heavy traces of it in his urine. But that wouldn't be surprising considering the poor chap was suffering with his glaucoma. The drops would be absorbed into the system and excreted via the bladder.'

'Hmmm. And this Pilocarpine stuff is perfectly harmless?'

'Well, yes. So long as you follow the directions. It's only meant for external usage.'

Jack said casually, 'What would happen if, say, he made a mistake and swallowed some?'

Hamish laughed. 'It would certainly have to be a mistake because Pilocarpine would taste pretty foul. You wouldn't swallow it voluntarily.' Hamish noticed Jack's arched eyebrow. 'What are you getting at?'

'Just bear with me for a minute, please, Hamish. Suppose you did take some internally, what would happen?' Hamish looked thoughtful. 'It would depend on how much you took but a few drops would make you pretty sick...pinpoint pupils...increased production of saliva...profuse sweating and weeping...'

'Could it kill you?'

Hamish eyed him curiously. 'Well, if you were in frail health, and if you took enough, yes.'

'About how much would be needed in the case of someone like, say Lancaster? Would it be possible to disguise enough of it in a cup of lunchtime coffee, say?'

'Well, I...'

'And, if it was, how long would it take to kill him?'

'Now, look here, Jack...'

Jack reached out and gripped Hamish's shoulder. 'Look, Hamish, I'm not accusing anyone. I'm just talking theoretically.

Could Lancaster have been slipped enough of this Pilocarpine over lunch to bring on heart failure?'

'You don't...honestly...believe..?'

'Hamish, could he..?'

Hamish replied flatly, 'I suppose so...'

Jack punched his palm. 'I knew it. That's how it was done. That's how Pelham got rid of the one man standing in the way of his grand scheme. He just dosed him with the very substance he'd already been prescribed by his doctor. He knew that when it came to the autopsy, nothing out-of-the-ordinary would be discovered. Brilliant. But now we know, we've got the bastard.'

Hamish was regarding Jack with an expression of awe mixed with incredulity. Eventually he said, 'Absolutely out of the question. Pelham, you say? Pelham a murderer?' He shook his head sorrowfully. 'I think you may have been overdoing it, Jack. And, in any case, whatever you think might have happened there's no way of proving it.'

Jack said perplexedly, 'But, surely...'

'Look, my old friend, I don't know what you think you've stumbled on but my advice is, forget it. You see, even if it was true that Lancaster was...um...poisoned, there's no way on earth to prove it.'

Hamish explained, 'Pilocarpine is one of the few substances that leaves no trace in the blood. The presence in the urine, even of an unusually high proportion, would not prove it had been ingested in any other way than via legitimate use as eye medication.

'While about 60 milligrams would kill a healthy adult, the residue in the urine could be a quite normal amount. The rest could have been excreted via the sweat glands.'

Jack said, 'But what about the stomach contents? Surely,

you found evidence of this Pilocarpine there?'

Hamish replied, 'I said just now that Pilocarpine has rare properties - no evidence in the blood, etc. Well, we did uncover traces of it in the stomach but it was assumed it had found its way there via the nasal passages--'

'But there must have been ten times what you would expect to find through normal usage?'

Hamish said awkwardly, 'Pilocarpine is difficult to test for volume. We assumed that the traces we found were from the Prime Minister's regular application of the eye-drop dispenser.'

Jack said, 'So there's no way we can prove if the chemical was administered deliberately?'

Hamish shrugged. 'If your theory's right, Inspector...and it's a big "if"... Lancaster's death would add up to the perfect murder.'

Tessa was humming to herself as she put her key in the latch that night. Josh and she weren't rowing any more. Ironically, since they had both agreed to go their separate ways, they had never got on better.

She said Josh could stay at the flat until he had found somewhere else. And he had repaid her reasonableness by cooking the meals for them after she got home from The Examiner.

'Hi, Tess.' Josh gave her a welcome home peck on the cheek. 'How's the world of the harlot?'

'Sorry?'

'You know. Wasn't it Baldwin who said of newspaper barons: they had power without responsibility, which had been the prerogative of the harlot throughout the ages?'

Tessa eyed him archly. 'Actually, I think you'll find it was

Kipling who said it first.'

Josh gave a small bow. 'Oh, how ignorant of me. I stand corrected.'

Tessa grinned at him. 'Well, you wait till tomorrow's paper hits the streets. I think you'll find we've taken on a fair bit of responsibility. And, if we've miscalculated...' Tessa made a cutting gesture across her throat.

Josh looked at her quizzically. 'Do or die, Eh?'

'I'll tell you all about it over dinner. Because, if it hadn't been for you and your inspired guess about elite registrations, none of this would have been possible. So you deserve the full, unexpurgated version.'

Over a spicy spaghetti bolognese and a cool bottle of Pouilly Fume she told Josh the whole story, from the meeting that morning in Jack's flat to the tipoff from the Palace and then her and Frank's scramble to put some kind of story together that The Examiner's lawyers would approve.

At last the front page had been finished. 'It's really sensational,' Tessa said proudly. 'It's going to be the talk of the trade for years.' She described the paper's final design. Over a composite picture of various royals, superimposed on a large RIP headstone, was the headline: 'PELHAM TO DITCH CROWN - END OF LINE FOR WINDSORS.'

Beneath was the story of the Acting Prime Minister's plans as presented that morning to Charles at Highgrove. Woven into it were hints that Pelham had ruthlessly pursued his life's ambition.

And that police were still investigating the murders of two women who were now known to have associated with a mysterious American believed, in turn, to have government connections.

The front-page lead also examined suggestions of covert

discussions between Pelham and the United States aimed at achieving a 'confederation of the republics.'

'Jeezus!' Exclaimed Josh, 'that's going to rate as the scoop of the century.'

Tessa beamed. 'Not bad, eh? For a woman editor.' Their combined chortles were interrupted by the phone. 'If that's transport telling me they've missed another train connection again, I'll personally sack the lot of them.' She picked up the instrument. 'Tessa Jordan.'

'Tess, it's Frank. I'm sorry, Tess, I really am...'

'Frank what is it? What's happened?'

A devastated Frank said flatly down the line. 'Our story's been pulled...'

'Pulled? Who the hell by?'

'El Supremo himself. Apparently, one of the lawyers wanted to cover his own back, so went up to the Penthouse with the proofs. The next thing was, Hobart ordered me to strip out something from inside and run it as the splash instead. I tried to argue him out of it, but you know what he's like...'

Tessa felt the rising bile of defeat in her throat. She said softly, 'Don't worry, Frank, it wasn't your fault. Do as he says.'

'I'm sorry, Tess, but that's not all.'

Tess sighed. 'OK, out with it Frank.'

Frank's said miserably, 'He told me to tell you you're fired. He says you not only disobeyed a direct order, but if it wasn't for his quick action in stopping publication we would be liable for millions in libel damages.

'He said he was backing Pelham to the hilt and wasn't going to stand for any more sabotage stories in one of his own papers. And your firing would be a lesson to anyone else who might fancy his chances.'

Twenty-eight

The reason why the IRA's England Department had carried out its post-Brexit bombing campaigns on the British mainland with such conspicuous success was not so much their brilliant planning as the lamentable breakdown of communications among the British anti-terrorist community.

Ever since the rise of Islamist terrorism each security organisation had been given priority status by the Treasury when it came to budgets. As a result every security silo had developed their own system, jealously guarding their most successful practices from each other.

So, it might seem to a casual observer that, had those in the security apparatus spent more time combining their resources against a common enemy and less time ignoring each other, one of the world's most sophisticated terrorist organisations might have been tamed.

In Northern Ireland the Good Friday Agreement, which had brought peace to the Province for two decades, was now but a fond memory. All the sectarian fault-lines had fractured into a renewed orgy of violence. In trying to keep some kind of democratic control a struggle for power raged daily between the Police Service of Northern Ireland's E4 and E4A surveillance and bugging departments and its own Special Branch. These, in turn, vied with MI5's A1A and A2A break-in and transcription specialists who kept an arms-length relationship with the F3 and F5 political and analysis units.

An even more secret set-up in the Province was 'Five's FX group, who ran agents in subversive organisations. Often these operatives worked for several masters without any of them knowing. Add to all this the activities of the SAS, activated 'sleepers' with MI6, plus mercenaries employed directly by the Home Office, and the inevitable happens. Confusion. Which was adroitly exploited by the Republican Godfathers.

Over-arching all Britain's security apparatus was Britain's 'listening post' GCHQ, based in Cheltenham with offshoots in Bude and Scarborough. Each institution jealously guarded its own piece of the jigsaw. Had they pooled their knowledge, the overall picture would have been a lot clearer

On the British mainland the Ulster rivalries were mirrored by the Army, MI5, MI6, Special Branch, the National Crime Agency, regional police forces and a slimmed-down Scotland Yard Anti-Terrorist Squad. The squad's role in the front line fight against the bombers and gunmen had been taken over by Military Intelligence.

But after the rise of the Islamist threat the Metropolitan Police Commissioner had refused to disband his department entirely, so there were still a few relics with their fingers in the IRA and terrorism pie.

Jack Lockyer's office was just one floor up from where these counter-terrorist veterans spent their days sifting information from tip-offs, wire-taps, intercepts, social media postings and agents in the field. This was why Jack was surprised to hear something first from Keith Passmore which, by rights, should have been on all the noticeboards in the building.

Keith had rung to find out why he had been told that,

from now on, he should liaise with Superintendent Gorringe on the Wiltshire murder. Jack had thought it simpler to tell him it was a re-distribution of work-load. Passmore had sounded unconvinced but changed the subject before his scepticism showed.

'Catching the killer's dropped down the agenda here, anyway, Jack. There's a Hell of a flap on. Apparently F Branch reckons the IRA are planning an operation to co-incide with the PM's funeral.'

Jack raised both eyebrows. 'Are they now? It's good to be kept informed of these things.' Passmore did not seemed to notice the irony in Jack's voice.

'Yeah, we've been alerted because of all the royals on our patch. The security threat level's Critical and we're on Status Black and all leave's been cancelled.'

Jack thought about it for a moment. He didn't envy the security forces their jobs over the next few days. It was going to be a nightmare. He smiled grimly to himself. Perhaps Commander Forsyth's insistence on his bringing the paperwork up to date was actually doing him a favour. I'll be well out of it, Lockyer reflected.

'I appreciate your call, Keith, but as I say if you want any more on the Burchfield case. Mr Gorringe's your man.'

'So, what are you going to do now?' Jack asked. Tessa shrugged. 'A journalist can always find work - even an ex-editor. I'll take some time out and then, if necessary, I'll freelance. I've got enough contacts on non-Hobart papers to get by.'

The two were strolling round Regent's Park. The early morning was overcast with the threat of thunder in the air.

Mist still floated in wisps on the canal and some had drifted to curl among the rose beds. Tessa had rung Lockyer at home last night to tell him about the call from Frank.

Jack had sounded oddly cheerful at her news and had suggested an early meeting the following day, somewhere close to her flat in St John's Wood.

Josh and Tessa had talked into the early hours. Josh had been wonderful; sympathetic, understanding. This morning she had left him a snoring lump under the duvet and had slipped out to find Lockyer already waiting for her on the footbridge over the canal.

'I must say I expected a bit more sympathy on the phone.' Tessa's smile took the edge off her annoyance.

Lockyer said contritely. 'Sorry, Tessa. I suppose I was so wrapped up in a stroke of genius I'd just had.'

'Oh?'

'Yes. I think I've found a way of exposing Pelham.'

Tessa regarded Lockyer anxiously. 'You must be careful Jack. The man's obviously cunning and ruthless, with some very powerful and resourceful friends.' She couldn't keep the note of admiration out of her voice. 'You've got to admit he's been one step ahead all along the line.' She looked at Jack uncertainly. 'There are times when the most sensible thing to do is admit defeat and get on with life. Maybe this is one of those times.'

Lockyer shook his head solemnly, 'Sorry, Tess. I can't do that. I know this is going to sound pompous, but it's my job. It's what I've spent my life doing, bringing criminals to justice. Just because this particular criminal happens to be the Acting Prime Minister of the United Kingdom is not a good enough reason for me to back off. The law's the law. I have to see this thing through.'

Lockyer added with a twinkle in his eye, 'Besides, you've just said you might have been fired as an editor, but you're still a journalist. You may still get the scoop of the century. And as you pointed out, Hobart doesn't own all the media.'

Tessa sighed resignedly, 'OK, so, how's the Met's David going to slay Westminster's Goliath?'

While Lockyer talked the two of them walked slowly along the path which threaded its way past colourful beds of aquilegia, wallflowers and polyanthus. By the time they had reached the lake, Lockyer had unfolded the entire plan which he and James Sherborne had worked out the previous evening.

When he finished Tess gazed at him uncertainly. Then she gave him a wide grin. 'You know, I think Goliath had better watch out.'

James Sherborne paced his study nervously. Sitting coolly in the chair behind James's desk was Harry Dresner, who was watching him with wry amusement.

James said agitatedly, 'As I told Pelham on the phone, I can't go through with it. I didn't realise I'd be filled with such self-loathing. I can't live with it, I'm sorry. I thought I could but I can't. I've talked it over with Elizabeth and she agrees. We've decided I should go to the police and make a clean breast of things.'

Dresner said mockingly. 'And they'll just say: "Thank you Mr Sherborne for being so obliging. We'll just take a statement and then you can run along."' Dresner's face darkened. 'You dumb-ass. They'll throw the book at you. You'll be locked up for at least 10 years. Have you thought, really thought, what that would do to you and your beloved family?'

Dresner looked at James searchingly. 'No, I thought not.

Your kids will grow up trying not to mention their father the murderer. As for your wife - she'll do her best to stay loyal. But, gradually, nature will take its course and she'll turn elsewhere for comfort. You? You'll finally emerge from prison with no job, no family and no nothing.'

James replied angrily. 'I might not be jailed if I tell them that it was a plot. That you tricked me into picking that girl up. That you and Pelham are involved in some sort of blackmail conspiracy. I shall tell them everything I know.'

Dresner sneered, 'And who do you think the police are going to believe? The ravings of an accused murderer, or the Prime Minister? Come on, Sherborne, get real.'

Dresner toyed with a glass paperweight as he added soothingly, 'On the other hand, if you do as we suggest...keep your head low until it all blows over...Well, everything'll work out just fine. You'll see. And, maybe your career'll get a boost, too. Robert's got a lot of influence on both sides of the House, you know.'

James rung his hands and bowed his head. 'I don't know...Everything's such a mess. First that poor girl, then her friend's murdered. Then, out of the blue Lancaster dies...'

He jerked his head up, 'I may be weak, Dresner, but I'm not a fool. I've been thinking about things. It's very convenient, isn't it, that the Prime Minister just happens to keel over at precisely the same time that Pelham's ready to launch his master plan?'

Dresner slammed the paperweight down on the desk and said menacingly, 'If I was you, Sherborne, I'd keep that kind of talk to yourself. The PM died of overwork. His heart just gave out. Another dedicated servant of the people killed by the burdens of office.'

'Dresner, you sicken me. You and Pelham are involved in

murder, blackmail, coercion and God knows what else and you salve whatever conscience you might have with claptrap about working for the overall good. People like you can't see that the means can never justify the ends.'

James's eyes shone with fervour. 'If you're prepared to kill, terrorise, cheat and lie to get your way, then however noble the cause it's not worth a light--'

Dresner's lip curled contemptuously. 'You pathetic jerk. Haven't you worked out yet that the only way to achieve anything in this world is by grabbing power. The more power you have, the more you can do with it.

'Do you really think words like "please" and "thank you" cut any ice in that jungle out there? It's the survival of the fittest. It always has been and always will be.'

He said, 'Robert understands that. He's a great man with big ideas. His name's gonna be written big on the billboard of history while people like you won't even rate a footnote.'

James retorted, 'I don't care what you say, Dresner, nothing justifies murder. The day that we say it does will be the day we crawl back into the primeval slime--'

'Murder? Snuffing out two hookers and giving a played-out old guy a helping hand to meet his maker? In my book that's no more murder than putting down a couple of alley cats and an old dog.'

James said steadily, 'So you actually admit you...you...assassinated the Prime Minister of England.' Dresner grinned at him. 'Yeah, well, no-one can prove a thing. And, it's small potatoes in the big picture.'

James's shoulders slumped in defeat. He murmured, 'I...I...can't fight you. I'll...do as you say...I won't cause any trouble.'

Dresner smiled at him genially. 'That's my boy. Robert

thought you might be persuaded to change your mind if I pointed out a few facts of life. Don't get up, James, I'll see myself out.'

After Dresner's car drove through the gates at the end of the drive, Lockyer and Tessa stepped into the room.

Lockyer beamed. 'Well done, Mr Sherborne. Went like a dream. I've just checked back the tape. It's all there. You'd think that someone who's used to blackmailing people with hidden cameras would be a mite more suspicious when it came to their own situation, wouldn't you?'

Tessa said drily to James, 'When you started hamming it up talking about...crawling back into the primeval slime...I wondered if he would rumble you.'

Jack said, 'Well, it doesn't matter now. We've got enough to confront Pelham and arrest them both on suspicion of murder.' He looked at James. 'And did you notice something else when he slammed that paperweight down? I was looking through a crack in the door. The man's left-handed.'

James looked at Jack carefully. 'You mean, he could be the one who followed me that night and killed Linda?'

Jack nodded. 'Could be. The perpetrator was left-handed, remember.' He added briskly, 'So, on with phase two. Ring Pelham and say that Dresner didn't change your mind and that you still intend going to the authorities.

'But, before you do, you insist on meeting them both at the House at, say, seven o'clock tonight. By then I'll have briefed Sergeant Bishop and we'll both be with you.'

'Excuse me!' Lockyer and James looked towards Tessa. 'I'd like to be at this meeting, too.'

Lockyer shook his head. 'Sorry, Tessa. But don't forget, he is the Acting PM. It'll be difficult enough for us to get through his security without a journalist tagging along as well.'

Tessa eyed Jack determinedly. 'It might be - if I was a journalist. But not if I had a police officer's warrant card.'

Lockyer looked at her sternly. 'Impersonating a police officer, Miss Jordan, is an offence. I could not possibly condone it.'

James said, 'You did say earlier, Inspector, that it wouldn't be a bad thing if there was an independent witness to hand. I think I can arrange a temporary visitor's pass that'll get Tessa past front-of-House security. After that we'll have to bluff her through.'

Lockyer looked unconvinced. He said reluctantly, 'Alright, I suppose Tess does deserve to be in at the kill.' He looked at his watch. It was 3.30pm. 'Just about enough time to get everything in place.'

He grinned and as an afterthought added, 'Pelham's enforced absence is going to play merry hell with tomorrow's state funeral...'

Twenty-nine

When Lockyer, Claire, Tessa and Sherborne walked into Pelham's inner sanctum in the Palace of Westminster, the last thing Jack expected was to be greeted warmly.

Pelham emerged from behind his desk and shook his hand. 'Inspector Lockyer, a pleasure to meet you at last.' The Acting Prime Minister introduced Harry Dresner, who was standing impassively at his side. Pelham surveyed Lockyer's companions. 'Hmmm, quite a deputation. Please, everyone, do make yourselves comfortable.'

Jack remained standing. Claire took up a position behind her boss, Tessa perched by the coffee table and James leaned on the mantelpiece.

Out of courtesy a frowning Lockyer briefly introduced Claire and Tessa before saying severely, 'Mr Pelham, this is not a social call. I am here on a most serious matter.'

Pelham smiled genially. 'Then to business, Inspector, I am all ears.' He returned to his seat and leaned with his elbows on the desk his clenched hands pointing to the ceiling.

Lockyer dug into his jacket, sat down and balanced a smart phone on his knee. 'Sir, I should like you to listen to this recording very carefully. It is of a conversation Mr Sherborne had earlier today at his home with Mr Dresner.'

Abruptly, Lockyer pushed the 'on' button and a flattened version of James's voice emerged...'As I told Pelham on the phone, I can't go through with it...' Everyone in the room heard Dresner's voice sneeringly pointing out what effect James's confession would eventually have on his wife and children.

Tessa shivered as she heard again Dresner talking of 'snuffing out two hookers and giving a played-out old guy a helping hand to meet his maker.' Jack stared intently at Pelham's face as an angry Dresner spoke of 'putting down a couple of alley cats and an old dog.' Apart from a smile playing about the edges of his mouth, the Acting PM displayed no emotion.

After James's show of defeat, Lockyer switched the recording App off and the room fell silent. Finally, Lockyer cleared his throat again. 'Before I formally caution you both, would you care to say anything..?' He glanced at Dresner and back to Pelham.

Neither man was exhibiting any signs of concern. By now all Hell should have broken loose. Lockyer had even stationed a constable in the vicinity to ensure Dresner did not escape should he make a run for it.

His eyes swivelled back to Pelham who seemed absorbed in the symmetry of his fingers. When he seemed satisfied he had made a perfect steeple, he said laconically, 'My dear Inspector, I fear you have come on a fool's errand. There is nothing for you here.'

Lockyer replied firmly. 'Now don't let's play games, Mr Pelham. I am perfectly satisfied...' He gestured to the mobile phone, now on the corner of the desk '...that you and Dresner here are implicated in at least one murder, but probably three if the truth were known.'

Tessa said, 'And, in case you're thinking of throwing that phone out of the window, or flushing it down the toilet, the conversation is, of course, stored elsewhere, in a safe place. I'm actually a journalist and I shall be using the original when I come to write this story up. If there's any justice at all, it should get headlines around the world - despite Ben Hobart.'

Dresner, who up to now had remained silent, chortled mirthlessly. 'Go on, tell 'em Bob.'

Pelham looked from one to the other. 'Oh dear, Oh dear, Oh dear! This is all really quite pathetic, Inspector. Dresner here was fully aware that this afternoon was a bit...ah...unlikely. James's call to me didn't quite ring true.

'So Harry and I decided that if there was some kind of plot afoot, we'd better find out rather pronto who was behind it. We couldn't afford a slip-up at this late stage could we?'

Pelham smiled benevolently. 'Now that we have flushed out the opposition, which turns out to be a mere police inspector, who has been removed from the case for insubordination, a junior officer, a murder suspect and one sacked journalist, I am much reassured.'

Lockyer retorted uncertainly, 'That's how you may see it, but the law may take a different view.'

Pelham replied, 'Of course, Inspector. You must do your duty. In fact, come to think of it, I insist upon it.' Pelham turned to Dresner. 'Harry, answer me truthfully now. Have you been involved in murder?'

Dresner looked contrite. 'Yes, I have sir.'

In fact, did you...er...strangle that poor Linda Burchfield?'

Dresner nodded. 'Yes, Mr Prime Minister, I did.'

Tessa, Claire and James gaped in astonishment. Lockyer sat silent. Pelham continued evenly, 'And, did you have that girl outside The Examiner's office killed, too?'

'Mea Culpa, PM.'

And have you been involved in blackmailing senior

members of Her Majesty's Government?'

"Fraid so...'

Lockyer exploded, 'What the Hell's all this? Does he realise what he's confessing to? And, in front of four witnesses?'

Pelham replied silkily, 'But of course. Isn't that what you want, Inspector?'

'What I want, sir, and what I intend to do, is arrest you both and charge you with murder.'

'Me, Inspector? Good Lord, you want to arrest me? What ever for?'

'I've just told you...for murder.'

Pelham drew in a deep breath and expelled it in a long sigh. 'But, Inspector, arrest the Prime Minister of England on such a charge, without a shred of evidence, when the real culprit has just confessed?'

He turned back to Dresner. 'Harry, have I been in any way involved in any of these crimes?'

Dresner shook his head vigorously. 'Absolutely not, Prime Minister. Whatever I did, I did entirely under my own volition and without your knowledge.'

Pelham swivelled back to Lockyer. 'There, Inspector, you have not only the perpetrator's admission of guilt but his denial of any involvement by myself. And, indeed, I'd like to re-inforce that statement. I had no idea my temporary assistant, on attachment from the United States, was such a...Jekyll and Hyde. I shall protest to the Embassy, in the strongest terms, I can assure you.'

Lockyer glared at Pelham in disbelief. At last he said, 'What about the late Prime Minister. Did Dresner have a hand in his murder, too?'

Pelham looked askance. 'Murder? Old Ted murdered?

Come on, Inspector, this is England. No-one murders the Prime Minister. I am assured the pathologists performed a very thorough examination at the autopsy. No, alas, heart failure, plain and simple, was what killed him.'

'Not the eye drops you laced his coffee with?'

'Inspector, I have been commendably patient with your outlandish attacks on my integrity. Have a care, that patience is now wearing thin.' He opened a drawer on the right-hand side of his desk and took out a tiny Philips DVT voice recorder. 'As you may observe, two can play at your little game. Our conversation's already stored on the cloud, as they say, and I shall keep this version for handy future reference, should I need to defend any more wild allegations.'

He gazed at Lockyer thoughtfully, as a thought struck him. 'Or perhaps I'll send a copy to Commander Forsyth. I'm sure he'll want to know his loose cannon is still crashing about his Division.'

Lockyer looked at Pelham defiantly. 'In the light of what Dresner, here, has said I admit I cannot, at this stage, place you in custody.' Turning to Dresner he continued formally, 'But as for you... Harry Dresner, I arrest you for the murders of Linda Burchfield, known as Lucinda and Rebecca Ward, known as...'

'Inspector, Inspector...' Pelham's interruption stopped Lockyer in mid-flow. '...you cannot arrest Dresner.'

'Can't arrest him? He's just confessed to murder, man.'

Pelham nodded slowly. 'I agree, Inspector, but you have no authority to take him into custody. Extra-territoriality, you see.'

Lockyer's face suffused the colour of an egg-plant. 'I've just about had enough of this. What are you talking about now?'

'Territoriality. Extra-territoriality. To you and me,

Inspector, Diplomatic Immunity. Under the terms of the Vienna Convention of 1961 any diplomatic agent is exempt from the criminal or civil jurisdiction of his host country.'

Lockyer stuttered, 'Diplomatic..?'

'...And as the accredited agent of the USA, attached by the specific authority of Sam McGovern himself to the American Embassy here Dresner is, regrettably, immune from prosecution.'

Pelham added placatingly, 'I shall, of course, have him deported instantly - at least as soon as is practicable after tomorrow's funeral.'

Thirty

As Lockyer sat in the driver's seat of his car he pounded the steering wheel in frustration. All three of his passengers silently fumed in sympathy. At length Tessa broke the silence. 'Talk about cunning...He's going to get away with it, isn't he?'

Claire said grudgingly, 'I know all politicians are supposed to be duplicitous, but he's positively Machiavellian. He's the most unscrupulous, devious, treacherous, brilliant bastard I've ever come across.'

'And he's beaten us, hands down. He's matched us move for move until finally we've run into the sand,' said Lockyer.

Tessa ran the fingers of both hands through her hair and then cradled her head. 'I hate to agree. You've got to hand it to him...Maybe he's just the sort we need to run the country.'

'A criminal mastermind who just happens to be our Prime Minister - quite a combination,' observed Claire wryly.

Wearily, Lockyer lifted his head from the wheel. He said, 'And, after tomorrow's State funeral he launches his new world order. Once that happens there'll be no chance of bringing him to justice. What he's got away with beggars belief.'

'Well, he might not get away with it.' It was James who, up to now, had been sitting silently in the back of the car. They all looked at him doubtfully.

'What's to stop him now?' Said Jack. 'There's nothing left. We've run out of ideas.'

'Not quite,' replied James. 'There's one possibility.' James's face cleared and took on a wide grin. 'In fact I've been such a bloody idiot, not thinking of it before.'

Tessa yelled, 'James, for God's sake, what is it?'

James said soberly, 'We can sink him with a resignation speech. My resignation speech.'

'Resignation...I don't understand,' said Claire.

'Quiet Claire. Let him finish,' rumbled Lockyer.

'I had intended to resign my seat anyway. Both Elizabeth and I didn't think I should carry on as an MP after...you know...Linda etc comes out.

'I don't know whether you realise this, but whenever a minister or shadow minister resigns, it's customary to hear him out in silence. None of the usual bear-garden stuff.

'So, I shall ask the Speaker's indulgence, saying that for personal reasons I wish to deliver my farewell speech on Tuesday before Pelham is due to address the House.'

As James outlined his plan the others listened with rapt attention. 'In giving my reasons, I shall simply recount events: the murders of two women, my own culpability, then the blackmail, my suspicions of Pelham's involvement, the possible assassination of the Prime Minister, and the employing of diplomatic immunity to cover everything up.'

Tessa said excitedly, 'My God. You'll cause a sensation! All the world's media will be there to record the new PM's first appearance. Once you stand up, everything you say will hurtle round the world in minutes. Pelham will be finished.'

James nodded soberly. 'And no-one to sue me for libel because I'm protected by Parliamentary privilege.'

Lockyer said, 'Hang on, it can't be that simple. You mean you catch the Speaker's eye, stand on your hind legs and just reveal everything. And no-one can stop you? Not even the

Prime Minister?'

James said, 'I don't know about catching the Speaker's eye. Probably the safest thing will be to telephone Bellinger in advance and set it all up. But, yes, once on my feet I can say what I like.'

Lockyer thumped the steering wheel again, this time with exuberance. 'I can't believe it. By God, I must get myself a place in the Visitors' Gallery, just to see Pelham's face.'

That evening, Jack and Tessa made love. Tentatively at first, each being aware of the other's emotional sensitivities. Later, as they grew in confidence, their mutual passion flared into an all-consuming conflagration which left them both exhausted but at peace with the world.

Now as Jack lay awake in the darkness, looking at the ceiling of his bedroom and listening to Tessa's steady breathing beside him, all the walls he had built around his inner self over the years, began to crumble away.

He knew that from now on his life would have a new meaning. He had a future once again. With a woman he knew he could grow to love deeply. And for always. Suddenly, he was flooded with a happiness he didn't know was possible.

After the State Funeral, which filled the capital with world leaders, accompanied by armies of secret service personnel, everyone breathed a sigh of relief. There were no security scares. The IRA threat had not materialised.

Pelham and McGovern had their meeting and, as McGovern had calculated, no-one thought it strange that the President of the United States should wish to express, in private, his sincere condolences to the acting Prime Minister of

Great Britain on the tragic loss of a much-respected statesman.

To make certain the Limey knew his place, and that Dunkirk would be dead in the water without Uncle Sam, McGovern insisted on covering, in painstaking detail, the role his countrymen had played in achieving lift-off status.

Then he followed up his 'hard man' routine with a 'soft man' sucker punch. 'This is deep background material, Bob, but you oughta know I've set aside an initial 100 billion dollars to bail you out of Europe. So your manufacturing infrastructure's secure and so's any guarantee you have to make good to Brussels.

'After that it'll be just us and you, equal partners, trading freely with the rest of the world. You'll have our South American and Pacific markets and we'll have Europe and Scandinavia.'

McGovern failed to mention that when Britain had burned its boats there would be unexpected problems with Congress over funding. The Brits would be bankrupted and obliged to change their treaty arrangements. Within a few years they would be begging to become the 51st state of the Union.

And he, Sam McGovern, would be seen as the architect of the mother country's return to the fold. Yeah, to achieve his place in history had been worth a few murders and a little blackmail along the way.

Pelham looked suitably grateful as he shook McGovern's hand and led him back into the limelight of Number 10's reception room. Observers who noticed the Prime Minister patting his jacket pocket would have put the gesture down to a rare nervous mannerism perhaps.

They were not to know it for what it was: a gesture of silent appreciation to the Matsui pocket recorder, whose tiny condenser microphone had captured every incriminating word the President had spoken and the even tinier transmitter had relayed the exchange to be stored in a safe place in his Government office.

As the Heads of State took their leave they all pledged their comradeship in the trying times ahead as a nation struggled to put its grief behind it. Pelham inclined his head graciously and said their words meant more to him than they will ever know.

After the last had gone the new Prime Minister read through, once again, his address to the Commons, due to be delivered to an expectant House the next day. It really was a tour de force, he thought. Gravitas combined with optimism. A future full of hope, with himself centre stage.

It began with the grave news of Her Majesty's terminal condition, but ended on a unifying and upbeat note, pointing the people to new, sunny uplands which awaited a born-again Britain welcomed into new nationhood by our kith and kin across the sea.

Schmaltzy, as that bone-head McGovern might say. But appropriate to the mood of the moment, he thought.

Pelham smiled to himself and drummed his fingers on the arm of his chair. After Mr Speaker Bellinger's quiet word in the cathedral earlier, there remained one last, small problem.

James was late - this day of all days. Yesterday he had managed to pluck Mr Speaker from the pomp of the funeral for just long enough to explain, in confidence, that he was intending to resign. He had hinted that it was for a tragic, family reason.

Mr Speaker Bellinger had been sympathetic. It was not usual to pre-empt a Prime Ministerial address. But, in the circumstances...The Speaker had promised he would allow James to catch his eye a few minutes before the PM was due to get to his feet. And, scheduled that way, James's statement would not appear an anti-climax to an exhilarated House, Mr Speaker had suggested kindly.

So, what a time to have a puncture, cursed James as he struggled to change the tyre. Luckily, Elizabeth who had come to the door to kiss him goodbye had spotted it as soon as he had got in the car. So it could have been worse. He could have been stuck on a hard shoulder somewhere.

James did up the last wheelnut, dashed indoors to wash his hands. A hug from Elizabeth to wish him luck. He looked at his watch. Thank God he'd had the foresight to build into his plan plenty of room for the unexpected. He'd still get there comfortably before Pelham was due to speak.

Trouble was, on days like this, the Commons was filled to overflowing - even his usual place on the Opposition Front Benches would be commandeered if he didn't step on it now.

He started the engine and drove a little faster than usual down the drive towards the open double gates. With about 20 feet to go, he braked hard to avoid shooting out into the busy road that ran the length of Hinton Magna.

While the Daimler's Automatic Braking System brought the vehicle to a smooth, safe halt, it did nothing to impede the forward motion of a globule of mercury trapped in a narrow pipette. As it surged onwards, one end of the glass tube became heavier than the other and tilted downwards.

This brought a copper wire, heat-sealed to the tip, into contact with the positive electrode of a small battery. The resultant amperage was all that was required to set off a small detonator. This, in turn, caused an odourless, colourless plasticine-like material moulded to the exhaust pipe, to explode.

Within a nano-second the sleek outline of the Daimler was reduced to liquid by the effects of a 3,000 degrees Celcius fireball.

The blast was heard over five miles away. It took the Wiltshire police two hours to discover what had happened. Later, a white-faced police constable found the car's steering wheel, still in perfect condition, but minus its column, up a tree 300 yards down the road.

Of the driver of the car, there was no sign. Forensic scientists, working with tweezers, eventually recovered just about enough human remains to fit into a shoe box.

An investigation established that the bomb type, and the methodology, pinpointed the outrage as the work of the IRA. Which puzzled Fergal MacStiofain, Chief of its England Department, as none of his active units on the mainland had been within 100 miles of the scene at the time.

His brigade had decided that, with the heavy security associated with the former Prime Minister's funeral, it would be wiser to keep their heads down. He did not know where the rumour about a high-profile IRA operation had come from, either. He shrugged to himself. Probably Loyalist disinformation, he thought.

About two hours after the assassination of one of Britain's most promising MP's, Harry Dresner, accompanied by the DOI's chief explosives expert, boarded a CIA Gulfstream G550 at Heathrow Airport, bound for Andrews Air Base in Maryland, USA.

As Dresner stood on the first step, he looked at his watch.

2pm. Just about now, a new era was beginning. And he had played his part. He shook his head in silent admiration. Robert had told him this morning that he'd bring his speech forward by half an hour to avoid any possible news of another terrorist outrage stealing his thunder.

The guy was a genius and it had been a real pleasure working with him.

He smiled and ducked into the aircraft. He was looking forward to renewing his acquaintance when the new President of the Republic of Great Britain was formally sworn in. In the meantime Sam McGovern had told Dresner to keep his head down. He didn't think a certain London cop would cause any ripples. But, if he did, they would be handled.

Across London, a hushed House of Commons waited for the new Prime Minister of the United Kingdom to speak.

Robert Pelham solemnly grasped the lectern. 'Mr Speaker, Right Honourable and Honourable Members, I have a grave and momentous announcement to make, one which will change the course of history...'

A word from the author

If you have enjoyed this book please consider writing a review
on the Amazon site because this will encourage others to enjoy
it too.

And if you are on Facebook and Twitter, please take a few
seconds to let your friends know about it. If it takes them
away, even for a few hours, from their stressful lives they'll be
grateful to you, as will I. And it may give them a forewarning
of events to come...

13364172R00136

Printed in Great Britain
by Amazon